BLOW ME OVER WITH A FEATHER

Based on a true story

Caroline Sherouse

To Joanie

Lots of love

Caroline xox Sherouse

For my daughter Lisa and husband C.G.

Every gun that is made, every warship launched, every rocket fired, signifies in the final sense a theft from those who hunger and are not fed, those who are cold and are not clothed............

Excerpt 'THE CHANCE FOR PEACE'

Dwight D. Eisenhower: 34th U.S. President
January 20, 1953 – January 20, 1961

CONTENTS

PROLOGUE

Today, thirteen months after Mum's funeral, I called my five brothers and two sisters in the UK. She was the cog in the middle of our family's wheel, and the spokes all fell off when she left us. At least that's how we all felt at the time. On reflection, we all pulled together rather well. Maybe her death permitted us to function together with a new found confidence in being centers of our own wheel.

When Mum was alive, my siblings were sometimes at odds with me. I knew too much. They didn't want to know anything. Now it's different. When no more logs fuel the fire, it goes out. Mum ignited fires by denying her part in any of the dysfunction in the family. She hated the smoldering smoke; she preferred a flare-up. That way everyone was so busy putting out the fire; no-one had time to see the real picture.

Our love for her was as individual as how we each miss her. Some of us have become closer. One sister sent me a surprise bouquet of delightful flowers at Christmas. She and I had long thought we didn't have much in common. We had what you might call an antagonistic relationship over the years. Since Mum died, I was surprised to hear her say she didn't know Mum very well until the last three or four years of her life. It dawned on me that maybe we had more in common than we thought.

Each sibling had willingly stepped into the gap as Mum began losing her memory and self-confidence. My older brother had been going in daily to dispense medications, but it wasn't enough. Everyone was afraid she might burn the house down if she forgot about the cooker being on.

At a family meeting everyone spoke up about feeling helpless, some wanted to be there full time for her, but they did not have the room or the means. I was out of the picture, living five thousand miles west of the family and when I learned the outcome of their decision, I kept thinking, 'eight children and not one of us able to take her in.' So she went into a home run by a private insurance company. At least she had plenty of visitors, more than anyone else there.

Mum's ovary developed a tumor, but when removed, the surgery somehow affected her colon which became twisted and blocked. I kept imagining a pair of careless hands dumping her entrails on the table beside her unconscious body and not putting them back with loving care. A section of colon died. Another surgery removed it and a Stoma-bag was attached to the upper part of her colon.

Naturally, Mum hated it and would not acknowledge its existence. She became over-anxious, cantankerous and her memory worsened. Over-full bag accidents became the new norm, nurses and family members had to help her many times.

I remember taking Mum for lunch to the pub across the street from the nursing home. Before we ate, I helped empty her bag in one of the cubicle toilets. It did not smell thank goodness, being on the upper colon, but it was not what I cared to do just before lunch. I felt her squirming embarrassment at having to be helped, so I just got on with it with kindness, remembering all the times she cared for our toilet habits without a thought for her own discomfort.

Mum's dementia was so sad, a challenge for everyone, as were her angry words at times. My sister told me about an incident in the nursing home that made us laugh out loud. If I hadn't laughed so hard, I might have cried for her.

"Whose clothes are those in my wardrobe? They're not mine," said Mum. It was a repetitive question and statement they all heard frequently. My sister calmly told her they were her clothes. On this particular occasion, Mum was having none of it.

"Those are not my things. Some bastard has put my name on everything in that wardrobe."

"Well, that bastard must be me because I ironed every single one of those name tabs on your clothes," replied my sister.

"Okay. So who in the hell is Mark Spencer? He's put his name on a few of those things in there."

"Mum. It's Marks and Spencer, not Mark Spencer. You know; Marks and Spencer the shop."

Tears ran down our cheeks, and my sides ached. It was a good few minutes before I could speak.

"You know Mum appreciated all you did for her Nat. She said to me, 'You know, I don't know what I would have done without our Natalie this past couple of years.' "

"Yes, she said that to me too," replied my sister. "One day I said to her, 'Aha! So that's why I was born.' "

My heart bled for her.

"Did you say that to Mum?"

"Yes, I did. I've often wondered why I was born."

Yes, we have a lot more in common than we thought.

I had some anger when I got back home after Mum's funeral, and didn't know what it was about until later. I'm mourning Mum's death, yes, but I'm also mourning everything I didn't have with Mum. Everything I can never have now. My sister summed it up.

"We all had very different relationships with Mum, and all of us are angry with her about some things, but we just have to face it and get over it I guess. We all have things we need to forgive."

I enjoyed my talk with her today. It's like we never saw each other properly before. We ended our conversation saying we loved each other.

* * *

CHAPTER 1: 1956 MARY: A NEW WAR TO FIGHT

Hosea 2:5-6, Their mother has been unfaithful and has conceived them in disgrace. She said, 'I will go after my lovers, who give me my food and my water, my wool and my linen, my olive oil and my drink.' Therefore I will block her path with thorn bushes; I will wall her in so that she cannot find her way.

I open the front door to find a policeman looking straight at me with a piece of paper in his hand. I'm in shock. First of all, he's the tallest man I've ever seen. I'm on the top step, and he's three steps down and at eye level. Secondly, in the war years, the only reason a policeman came to your door was to tell you the worst news you ever heard in your life. I witnessed policemen telling friends or coworkers that their men had been killed in action, or were missing, believed dead. My Bertie died in action. That news was the first and last time I ever saw a policeman at my door.

His expression is grim. His brown speckled eyes stare right into mine. I'm speechless. His dark brows rise.

"I'm looking for Mrs. Krupp, Mrs. Mary Krupp?"

"I'm Mrs. Mary Krupp." My voice sounds like a timid bird, barely able to chirp.

"Are you the mother of Elizabeth Caradine?"

"I am. Why? What's wrong with Beth?"

My voice is back but sounds like a screech. He remains calm and asks,

"You call her Beth?"

I nod, tears spring to my eyes.

"Beth has been taken to Manchester Infirmary Mrs. Krupp. She appears to have taken an overdose of pills and is in critical condition. She's also gone into labor."

"My God," I scream, "What about the children? Where are they?"

He squeezes my arm to reassure me.

"They're with her neighbor. They're ok. We can pick them up later. Go and get your coat and keys and I'll take you to the hospital. Is your husband home?"

"No, he's at work; I'll hurry."

I run into the hallway, grab my coat, throw off my slippers and with the shoe-horn's help, force my feet into walking shoes without untying the laces. My race into the kitchen takes about five seconds to complete. I grab my bag off the armchair and hitch the keys off a hook on the wall. The stove is already banked up with coke, so hopefully it will not go out before I get back. Then remembering Mama, I fly into the back kitchen, fill a cup with water and visit her in the front room, telling her I have to go to the shops and will be back soon. She's sleepy and has put her feet up. She'll not need me this afternoon.

By the time I'm out of the house and lock the door, the policeman has started the car, and we are away as fast as he can drive, bell-sirens blaring which serve to feed my panic.

"Is she going to be ok? She's not going to die, is she? What did they say at the hospital?"

"She's had her stomach pumped, they think they may have got her in time, but I'm not sure about the baby. They said labor had started when I left there."

My stomach lurches. I think I may throw up and guilt clouds my thinking. Our last discussion had been two days ago, and I had said what a trollop she was, having a third child and no man in the house.

"You can hardly cope with the two kids you already have," I told her, "How in hell's teeth will you cope with another?"

I had slammed out of the house, our other house in town. No rent again from her this week. My husband John was furious. He spat feathers at me. John is a hard man to please at the best of times. Polish-German, dour faced and sour tempered. We had enough to cope with when we brought his mother over after the war, hidden under a blanket on the floor between the car seats.

I had been beside myself to know Beth was pregnant again. I said sterilization should be her next option and her response, quick and sharp, walloped me.

"Why, is that what you did after Maureen?"

I slapped her face.

Bertie, my fiancé, died before my second daughter, Maureen was born. It was such a hard time for me. I brought the two girls up thinking they were full sisters and had the same dad. Beth never asked any questions. Why would she? What does a seven-year-old know?

Mad as hell I am at her, but I don't want her to die. I like her two kids; they are canny, especially the girl Lizzie.

I had suggested that we pass the name Elizabeth down the family line.

"Okay," Beth had replied, "But if I do, I never want to hear her called Elizabeth. It's too formal a name to put on a little girl's shoulders. She'll be Lizzie for short."

It had pleased me because I'd felt it unfair that women lose their last name when marrying. We are the ones holding house and home together. My mother is called Elizabeth. She christened me Mary. I never liked my name, too Catholic. Mother told me it was after Mary Queen of Scots. I gave up asking questions. I had no idea where Scotland came into the picture, never mind a Catholic Queen. Maybe she just liked having two Queens' names in the family. She can get a bit above herself at times.

I felt I was getting a second chance with Lizzie, of knowing how to love her. God knows I barely like my daughter, Beth at times. But that is because of the war and me having to go to Lancashire to build bombs and leave my two girls with my mother. I hardly ever saw them.

I had tried to get to know Beth better. When she was fourteen, I had her come live with me. She was a good worker and brought in some handy money. But we never really bonded. We were stuck together like flour and water paste, messy and easily broken apart. It wasn't long before Beth went back to Glenridding to live with her Gran. Later she went to be a nanny down south. That's how she eventually came to meet Lonnie Caradine, the US military jock who got her pregnant. Not once, but twice.

In the police car, I'm so deep in thought that our arrival at the hospital startles me. As we turn quickly into the grounds of what had once been a wealthy landowner's mansion, I see the magnificence of the Victorian building. At any other time, on any other day, I'd have admired it's every architectural nuance. Today I'm in too much of a rush.

The policeman switches off the engine and like the gentleman he is, springs out of the car and strides quickly to open my door. I notice his huge, black, shiny shoes. My mother had drilled into me that you can tell much about a person by the shine on their shoes. He leads the way through the massive open front doors. I recoil at the smell of Dettol disinfectant. After talking with a nurse, we make our way to the ward. He stands at the door and ushers me into the Ward Sister's office.

The Matron's there; a stumpy little thing with a white matron's cap that makes her look taller and like a nun. She reminds me of a Mother Superior, holding her hands together center front as she piously explains all the facts to me. I can tell she thinks very little of me, mother to a pregnant girl who has attempted suicide. I feel shame cover me like a shroud.

"You can probably see her tomorrow," she says. "We think we got her in time. Call the hospital in the morning, and we'll have more to tell you then. I hope for her sake the child lives, or she could be looking at going to prison. It's not just herself that she tried to kill, but her baby too."

"Well she's a big chip off the old block then," I tell her, "Her father killed himself as well; hung himself in the hold of a ship. Left us high and dry. She's of the same mettle. Oh, my good God, I don't know what to do with her."

The Matron raises her eyebrows and doesn't even blink.

"Does your daughter have somewhere to go where she'll not be alone when she gets out? If the baby lives, she'll need some help for a while."

"Yes, we have plenty of room."

"Good then. Call the ward tomorrow. She'll probably stay here for a week, just to be on the safe side with the baby and all."

"Can I see her tonight?"

"No, it's not a good idea. Call the ward tomorrow. Don't worry, if we need to get hold of you," she pauses and looks up at the policeman and nods, "we will."

I'm tempted to demand I see Beth. I don't like hearing 'no.' Something makes me look down at her shoes. Big buggers they are, shiny too. They move toward me. I look up. She has raised her arm, and her armpit is one foot closer to my face. She is showing me out. The policeman backs up and his right arm gestures toward the door. He smiles as I pass him. I feel daggers at my back from her. In the corridor, he touches my elbow.

"We'll go get your grandchildren and get you all home."

He seems very kindly after the sharp harangue from the Matron.

I'm reticent and don't speak as we drive to Edward St. I feel like a ton weight just landed on me, and John isn't even home from work. I know he'll have plenty to say. I say a silent prayer that the baby doesn't die. Not that I particularly care about it but if Beth goes to prison, Steven and Lizzie are my responsibility. I know I do not want that. John would not have it either.

My mother, settled as she is in a tiny village in the Lake District, still has my other daughter Maureen with her. God knows she won't want two more children. I'm in a quandary alright.

When we get to Edward St, I get myself together, all business and orders. We soon have clothing and everything we need to take Steven and Lizzie home. They seem puzzled and keep asking 'Why this and why that?' I tell them to climb into the back of the police car.

"You're coming to stay at Grandma's house for a little while. Your mummy is poorly in the hospital."

"Why Grandma?" asks Lizzie.

I turn to Ellen who has two children of her own demanding her attention.

"Thank you, Ellen. It was good of you to take them in. I appreciate your kindness."

"Think nothing of it, Mrs. Krupp. I just hope she'll be alright. Can I come to see Beth when she gets home to your house?"

"Yes of course. Just give it a week or two and then come. Here's the address."

I scribble into a small diary from my handbag and tear out the page for her.

By the time we get home, I still have an hour before John walks through the door. I poke up the stove and put in more coke, feed the children egg on toast at the kitchen table, visit Mama and sort out her commode while she eats supper, and then I get them all ready for bed. I don't remind the children about Mama because I just want them, and her, to settle down for the night. They can visit tomorrow.

Upstairs, in one of the small bedrooms, the chimney warms the whole wall alongside the bed. Steven and Lizzie snuggle in at each end of the bed and I sing a lullaby, one I remember my mother sang to me. As I finish the song, I hear John in the hallway downstairs. Lizzie peeps at me, so I shush her quietly and go down to meet him. We kiss.

"Guess what John?"

"Vot?"

"We have our two grandchildren tucked up in bed upstairs."

"Vy is dat?" He blurts out in his clipped accent.

"Beth took an overdose of pills and ended up in the hospital. She's very sick; they're not even sure if her baby will live."

He stares at me, his forehead furrowing. He shakes his head.

"Mine God. Vy she do this? Vot is up with your daughter?"

"I don't know John. She hasn't been right for a while. Maybe she's more desperate than she lets us know."

He embraces me.

"I'm so sorry she did this Mary. Such a shame. Ve just have to hope everything is going to be alright with her. Mine God. Are the childer asleep?"

"Probably not yet. I just tucked them both into bed."

He's grumpy about the whole thing but not as angry as I thought he would be. He seems sorry for the situation and follows me upstairs to check on the children. They're still awake, so he tells them some story about Ingrid, the cow, and has a smile as he tells it. Even Steven starts to giggle.

Well. You could blow me over with a feather.

CHAPTER 2: 1956 LIZZIE: THE LAST TIME I SAW HER

Matt 7:26, But everyone who hears these words of mine and does not put them into practice is like a foolish man who built his house on sand.

Staring at the curvy crack on the ceiling that looks like Mummy, I'm trying to remember the last time I saw her. Two pictures of her sleeping face come to me. One is scary, her mouth a strange shape. I don't want to remember her like that, so I think harder about her peaceful face.

I was in my crib, sitting up and watching her sleep in her big bed. I liked looking at her face and her black, wavy hair all over the pillow. Her eyes flickered, and a sparkle slid onto her cheek before it disappeared into her hair. Another one peeped between her eyelashes and followed the same trail. Still more appeared and disappeared until she lifted soft fingers and wiped her cheeks. I was puzzled.

"Mummy, why are you crying?"

Without opening her eyes or moving her head, she replied,

"No Lizzie, I'm not crying. My eyes sometimes water first thing in the morning. I'm just tired."

Sometimes she kidded me, so I was unsure. It looked like crying to me. I felt desperate to go to her.

I stood up and lifted my leg over the side of my crib. I looked to see if Mummy was aware, but her eyes stayed closed. I pulled on both my arms, a quick twist and I was halfway over, terrified I was going to fall. Soon I was on the outside of my crib with both feet between the bars, standing on the mattress. I bent my knees, allowing my hands to slide down the bars and stepped down onto the carpet.

Mummy opened her eyes and lifted her head.

"So Lizzie, you've learned how to climb out of your crib have you? Clever girl."

Sniffing, she lifted me into bed and settled the pillows behind us, hugging me close. She felt warm and smelled like flowers.

"Will you tell me a story Mummy?"

She knew my favorite. It was the one about the three pigs who made different houses out of different things.

"Once upon a time," she started.

I snuggled in closer as the whole scary story unfolded. We both huffed and puffed like the wolf and laughed out loud when he couldn't blow the third brick house down. The three pigs were once again safe.

"That naughty wolf can't blow our house down either hinny," she said as she wiped her cheeks again.

But that was not the last time I saw her.

It was in the front room of our house.

I was kneeling on the floor playing with my doll, when Steven, my older brother barged in through the front door. It thudded against the wall. He ignored me and marched up to the sofa where Mummy was sleeping. His voice was loud and demanding.

"When are we going to have something to eat? I'm hungry."

She did not stir. Steven patted her shoulder.

"Mummy, wake up. I'm hungry."

Steven's voice got louder as he patted her shoulder harder. Then he put both his grubby hands on her cheeks and pressed. Her lips pushed out in an ugly shape. Still, she didn't wake up. I didn't like that her mouth squashed like that, and she didn't know. So I stood up quickly and got right up to her, rubbing her arm with my hand.

"Mummy, Mummy, can you wake up please?"

Still, she slept. No amount of Steven squashing her face or shouting in her ear moved her.

"Lizzie, go and tell Aunty Ellen that Mummy won't wake up," said Steven. "Tell her to come and help us get her up."

Immediately, I ran into the street and knocked on the door next to ours. I stood on tiptoes and looked through the letterbox. Aunty Ellen often babysat us for a few hours when Mummy went to work. I could see her coming from the kitchen towards me. She opened the door.

"What are you up to Lizzie, looking through my letterbox?"

"Steven told me to," I replied. "Mummy's asleep and she won't wake up. Can you wake her up for us?"

Aunty Ellen picked me up and swung me on her hip. She left her front door wide open and rushed into our house. She saw Mummy on the sofa and put me down.

"Beth, Beth, can you hear me?" She knelt by her and shook her shoulder. "Beth. Wake up."

But Mummy stayed asleep.

Aunty Ellen jumped up, grabbed Steven and me by the hand and practically dragged us into her house She sat us on a big chair together and told us,

"Sit there and don't move. Your mummy's sick. I need to call an ambulance and get her to the doctor. I'm running to the phone booth, and I'm shutting this front door. Do not get up. I'll be back in a minute."

She left us sitting there, feeling like something was wrong with Mummy. Steven's stillness scared me. He was too quiet. Tears were stinging my eyes. Another minute passed, and the front door opened. Mrs. Jenny from across the street came in. She smiled at us, and said,

"Your mummy's sick. Auntie Ellen's calling an ambulance to take her to the hospital. They'll make her better."

Steven started wailing, "I want my mummy," over and over.

My memory of the day starts going away and coming back with little words said, faces appearing, strangers talking to each other in hushed whispers. I hear doors banging, bells ringing and the terrible noise of a heavy vehicle driving away. I think I remember the house shaking.

A policeman in his black uniform took off his hat and talked to Aunty Ellen outside her front door which she pulled half shut. I don't know what he said. I was scared. I kept twiddling with my fingers tapping them at each other. I felt aggravated and close to tears all the time. Steven kept getting off the chair and trying to look through the window. Whenever the front door opened or voices came close, he ran back and sat down, pretending he'd not moved.

When Aunty Ellen's two children came home, we ate egg sandwiches. They asked all kinds of questions that never got an answer; just that Mummy was not well.

Later the policeman came back with Grandma. She bossed us all around and wouldn't answer our questions either. She ordered us to get in the back of the police car. She went in and out of our house a couple of times, carrying bags before she said goodbye to Aunty Ellen. The policeman drove us all back to Grandma's house. He put the bells on a couple of times to stop us crying.

I keep seeing my Mummy's face, asleep, with her lips puckered by Steven. That was the last time I saw her. Grandma says she's in the hospital having a rest for a while. I wish she were here.

CHAPTER 3: 1956 BETH: STILL AROUND.

Gen 3:16, To the woman he said, "I will make your pains in childbearing very severe; with painful labor you will give birth to children.

Pain vibrates my cheek like a cymbal clash. My arms flail instinctively, and at the same time, I hear my name.

"Elizabeth, wake up. Elizabeth Caradine, come on now, wake up. That's it. Open your eyes. C'mon girl, wake up."

Everything's blurry. I see a white hat and a stern face. The eyes are blue and hard, and a thumb stretches my eyelids. Piercing light moves from one eye to the other.

"C'mon Elizabeth, we don't have time for this. You have to wake up. Your baby's coming."

My head feels like someone stuffed it with thick candy-floss and is taking bites out of it. I can smell antiseptic and my throat feels like a gobstopper's stuck in it. I can't tell what hurts most; my head, throat, or stomach.

"You have to wake up Elizabeth. Open your eyes," says the red mouth with the gap in the front teeth. Good grief, I can see the hairs in her nose.

"My name's Beth. Call me Beth." I feel angry but sound pathetic.

She sticks something under my tongue and a wooden spatula between my teeth and holds it there. I'm still around. Can't I do anything right? Did she say the baby's coming? I blink and try to raise my head.

"Stay still 'til we get your temperature, we don't want that thermometer broken."

Tears prick my eyes and overflow. They started days ago, got interrupted and now have free reign. My face and ears are wet and I can't stop. She takes away the offensive instruments, looks at the thermometer and shakes it before stretching to put it back on the wall behind me. Her stiff apron grazes my face.

"All the crying in the world's not going to change things. You'd better help us deliver this baby alive, or you'll be in a lot of trouble. What were you thinking girl?"

Two midwives hold a knee each and lift my legs back nearly up to my ears. I feel such shame. The blonde one 'tutts.' Do they have any idea how humiliating this is? I want to scream, 'Go to hell and let me die. No one asked you witches for your help.' But I don't feel able to say a word. The pain in my stomach and abdomen increases unbearably. Someone grabs my elbow.

"Sit up and push. Keep pushing. Take a deep breath and push again."

I bear down, aware that nothing I can do now can stop this baby coming. I already had two experiences of this. I know the harder my pushes, the better it will be for me in the long run. Warm urine comes out, feces escapes. I used to apologize when I did this with the other two; like it was my fault and I was disgusting. 'To hell with it,' I think; 'to hell with them all.'

I hear screams and shouts coming from the woman next door. I feel only scorn. She's another 'soft' woman who can't bear her child without drama, bringing attention to herself.

"Shut up," I say out loud.

My Gran had been 'the woman of the street' up in South Shields. She was the one everyone ran to when a baby was birthing. She had delivered umpteen babies, and she told me about the 'soft' women who made the most noise. I vowed back then she would never call me that. She had been with me when I gave birth to Steven and then Lizzie. Her steady blue eyes never left mine. Even though the trained midwives would not let her give instructions, and believe me she tried to; her presence gave me courage. I wish she were here now. The next pains make me grit my teeth. I call out through the spittle.

"Gran, where are you when I need you?"

Another fifteen minutes go by in constant labor, pushing and panting. I see Carl's face and hear his voice tell me ‘I'll not be seeing you again, it's over.' He's married and loves his wife. I scream his name in my head, ‘Carl, you bastard. I'll chop your dick off if I ever get the chance.'

I feel the baby's head lodged in my birth canal. I push like my life depends on it, because it probably does. There's a gush of fluid and then blessed relief.

"The heads out," says the dark haired nurse. "Just a couple more pushes like the last one, and we can tell you if it's a boy or a girl."

Three hard pushes later I feel something in my vagina give. A heavy sensation of bumps and knobbles squiggle out fast and warm. My baby is born. The relief is ecstasy.

"It's a girl, Mrs. Caradine." The formality in her voice is respectful. She picks up the gray, wet baby. She holds her upside down by the ankles and slaps her bottom.

What I can't get over is the baby’s unnatural color until she breathes.

"Is she alright, I mean will she be alright?"

I can see her color warming. At first, she lets out a kitten mew-sound. Then her mouth opens wide, and she begins a loud, incessant cry that builds up. More like a cat calling a mate.

"Well, she's premature, so we'll have to take care of her, but it sounds like she's got healthy lungs." Still wailing, they weigh her in a small towel, hanging her from a hand held spring.

“Four pounds eleven ounces,” says one midwife, “A healthy weight for seven months.”

Then, she wipes the baby all over. Her crying is louder and staccato. It’s strange that a dozen babies can be crying in a ward and you recognize your own instantly.

“Have you a name for her yet?” asks the nurse.

She places the wrapped bundle in my arms. Her wrinkled brow goes smooth, and she opens her eyes for a second or two. One arm is out of the blanket, her teeny hand wavering. I put my little finger under all of hers. She grips it. Her fingernails are no bigger than a doll’s. She’s bald, but for a little down and a single blond curl on the top of her head. I smile, and something brings to mind the story of The Three Bears.

"Hello Goldilocks," I whisper.

I wonder how I could have been so depressed that I would even think of harming this tiny, beautiful baby in my arms. I hadn't been thinking. There were only feelings that overwhelmed all sensible reckoning. I had turned my anger and brokenness on myself. Stamping out my existence would have done us all a favor.

Ironically, not even an hour after realizing death eluded me; my thoughts are on naming this angelic being in my arms. I remember a name from one of those mind-numbing, happily-ever-after romance novels.

"I'm calling her Natalie," I say, touching her tiny chin with the tip of my finger. Her bottom lip trembles, a bubble pops out. She has blond eyelashes and the teeniest pink nose. I whisper to her face, "I'm going to love you, Natalie; I'll make up for this. I promise."

I'm grateful.

"Come on then little Natalie," says the nurse. She takes her. "She'll be in an incubator for a few days. We'll maybe express some milk for her after we do a few tests."

I nod as an apology falls from my lips.

"I'm sorry for what I did. Thank you for all you've done."

The Sister looks at me as the midwife takes my baby away. I think she must have been an army nurse in the war with that stony look on her face. 'She wants to save lives,' I say to myself. 'Here I am trying to end life. She must hate me.'

"Your mother's been here and will be back tomorrow. The police have also been here and will want to talk to you. What you did was reprehensible, Mrs. Caradine. Attempted suicide is one thing, but your baby? You may go to prison."

I feel shame and look down at the medical tape wrapped around the ring Lonnie gave me. My fingers twist the blanket. He told me the ring had belonged to his mother. I start to pick at the edge of the tape. It reminds me of picking at a scab. Then I look up.

"I know I'm in a pickle, but I'll make it up to her. Honestly, I will. Did my mother say anything about my other two children?"

"Yes. The policeman took her to pick them up from your neighbor's house. You're fortunate to have a mother like yours. Be glad of what you've got. Some women don't have your luck; their children get taken away for good."

I don't want to see my mother at all, but I know I'll have to. I swallow hard, it hurts. I dislike even calling her Mother; it sticks in my throat. The Ward Sister steps towards me, her hand, palm up. She wants the medical tape I'm grinding between my fingers. I drop it like a nasty bug in her hand. She throws it away.

"We'll get you back to the ward. Your throat may be sore for a while. It's the tube we put down in your stomach. Before you go to sleep tonight, we'll take urine and a blood sample, then one again in the morning. We can't give Natalie your milk if it has the chemicals from the pills you took. We do have some milk from others; we may try that if we can't use yours. Hopefully, things will look differently in the morning. You get some sleep tonight. How do you feel?"

"Okay," I say. "My headache's bad. But at least I'm alive to feel it. How long will you keep me in, do you know?"

"Maybe a week. The doctor will see you on his rounds tomorrow. You can ask him."

With that, she's gone, her heavy footsteps fading down an echoing corridor.

An attendant wheels me to the ward. I realize that I'm happy to be here. I've been so tired and distressed lately, that having people look after me feels heavenly. I'm enjoying the attention. How sad is that? You know I can't remember the last time someone cared for my needs. It's been years; back to the times we lived in the Lake District and before then, South Shields when Gran made the best breakfasts ever.

I love my Gran even though she can be a harsh woman at times; but she's always been there for me. She's not too happy with me now though, having another baby. In Gran's day, most kids were grown and working by the time they were teens. Gran said she worked from being twelve. She was always saying, 'It's a hard life if you don't weaken.'

"What is it, if you do weaken?" I asked once.

"You're dead."

The nurse and orderly help me to bed and close the curtains around me. The nurse brings me a cup of tea and a couple of biscuits. I snuggle down into the crisp white sheets. I feel safer than I've felt in years in this hospital bed. The lights grow dim. I know the nurses want to take a blood test from me, so I don't even think about sleep.

The semi-gloom takes me back to South Shields and the memory of the big bombing raid that still haunts me. I've tried in the past to pray the memory away. I've told myself over and over to forget it. But it flashes up before my eyes. It's not like any other memory I have. I can still hear every sound and smell the changes in the air. I feel the absolute terror I felt back then, and it's all happening right here, in this hospital ward.

*

Gran's calling me in from the street.

"Your supper's ready Elizabeth. Bring your bike in and wash your hands. You can set the table quick."

I like that my name is the same as Gran's, we both do. The brake makes a whooshing sound as I pull up to the front step. I know what's coming. She simultaneously slaps my hand and switches off the light.

"You shouldn't be out on your bike at this time. What have I told you about not turning on your light? The Jerries will have your guts for garters." She shakes her head and turns to go inside.

"What are we having for supper?" I offer.

"Stewed bugs and onions. Now hurry up." She walks down the hall towards the kitchen. I try a bit of humor.

"Aw, we had them last night Gran. Can we have egg and beans with fried bread?"

She calls back over her shoulder more softly, "That's Sunday breakfast girl, not your supper. Now come in."

I get off my bike and roll it into the hallway careful not to scratch our walls. It was a new one for my eleventh birthday, the highlight of my whole year. Well, not brand new. Steel was in short supply for anything but ships, bombs and Anderson shelters, but Gran got it for a good price from the woman whose house she was wallpapering. All the iron fences and gates had been taken down by the government to go to the war effort, and lots of people had given in their old bikes as well. I was so happy when Gran got it for me.

As I enter the kitchen, my four-year-old sister Maureen is already sitting at the table kicking her legs with her spoon and fork all ready to go. She grins. I don't smile back. She's been irritating the life out of me lately. Wherever I go, Gran always tells me to take her, and I feel a goading, deep resentment. I wash and dry my hands.

"Do we need a spoon Gran for any pudding tonight?" I ask.

Before she can answer, the air splits with sirens going off in that intermittent whirring noise that signals a bombing raid by the Jerries. I swallow bile.

"Please God, not again," Gran cries. She flips off the oven and the whistling kettle and grabs Maureen and my arm. We fly into the front room. She gives me three small cushions and shoves me towards the back door.

"Quick, get you and Maureen into the shelter."

I grab Maureen's hand and bolt for the back door while Gran grabs the two blankets off the back of the armchairs.

"Gran, I'm scared," I yell.

This is the second air raid this week. Tuesday night was bad enough. It happened after we had fallen asleep. Gran had dragged us from our beds, and we awoke to a nightmare of noise and thundering planes. After it was all over, I was sick as a dog all night, shivering. I hardly slept a wink even though Gran had us both in her bed. The next afternoon I heard my Gran talking to our neighbor. She didn't know I was listening through the partially open front door.

"The bloody Jerries demolished High Shields Station and South Shields Market Place. Killed about twenty people. Mr. Newsham was one of them."

"I know," Mrs. Smith replied, "I heard. The rubble is terrible. Our Fran doesn't have any water, the mains shattered. Her family were all crouched down in their shelter, they heard the whistle of bombs, and they exploded so close they thought a whole street must have blown up. They were terrified."

I couldn't forget their words. I'd replayed them over and over.

Maureen screams. I let go of her hand to open the back door and just as quickly grab it again.

"Shush Maureen. Let's go, run quick."

My heart's pounding. We race into the halting darkness of the back yard. Gran has already shut all the black-out curtains in the house. Maureen wails. Gran runs past us as though she can see in the dark. She opens the Anderson shelter door before we get to it.

"Get in quick," she hisses. She's out of breath. "I knew I should have made supper earlier. Damn the Huns."

Gran had got two men from the docks to put the shelter up. Young stocky-built men who spat on their hands before lifting the pick-axes that flew down into the ground to pull up the dirt. The shelter was sunken, so Gran had to duck her head as she stepped down to get in. We had practiced enough times what we would do, but I never thought we would have to use it for real, you know, for real bombs falling on South Shields. But we were a port and a shipbuilding town, so the Jerries targeted us.

Gran pulls us into the shelter and pushes us to the back. She closes the thin metal door.

"Stand still while I light the lamp," she says. A couple of matchsticks spill out on the floor. "Damn and blast," she hisses, striking a match, I smell sulfur. She removes the glass dome from the lamp on the shelf, and soon the wick ignites to a tall flame, which she deftly makes smaller. "This bloody door is neither use nor ornament," she grouches, hooking the catch closed.

But it was the only one made for these shelters. We were lucky to have one at all. Mrs. Smith next door got her shelter later than us, and she still doesn't have a door, so she can't even light a lamp.

The semi-dark is spooky and oppressive. I smell damp earth and paraffin which catches my throat. We still hear sirens blaring above Maureen's stifled screams. I'm shaking and whimpering. Gran places the cushions on the bench and quickly lifts Maureen onto the middle one.

"Sit down Elizabeth, she orders, "And you know not to lean back on the walls; they'll get wet in a while." she wraps a blanket around our shoulders.

At school, we had lots of bomb-drills. We'd all torn off the gas masks the first time they showed us how to place them over our faces. They stank of rubber and made our breathing labored. The teachers said we'd die if we took them off when gas bombs dropped. I hated putting on the disgusting smelling mask as I crouched under my desk, but I somehow managed to make it bearable by pretending to be somewhere else. I daydreamed of being a baby elephant in the zoo, and the corrugated rubber hose was my trunk. The desk was mummy elephant towering over and protecting me. It was how I survived the ordeal.

Gran sits down wrapping her knees with a blanket. She squeezes us together. A sickening, droning noise gets louder and louder and seems to be coming very close to the top of our shelter. I go hysterical.

"Gran, the planes are above our street. We're going to get bombed."

"Whisht child," she shouts, "You're scaring Maureen."

The deafening planes drown us out, the sirens, crazy in the background make me put my hands on my ears and screw up my eyes. It's hard to describe, but I feel myself being whisked backwards, as though being sucked up through a little door into another place. There's no more noise. A bubble surrounds me with a tiny high pitch ringing; but nothing more. I feel invisible and safe. Opening my eyes, I realize Gran's mouth is moving wordlessly. The world has slowed down. Everything looks strangely grotesque.

Suddenly a massive quaking shoots through me and I'm back in the shelter with Gran and Maureen. Gargantuan blasts and thunderous explosions vibrate the very air we breathe. Maureen's screeches pierce my ears and heart. Gran puts both her arms around our heads and bends low over us.

"Be brave my lovely's. Be brave."

I know our shelter is rusting corrugated iron and is useless as a defense in a direct hit. My fearless Gran, who can peel paint off the walls with the right look, is afraid. I see agony in her face. We are overwhelmed with terror. I close my eyes again, my hands still over my ears. I go back to my bubble. It sounds like all hell is breaking loose out there, far away, but not in here. It's like I'm in two places; the crazy place and this safe place, where I feel wrapped in a big cotton wool ball. I'm pleading with God, over and over.

"Please keep the bombs away from all the children and their mummies and grannies."

Suddenly, I'm thrown back into this metal ark again, and our whole world is exploding into smithereens around us. It goes on and on. Rapid fire, air-raid sirens, fire bells, droning planes, our bench shaking with every explosion. Or maybe it's just me shaking. I can't tell anymore. I feel a warmth flood between my legs and creep under my bottom on the cushion. Maureen is screaming,

"Make it stop Gran, make it stop."

I drift away again. I don't know how long it all goes on. Eventually, the droning fades away. I hear Gran take a deep breath and her arms loosen their grip. Gran's head is back like she's trying to see the sky through the metal. I can still hear fire engines, but the sirens are fading. Maureen lifts her head from her knees and whispers,

"Have they gone, Gran?"

Gran puts her finger to her lips and shushes us. We all listen hard for the 'all-clear' siren, frozen, our heads cocked to one side. Then it goes off like a celebration bagpipe.

"Oh thank God," Gran cries. "Thank God we're safe."
Her face crumples, she bursts into sobbing. It scares me. I've never seen my Gran cry like this. It's not what she does. I place my hand gently on the back of her head and stroke her hair.

"Don't cry Gran, don't cry. I'll make you a nice cup of sweet tea shall I?"
Maureen stares at me. Gran heaves for air. Eventually she blows her nose on a hankie from her apron. Her voice splutters in little fits and bursts.

"It's okay. I'm just so glad I have you both. C'mon, let's get out of here."

I hold out my cushion.

"Gran, I wet my knickers. I'm sorry."

"It's alright Elizabeth. I almost wet mine too." Gran looks from me to Maureen and tries to sound cheerful. "Well. I think we should all get in the tin bath tonight after supper."
Maureen giggles and Gran gathers us up and leads us out of the shelter.

The sky in the distance is lit up blood-red and orange. Something excites me beyond reason, and I start to jump up and down, waving and pointing at the sky.

"Look at the sky Gran. It's red. Redder than I've ever seen. Wahoo."
I jump all over the yard like a rabid dog; the cushion flies into the dark. Gran grabs me and holds me tight. She 'shushes' me and gets down to look into my face. I start laughing and crying.

"But just look at the sky."

"Calm down Elizabeth. It's the fires." She taps my cheek hard three or four times. "Calm down, be quiet. It will be alright."

Mrs. Smith calls over the wall from next door. I jump.

"Elizabeth? You and the children alright then?"

"Yes, Brenda. Those bloody Jerries gave us a right hammering that's for sure. You alright too?"

"I'm shaken. I don't know how much more o' this I can take. So many bombs on the town tonight. Our Jimmy went for a drink in the pub. He said he didn't think the bombers would be back so soon. God, I hope he comes home alright? I'll not rest 'til I see him."

"Dear God," Gran says, "let him be alright. I wish to God my Will was here. The whole town's alight."

"Bloody Huns could ha' waited 'til we finished eating."

"I'll not be eating now. It's going to take us awhile to settle down again."

"You're right Elizabeth. I'll see you tomorrow. I pray to God Jimmy is home soon."

Gran gets us inside and looks around for damage. Two pictures have jumped off the wall, but it all seems to be ok. I'm quiet, in my haze, drifting in my bubble again. Gran tries to sound cheerful, but her voice has little strength.

"Can you make me that cup o' tea then Elizabeth? Put two sugars in and make it strong enough that my spoon stands up in the middle. I'll get your supper warmed up."

But I can't move. My legs are like jelly. The kitchen looks foggy. The Germans may have missed our house with their bombs, but they shattered my mind and heart. Maureen is clinging to Gran's legs.

"Elizabeth, you're as white as a sheet girl. Come on with your sister and lie down on the sofa. You're shocked hinnies. I'll make us all a sweet cup o' tea."

She leads us into the sitting room and helps us out of our underwear. She settles us at either ends of the sofa and covers us both. I curl up under the blankets.

Then, I'm back in my hospital bed, and a nurse is asking me if I can sit up, she wants to take my blood. My head feels like it's in a vice and I'm stiff. I stare at her as if I don't know what she's asking of me; tears stream down my cheeks. How many more times do I have to live this memory? Will it ever go away?

CHAPTER 4: BETH: CHEEKY BUGGER BRINGS ME A PRESENT

Exodus 20:17, "You shall not covet your neighbor's house. You shall not covet your neighbor's wife, or his male or female servant, his ox or donkey, or anything that belongs to your neighbor."

I awake the next morning in the ward. A nurse takes my temperature. She tells me I'll not be feeding Natalie, as chemicals are in my breast milk.

"She's doing well in her incubator, her breathing's normal, and we managed to get a few ounces of stored breast milk into her last night and this morning. Would you like to visit her before the Doctor's Round?"

"Yes, I would, very much."

She pulls back my covers and hands me my dressing gown.

"I'll show you where she is. You won't be able to go into the premature baby unit, but you can see her through the window."

I stand up and start to put on my gown. My knees give way. I grab the bed behind me and sit down again.

"I don't feel like I can walk just yet, I'm sorry."

"No, that's ok. It's too soon. You get right back in bed. Here let me help you."

She removes my gown and helps me back under the covers.

"I'll bring you some tea as soon as it comes up to the ward. Okay?"

"Thank you. You're very kind."

I settle back down. My head feels woozy and I close my eyes and drift. A voice calls and wakes me up suddenly.

"Come on now, Elizabeth, we'll sit you in a chair while we make your bed."

It's two other nurses. I remember that no-one ever rests in a hospital. They help me out of bed and into a chair and strip my bed while chatting about the weather and what they had for supper last night. They are so young and professional. I wonder at their energy and their cheerfulness at five thirty in the morning. I wish I could be as efficient and work as fast as they do making a bed, they amaze me. Soon I'm back in bed, propped up with three comfy pillows, holding my tea cup with my pinky raised, like I'm at the Ritz.

"Heavens above. Don't get too comfortable Beth," I say to myself. "Remember you're only in here a few days, a week if you're blessed."

There is a freshness and beautiful feel to the sheets of a newly made bed that pampers the mind and softens the unease of the day. When someone else has washed and ironed them, then smoothed them over the mattress, they leave something of their touch behind that caresses a body's soul. Something about the sheets and the supporting downy pillows takes me back to a happier time; the first day I met the love of my life, Lonnie. Steven and Lizzie's dad.

I was working in the commodities store at the local American air base. It was such fun meeting all those tall, handsome airmen. They always had such big, bright smiles and such alluring accents. One reminded me of John Wayne, with his heavy drawl and witty repartee. We weren't supposed to spend time chatting with them, but try as I might to stay quiet, one or the other of them would always manage to engage me in some small talk.

There was a handsome, blond man who seemed to come in every day to buy cigarettes. I wondered if he was married, he didn't wear a ring. It was one bright, sunny Tuesday morning in May, when something very different happened. The blond man came in earlier than usual. How I loved how he spoke. It was just so respectful.

"Howdy Ma'am, how are you today?"

"Very well thank you. How are you, Sir?"

"I'm as happy as a millionaire," he said.

"Well, that must be very happy indeed." I laughed.

He grinned and his white, even teeth, mesmerized me. All the American guys had beautiful teeth. I remember only ever seeing two of the men with teeth missing, and whatever their dentist did was a miracle, because when I saw them again, everything looked good as new when they smiled.

"How can I help you, Sir?"

"I brought you something," he said as he handed me a white package.

"Me? Why? I mean, what is it?"

"Open it and see." His eyes sparkled like a clear blue lake.

My hands shook as I pulled out a slim packet.

"Oh, how wonderful," I exclaimed.

There in my hand was a pair of the prettiest silk stockings, with a darker, straight line seam, running through their length. My mouth opened to speak as I stared at his gleeful face but no sound came out. He cocked his head to one side.

"I hope you like them."

"Like them? I love them. Thank you so much. I don't know what to say."

He started to reply but was interrupted by Marilyn, my supervisor who seemed to appear out of nowhere.

"Excuse me, Sir."

We both looked at her.

"My staff are not allowed to accept gifts." She put out her hand and fully expected me to hand them over to her. I held back.

"I'll take those Elizabeth. You can collect them at the end of your shift. This will not happen again, do you understand?"

Her mouth puckered tight. She looked down at the stockings, and then her eyes swept over my breasts and neck before landing on my face again, her disdain apparent. I handed them over and spluttered something about being sorry and not knowing. Then she turned to the airman.

"I'll thank you for not bringing in gifts for my staff sir. It's against the rules."

He tipped his hat.

"I apologize, Ma'am. I'm sorry for causing you any inconvenience."

Then he left. When he opened the door, he turned and winked at me. He had not even asked me for any cigarettes. Marilyn spoke again.

"Miss Borge, please get on with your work. You can have these later. If it happens again, I'll not be so lenient next time. You understand?"

"Yes, Miss Linton. It won't happen again."

I could have argued that I didn't even know the man, but it would be hard to convince her, after all, silk stockings are more provocative than a box of chocolates.

"Good. You must watch these Americans. They are away from their homes, wives, and kids and have a reputation for gadding-about. Don't mistake all that smarmy smiling, 'Yes Ma'am, No Ma'am, to be anything other than their showmanship. They are trying to get into your knickers my dear, and don't you forget it."

I was shocked. I put my hand to my mouth as though slapped.

"Now, I'll say no more about it. We'll forget this little incident."

She stalked off. I watched her disappear into her office. She closed the door. I did notice two very straight seams drawn in eye-pencil up the back of her calves. It struck me that maybe she would prefer me not to ask for the stockings at the end of my shift.

"Huh. Fat chance of that happening," I muttered, trying to sound more confident than I felt.

At five o'clock she was still being snippety and raised her eyes to the ceiling when I asked her for them. She stared hard at me as she handed them over. I felt my face flush with embarrassment and could not get out of the place fast enough. On the work bus home though, I hugged those stockings, replaying in my mind the moment when the Airman gave them to me.

Of course, the first thing I did when I got to my lodging house was to try them on. My mother had given me a white suspender belt which I hadn't worn for a couple of years. She had once managed to get a pair of stockings for me on the black-market; which was the cubby hole under the shopping counter of Jim Grimes the grocer. I wore those beauties out, and she sent me another pair for my birthday after that, but I never managed to get any more.

The 15th of March 1949, was when the use of clothing coupons came to an end. It was in all the papers. I had stood up and shouted three 'Hip Hoorays,' and danced around the living room. I'd be able to buy all the silk stockings I wanted, or so I thought, but they remained a luxury item, too expensive for the likes of me.

The gift from the handsome stranger meant more to me than all the tea in China. I took off my jacket, skirt, shoes and long black socks, and lifted my white satin underskirt to put on the suspender belt. I never could easily fasten it at the back, so I twirled it around to the front, and back again. I fed the satin straps down through my knickers and pulled them into place at the front and back of my thighs. I giggled as I remembered the first time I ever wore stockings. My mother had failed to instruct me on the finer points, like to wear the belt under my knickers, and not over the top. When I went to the loo, I soon found out why. What a carry-on. It was hilarious.

She did teach me one good thing though, and that was always to wear cotton gloves when handling silk stockings. I opened a drawer and found my pale blue gloves and put them on. I took the delicate stockings out of their packet as carefully as a bomb disposal expert would extract a fuse and detonator. There is something about owning new silk that raises the commoner from downstairs to upstairs in a moment. Life takes on a finer poignancy of deliciousness.

As I sat on the bed, smiling like a Cheshire cat, I luxuriated in the ritual of placing my thumbs into the tops and gently willing my fingers to gather up the silk, all the way to the toes. If it took me an hour to guide each stocking over my feet, then so be it. There was no way I was going to ladder this priceless gift that even a hangnail could destroy in a second.

Fastening the top band of stocking into the tiny metal suspenders became a challenge; my gloves got caught in them. So off came my gloves, I took a deep breath and gently eased the firm, minute button behind each stocking top. I was extra careful as I placed the metal slide on the outside of the stocking over each button, slipping the button to the tapered end of the fastener to keep everything in place. Such an intelligent invention and so simple in design; I marveled at how something so tiny could be so efficient at its job.

I stood up and savored the beautiful feel of silk on my legs, ignoring the uncomfortable tightness where the suspender belt dug into my waist. Sometimes beauty hurts. I took the mirror off the wall and lowered it to the floor, twisting this way and that, to see if the back seams were straight. One was, but the other was as crooked as a dog's hind leg. I would need more practice, for sure. I became aware that even the tiniest amount of hairs on my legs affected how they felt and moved. I made a note to shave my legs before I wore them again.

I owned one pair of high-heel shoes. It had been love at first sight on my part. They positively called out to me from the store window and were my size. I responded immediately by placing them on hold with a deposit. They lost their window view and were back in the shoe box faster than I could say 'I'll see you in a week.' I went back to the store regularly to put more money on them. Four weeks later, they were mine. Black, shiny patent leather, with a pointed toe, showed off three swirling leaves in plum, green and tan on the front. They were my most prized possession.

I felt like a million dollars as I slipped them on my silk-wrapped feet and strutted around in only my slip. I became a movie star, with an entourage of admirers. The thrill became sensual. I kept putting the mirror against furniture at different heights; posing and pouting; holding up my hair, showing off my legs.

"Elizabeth, you're beautiful," I told my reflection.

Then I stretched out on the bed, arms above my head on the pillow, floating on a sea of pleasure and joy. I felt a warm and sudden urge to pretend that the airman was stroking my ankle. Then his hand stroked higher and higher up my leg. I pushed his hand away, and he stopped for a moment before continuing to stroke my inner thigh. I could hear my heartbeat and a gentle thrumming sound in my ears. I heard Miss Linton's voice. 'He is only trying to get into your knickers.'

Wow. What a powerful thought that was.

Sadly, it still is.

When my landlady called upstairs to tell me supper was ready, I'd put everything away and was dressed casually in my comfortable loose dress and slippers. I'd also checked the bus timetable for Saturday. There was a bus that would get me to the base by twenty-five minutes past seven in the evening, and one that would get me back by five minutes after midnight.

After supper, I turned down an invitation to stay in the sitting room and listen to the radio with the other guest, an older woman. All I wanted to do was to be alone in my daydream with my American admirer. I didn't even know his name.

The next day was cloudy, but the sun forced a smile through the clouds at irregular intervals. I felt perky and had a sturdy blue umbrella, ready for whatever the heavens could throw at me. I don't think I'd ever looked forward to going to work as much as I did that morning. Diane and Judy started work earlier than I did as I never saw them at the bus-stop that, or any other morning. I noticed a few cheerful faces on the bus. Maybe my bright mood caused me to look more carefully at those people around me instead of just staring out of the window as I usually did. At work, even Marilyn's snootiness washed over me like water off a duck's back. Each time the door opened in the store, I glanced to see if it was him. I didn't even care that Marilyn might be close by if he did come in. I felt as though that day, all bets were off.

He never came. As the day evolved, determined my happiness would not dissolve, I smiled at every customer, wished them a great day as they left, even hummed a little tune. Marilyn remarked how chirpy I seemed and could she see a bit more of that from me, on a daily basis if you please.

As I inspected the shelves looking for gaps in the display of tins, I didn't feel my usual annoyance at those empty spaces. That day the boxes seemed lighter as I happily breezed through each hour as though I was on ice skates. I took swift, secretive glances at the door but he never came. Disappointed beyond measure, I still managed to put extra cheer in my voice as I left.

"Have a fun evening Miss Linton. I'll see you in the morning."

As I walked to the bus, I saw him there, looking towards me. I wanted to leap. He smiled, and I could not stop myself from positively beaming. He had not forgotten me after all.

"Hi, lady. How're you doing this evening? I don't believe we know each other's names."

He held out his hand to shake mine. Suddenly shyness caused my face to blush.

"I'm Lonnie Caradine. Pleased to meet you."

'Wow. What a great name,' I thought.

"I'm Elizabeth Borge. I'm pleased to meet you again." I shook his hand. Lonnie held mine for just a second longer than I was comfortable with, I let go first and spoke.

"It seemed strange yesterday that I should accept a gift from a stranger. My supervisor didn't give me a minute to ask your name."

"Yeah, I'm sorry about that. I didn't mean to get you in trouble or nothing."

"It's fine. Just don't do it again." I laughed. "Thank you so much for your kind present. I was a bit taken aback. I mean, I don't even know you."

"Well, I come by the store every day. I'd seen you working there, and it's only natural that a gal as pretty as you would attract attention. I wanted to speak to you every time I came in. I just couldn't find the right words. I told myself you probably have a string of guys lining up to ask you for a date. Are you going out with anyone special?"

I smiled and shook my head.

"Not right now. I did think that you are probably married yourself. Do you have someone back in America?"

He shook his head.

"No-one I'm dying to get back to anyway."

"What does that mean?"

"I had a girl, but then she sent me a ‘Dear John' letter."

"John? You said your name is Lonnie?"

He laughed.

"It is Ma'am. I just meant, she wrote and told me she met someone else."

He stopped grinning, looked down and shook his head. I spoke quietly.

"I'm sorry. I didn't mean to pry."

"Oh no Ma'am, you ain't prying'. It happens all the time. It's hard for the gals back home to keep waiting, especially for two years."

His face brightened again.

"Enough of that anyway. Life's too short to have regrets. There's a dance-band on at the base this Saturday night. I'd be mighty proud if you'd accompany me, Ma'am."

He took off his hat, and for a split second, I saw a glint, a mischievous look in his eyes, like he was grinning in his soul. Tingles rose up in my hair and neck. I blushed.

"Oh. Um, I don't know. I'm not sure. My landlady has rules about not coming in late. I would have to be back for ten thirty or so, and I don't know the bus times. But I could find out and let you know tomorrow."

"Ten-thirty? The dance is just starting to get going by then. We got a band, and they do all the swing numbers. Could you ask your landlady for a key maybe? That way, if you are real quiet, she won't know what time you get back."

Astounded, I retorted, "Cheeky Bugger."

He just grinned wider.

Just then the bus driver started up the engine.

"My bus is leaving. I'll let you know tomorrow."

I fled. My heartbeat felt like a drum in my chest. I felt scared. Not like afraid-scared. More like excited-scared. Like I was just about to get on one of those big fair rides at Blackpool or Skegness. I heard him call to me,

"You just let me know. See you tomorrow Ma'am."

His eyes followed me as I walked to my seat. I sat by the window and waved as the bus pulled away. Two blond women in front of me looked at each other, and one whispered something. They giggled. Then one of them turned to me and spoke.

"Are you going to the dance on Saturday?"

"I, er, don't know. I'm thinking about it. Why? Are you going?"

"We both are," she grinned.

Then her friend turned around to speak.

"We never miss. It's the most fun we've ever had. That your boyfriend then?"

"No, not exactly. We just met. He's asked me to the dance. I'll need to see if my landlady will give me a key. She's strict about coming in no later than ten thirty."

They exchanged a look.

"Bugger that," said the other. "We never get in before early morning. Those guys are just warming up at ten thirty."

I smiled and shifted in my seat. Something about the conversation was making me uncomfortable. I felt in ignorance somehow.

"Yes. Lonnie said the same thing," I faltered.

The first woman who spoke must have sensed my embarrassment. She smiled and put out her right hand.

"I'm Diane. This is my friend, Judy. What's your name?"

"Elizabeth. Pleased to meet you both. Where are you staying?"

"We've got a flat above Durden's, the haberdasher on Grant Street. Where do you live?"

"On Linfield Road. Do you know where that is?"

"You're not too far from us. It's about a fifteen-minute walk, that's all."

"Lucky you," I said. "I can't afford to rent. Not on my wages. Having a landlady is as bad as living with my mother."

"Yes, who needs that?" Judy retorted.

We chatted all the way to town. They worked in the canteen and said they loved it as they got to see their boyfriends every day. We said goodbye as we got off the bus and went our separate ways. They seemed very sure of themselves, but giddy too. Like they were trying to be all grown up but were like excited teenagers at the same time. I liked them both. They were from the north like me and had come south seeking work at the base. They seemed to know what they wanted.

"See you Saturday we hope," Diane called as we parted.

"Yes, I hope so," I replied.

I watched them link arms as they walked around the corner. I suddenly felt very lonely. I meandered to my lodgings feeling slightly envious.

I'd left my best friend behind when I left Gran's cottage in the Lake District for the first time. We'd caught up again when I went back, and we met regularly, but then I moved down South. I felt homesick. Maybe I would visit Gran in the summer for a few days, try to catch up with Olive again, see if she got engaged to William yet.

I felt sad until I got into my room again, then I remembered the stockings and opened the drawer, just to make sure they were still there. My heart skipped a beat, and I ran downstairs to ask Mrs. Maxwell about having a key. She wasn't keen at first, but I said I'd get home by midnight and no later.

"I don't allow visitors in your room, Miss Borge. So as long as you understand the rules of the house and abide by them, it should be ok. And don't be bringing in any of those Americans now. My husband and I are very strict about the people we allow in our home, and those Yanks are not welcome. Not that we have anything against them. It's just they've got very free ways about them if you know what I mean? We aren't into all that liberalism. It spells trouble."

I don't know which films they'd been watching, but I had no clue what she meant. Sure, I'd heard prejudice and sweeping statements about the American soldiers over the last few years. Everyone called them 'Yanks,' whether they were from the North or the South. I had no idea why, but I thought it might be because 'Yank' rhymed with 'Wank.'

All the British women were attracted to the clean-cut men in American uniforms. Who could blame them? Most of them were taller than our menfolk, and we all loved to hear them talk. They appeared confident and were very friendly. They brought to mind some of those handsome movie stars.

British men were jealous. Quite a few fist fights broke out on weekends in the town's bars. Our lads usually started arguments, then, controversial remarks from the Yanks, who said they won the war for us, would cause a severe reaction from our men.

"You won the war for us? You're living in an 'ollywood picture mate. It's only when the Japs zapped your fleet, which by the way was taking a long 'oliday in Pearl 'arbor, instead of being out there with the rest of the bloody world's navy, that you sprang into action mate."

That would start an immediate fight.

Or, some of our lads dared to accuse Americans of earlier years of hob-knobbing with the Germans. Then the Americans would bring up the sensitive subject of our 'namby-pamby' King Edward who preferred getting a leg over an American divorcee, to doing his job, and how he and Mrs. Simpson did their fair share of hob-knobbing with the Germans.

That's when fists would fly, bottles and chairs got smashed, and all hell broke loose until the police and the military PM's showed up and arrested everyone. Our lads usually managed to run off, or get bailed out the next day. I never knew what happened to the Americans. But the fights did nothing for their reputation with the local community; hence my landlady's hesitance.

"Mrs. Maxwell," I said in my best Queen's English. "I would never invite anyone into your home; you needn't worry about that. I'll get the last bus home and be in by 11:45 to midnight at the latest."

"Well alright then. We'll give it a try. But if you come in after midnight and we get wakened up, I know my husband will not be happy. If he's not happy, believe me, dear girl, I'll not be happy either. I have to live with him."

She took a key from somewhere in the back kitchen and dangled it like a carrot.

"It's on a key-ring, so don't lose it. Spare keys are precious. Now mind what I said," she added, as she put the key into my waiting open hand.

"Thank you so much, Mrs. Maxwell. I promise I'll take good care of it."

I was so excited; I couldn't eat my supper that night. I excused myself early and ran upstairs to grab the bathroom all to myself. I luxuriated in bathing, washing my hair, shaving my legs and under my arms. There was a sudden rapping on the door to let me know others were anxious to share the facilities. In my bedroom, I plucked my eyebrows, manicured my toes and fingers and put a few curlers in my hair before retiring. I had to take them out in the middle of the night, the pain was too excruciating, like sleeping on cacti.

The next day at work I kept tweaking my hair and refreshing my lipstick. In the afternoon, I had just got back to my cash-till when Lonnie walked through the door. He winked at me and asked for his usual brand of cigarettes so Marilyn could hear. Then as I opened the cash drawer, he whispered, "I'll see you later on, at the bus-stop."

"Thank you, Ma'am," he called casually over his shoulder as he walked away.

"Thank you, have a great day," was my cheery response.

I heard Marilyn's steady tap of shoes approaching. I bent down under the till pretending to tidy a shelf. The shoes stopped to my left. Taking a deep breath, I straightened and there she stood, with her narrowed eyes and her unsmiling, red lipstick mouth. She cocked her head to one side and spoke.

"You aren't fooling anyone, my dear. Neither's your admirer. I've seen it all before. It will end in tears; you mark my words. And it won't be him doing the crying."

Then she lifted her nose up as she turned away and disappeared to the other side of the store. I never heard another peep out of her all day.

I did think about what she said though. I wondered if she had been let down herself through dating one of the Americans. I also wondered about some of my disquieting thoughts about Lonnie. Just as Mrs. Maxwell said last night about their 'free ways,' I had to admit that Lonnie did appear very sure of himself. He'd not even asked my name before he decided it was okay to bring me a gift. And not just any gift either, if I was honest with myself, it was kind of intimate. He did seem to be what my Gran would call 'a cheeky bugger,' I'd even said it to him myself. So it's not as though I dismissed Marilyn's words completely. They did float around all that afternoon as I stacked shelves and counted inventory, but like the commodities I was handling, I shelved my misgivings to the lower shelves. Only the prominent, exciting sale products were at eye-level and available for real consideration.

*

Lonnie was at the bus-stop waiting for me. My goodness, it cheered me up to see him.

"Well howdy, Miss Elizabeth. You're looking mighty pretty again today."

"Thank you, kind sir. How are you, Lonnie?"

"On top of the world. How d'ya pronounce my name again?"

"Lonnie, that's right isn't it?"

"I like the way you say it." He mimicked me, "Lonnie."

"How do you say it?" I asked him.

His dialect softened and extended the ‘o,' so it sounded more like ‘Larnie.' We both laughed.

"I was wondering," he paused, "did you get a chance to think about the dance on Saturday? Will you be coming?"

"I most certainly will. I wouldn't miss it for the world."

"Well, that makes me very happy Miss Elizabeth, Ma'am. Does anyone ever shorten your name? Or do you prefer your full name?"

"Well, everyone calls me Elizabeth, like my Gran, she's Elizabeth too."

"Like Princess Elizabeth," he said.

Lonnie put out his right hand. I thought he wanted to shake mine again. Instead of the formal approach, he lifted my fingers gently and kissed them. This time my blush was hot. I withdrew my hand and placed it flat on my chest, shocked. Well, not just shocked, pleased, and shocked. No-one had ever kissed my hand like that.

"Mr. C- Caradine. Er L- Lonnie I mean."

"Miss Elizabeth. I didn't mean to embarrass you. I apologize, that was not my intent at all."

"No, I'm not embarrassed. Well, just a little. Look, everyone on the bus is staring at us."

"Well. I like that about you, Ma'am. I'm glad you're shy. That's a good thing to be, right?"

I looked over at the bus. Judy and Diane were beaming their smiles at me through the window. Lonnie spoke again.

"Well tell me, Ma'am. How'd you get on with your landlady yesterday? Did she give you a key?"

"Oh my goodness Lonnie, is there no end to your cheekiness? That's for me to know." I told him. "I will be on the last bus back; that I do know."

Lonnie gave me his full-on, handsome grin. My irritation melted like snowflakes on water as he spoke.

"Great. So be at the gate at seven-thirty Saturday night. I'll meet you. We'll have a blast. D'ya like to dance?"

"I love dancing. I may need time to warm up though. I know you Americans do all that swing dance routine. It's been a while since I practiced."

"I'll sure be happy to teach you Miss Elizabeth. Someone told me, I got some twinkle toes and a good lead."

"I can't wait," I replied.

"I know you're gonna love it. After this Saturday, there ain't no other place you'll wanna be on any Saturday night in the future."

Inside my head, another alarm bell tinkled. I switched it off, but it kept bothering me.

"Goodbye Lonnie," I replied and turned to walk to the bus. In my head, I was not quite at peace with myself.

I purposely sat further back on the bus from Judy and Diane, although I did greet them as I passed. I didn't want to discuss Lonnie with them, nor whether or not I would be at the dance. I needed to think. As I rode the bus back to town, I contemplated how cocky Lonnie was. I'd never met anyone like him before. Try as I might I couldn't imagine me introducing him to my family, who seemed so far removed from this man's view of the world. Gran would say, 'He's too big for his boots that one,' and she'd be right.

I thought about his words, 'Someone told me, I got some twinkle toes and a good lead?'

I mean, who brags like that? Who's this someone he's been dancing with anyway? Is she his girl back home, or maybe someone he's recently dated? I wasn't interested in what he thought about himself. Gran would say, 'Let someone else praise you, not yourself.' Nor did I care what he said other women thought about him.

I don't know why I started feeling negatively towards Lonnie; maybe I was getting cold feet. Anyway, it was only one date. I reasoned that if I didn't enjoy myself with him, I could end it right then. As the bus pulled away, I glanced out of the window. Lonnie was still there. He waved as I left.

*

Coming back to the reality of my whereabouts in the hospital, and taking one last sip of tea, I notice my hands shaking.

"Bloody cheeky bugger," I whisper to myself as I shut my eyes.

CHAPTER 5: LIZZIE: A TASTE OF THE GOOD LIFE.

Deuteronomy 10:18, He defends the cause of the fatherless and the widow, and loves the foreigner residing among you, giving them food and clothing.

I open my eyes, and for a little moment, I wonder where I am. The room looks unrecognizable. I feel warm and dreamy and a little excited. There's a crack in the ceiling that looks like my mummy in a tight dress, all curvy.

"This is Grandma's house."

My whisper reminds me that Steven and I are head to toe in one of the beds upstairs. Sunlight's dancing through orange and brown curtains. The room looks as happy as I feel. So many birds sing outside. There's a dressing table that looks almost like the one we have in our bedroom at home, except it has two drawers either side of the arch where mummy's feet go, and its mirror has no crack in it. I like the round shapes of the white handles; lines explode from the center like stars. They are the same color as Grandma's brooch, which she says is from an elephant's tusk.

I love drawers. They hold lots of interesting objects. I slide quietly out of bed and tiptoe across the rugs to the dressing table and sit on the small round stool, looking at myself in the mirror. My hair sticks up everywhere. I giggle and start to pull on a drawer. Inside I see lots of light, wispy, bright colors; they're scarves.

The bedroom door handle turns, and I quickly shut the drawer. It's Grandma standing there. She looks surprised to see me sitting at the dressing table and smiles. I grin back. She looks over at the bed. Steven is still asleep. She puts a finger up to her mouth for me to stay quiet and tiptoes into the room, picks up my slippers and gently lifts me off the stool to leave. We close the door softly behind us.

"Now hold the handrail and my hand," she whispers.

I love visiting my Grandma; she's always giving me attention and lots of smiles. I feel excited that I stayed overnight in her house. It's a new adventure, and right now we are on our own, without Steven.

As I hold onto the smooth wood with one hand and step carefully down large steps onto the dark red carpet, I notice how far away the shiny red hallway floor is below. These stairs go much higher than ours at home. Above the front door, I'm thrilled to see a semi-circle of blue sky and fluffy clouds; the window is the same arched shape as the dressing table mirror I just looked in.

"I can see rooftops Grandma, look." I let go and point.

She puts her finger to her lips and whispers again.

"Yes Lizzie, watch where you put your feet on these stairs, we don't want you to fall."

I take another step down, then, look at the light shining into Grandma's hallway through my most favorite glass door in the whole world. The upper half of the vestibule door is not clear glass like the other windows. It looks frosty and has clear, 'pretend' raindrops bobbled all over its surface, making the light dance and shine like the sun on wet leaves. It makes me feel glad inside. The red hallway floor looks stunning with the shafts and speckles of light on it. I know I'll return later and sit on my favorite step, halfway up, to enjoy the experience of just sitting and looking at everything in the hallway. Above the vestibule door is another clear glass and above that, a narrow rectangle window of red glass. Down each side of the door frame is yellow glass. Steven and I sometimes press our face to the sunny color and stare through it for ages.

I never sit on our stairs at home because all I can see is a tall narrow wall, which is not very exciting. No pictures or mirrors, not like here. This house is so much bigger than ours too. Everything looks like wide open space to me.

When my feet feel the cool hallway floor, Grandma tells me to sit on the bottom stair so she can put on my slippers. I see Grandpa and

Grandma's coats on the hooks on the hallstand. There are two umbrellas either side of the middle drawer; one black and large, the other, blue and smaller. They stand in the two square tin trays at the bottom of the stand. On each hook above the umbrellas is a coat. One is mine, and one belongs to Steven. Everything's in two's, in their place. We don't have a coat-stand or a hallway in our house. We have a dark cubbyhole under the stairs that is covered over with a blue curtain. It's scary. Once, mummy screamed, got a shoe and started hitting the wall and floor with it, still screaming. She killed the spider that was hiding under her coat. I never went near the blue curtain after that and Mummy always shook out our things before we put them on, just in case.

I love looking at everything in this house; it's so different and has such interesting patterns everywhere. The doors all have four panels in them with beautiful curved edges all around. I can reach the lower panels and like to run my finger down the soft grooves around each. The centers are flat and smooth with beautiful lines flowing close to each other, but never touching. Grandma told me the lines are called wood-grain lines. One day I want to be so good at drawing lines that mine never collide either.

I jump up with my slippers on and ask Grandma in a slightly louder whisper if I can open the dining room door. I always ask her permission to do things because she's stern sometimes. We have to go through the dining room to get to the stove-kitchen, and it is one of my greatest pleasures to open every door myself. This morning I can see my face in the shiny black knob on the hallway side of the dining room door. I giggle.

"Grandma, look at my nose, it looks wide. I look funny."

She looks down and laughs.

"Yes, your cheeks are puffed out like a hamster."

"Why is this knob so cold Grandma?"

"It's made of porcelain, which comes from the ground."

"Are all the knobs made of porcelain?"

"Yes, the round ones are anyway. Some are white, and some are black."

I push open the door into their large dining room. It's a lot dimmer in here, although there is a window surrounded by dark green pattern curtains. A shaft of light slants down onto the hearth, and I see dust motes dancing in it. The fireplace is tall and shiny black.

"Is the fireplace porcelain?" I ask.

"No, that's marble. It comes from the ground too."

There's a handsome, long table in the middle of the room with the most unusual and pretty looking chairs I've ever seen.

"Are these your new chairs Grandma? I like these." I run over to them.

"Yes, I told you last night they are new when you first asked me."

Each chair has a lovely square, bright green, velvet seat surrounded by rounded, shiny metal studs. I love the back of the chairs. Each has two long, straight back panels of the same bright green velvet set inside rectangular panels of wood. On the top of each chair-back, on each corner sits a tiny, carved pointed tower. I can't help touching them. I run my hands on the velvet seat, magically, lighter lines appear.

"Look, Grandma, I can draw pictures on your chair."

"Well just do not draw pictures on those chairs when Grandpa is around, or he'll chop your fingers off."

My grandpa chases chickens with an axe in their backyard. I can't bear to watch; he scares me. Grandma says he chops off a chicken's head to kill it so they can cook it for supper. When I run away, Grandma roars laughing.

I take my fingers off the chair and skip to the kitchen door. There is a round, black, shiny knob but it does not turn to open the door. Instead, I have to lift up a small metal bar that latches into a 'v' shape piece on the surround. The door is painted green to match the chair seats. I love this fascinating and fun house with its nine rooms; it's front and back gardens and backyard. So many doors, knobs that turn, latches that lift, bolts that slide, keys that go into locks and hooks that slip down into little circles. I'm so excited to be here.

As I open the green door, I feel a warm flow of bread scented air waft around my face. It smells delicious. The facing wall has a large rectangular space cut out of it where a fireplace used to be. Inside, there's a cream colored stove with four short legs and curved feet, standing on a stone ledge; a round, black chimney disappears into the ceiling. The four windows of the stove glow red-hot with all the coke packed in there. There are tins covered with white cloths all around the stove on ledges and two short stools. My grandma once told me she would let the bread rise in tins around the stove before she put them in the oven and here they are.

"Is that your bread?" I ask.

"Clever girl Lizzie," she says. "You remembered what I told you. Yes, I'm baking today."

I go to our favorite chair, right next to the warm stove. It's a big chair with a back that Grandma can move forward or back. It has broad, flat, wooden arm rests either side. Its seat is of soft, crackled leather. I scoot all the way to the back and rest my head on the padded backrest with my feet just over the edge of the seat. I feel happy.

Then we hear dull thuds above our heads all the way across the ceiling.

"Oh, Oh, Steven just got up," says Grandma.

Then the noises come down in two's as Steven jumps onto each stair. The dining room door opens, we hear footsteps coming nearer, and the latch picks up on the other side of the green door. Steven walks into the kitchen and has a scowl on his face.

"Well good morning young man," says Gran. "Close the door please."

"Where's Mummy?" Steven mumbles with his head down. His eyes are looking up at Grandma. "Is she coming home today?"

"Not today poppet. Your mummy's in the hospital. She's poorly. I'm going to see her today though, and I'll find out when she's coming home."

Steven's face crumples, and he puts his fists up to his eyes and starts bawling.

"I want my Mummy," he repeats over and over.

"Oh dear, someone got up the wrong side of the bed this morning," says Grandma.

She goes to him, pulls his arm and takes him to the table and chairs under the window in the corner. She kisses him on the top of his head.

“Your mummy will be home soon when she feels better. Come on now sit on this chair, and I'll get you some breakfast."

She lifts him onto the chair and then goes through the open doorway of the back kitchen where the electric stove, food cupboards, and sink are.

I watch as Steven calms down, rubs his eyes and then put his fists on his cheeks, his elbows on the table. He stares ahead. I get off my comfy chair and go and sit near him on one of the kitchen chairs nearest the door. I don't speak, but still looking at Steven, I too put my fists on my cheeks and rest my arms on the table. Eventually, Steven looks at me and puts both of his little fingers up into his nose. I do the same. I giggle as he pushes his nostrils up like a pig. Steven then pulls down on his cheeks just below his eyes with two more fingers. I can see the red rim inside his lower eyelids. He sticks out his tongue as far as he can.

I laugh out loud.

"You look ugly Steven, like a pig." I squeal.

I try to do it too. Steven laughs and tells me,

"You can't do it properly."

"I can do it better than you."

"No you can't, you're a sissy girl. You can't do anything I can."

"Well, you're a goofy boy made of puppy dogs' tails."

Steven lashes out and hits me on my arm. I scream out.

"Grandma, Steven hit me."

Grandma flies into the front kitchen just as the green kitchen door opens to my right and Grandpa Krupp strides into the room. He has a huge presence.

"Stop all this noise," he bellows with his distinctive accent. "Mama is still asleep. Be quiet."

There is absolute silence; his whole being invokes obedience. It's not that he is very tall, although he is wide; he has the largest head and face. His eyebrows are bushy and make him look fierce when he glowers. He has a big forehead with bony curves in his eyebrows.

There's always a blue-grey shadow over his entire chin, spreading down into his neck, and up the sides of his face. He has large ears. I have never seen such big ears. And that voice. It seems to come up from his feet in his big brown, shiny shoes. He almost makes the windows rattle. Even Grandma is quiet and retreats into the back kitchen to carry on making our breakfast. He follows her in there, they say good morning to each other, and we hear them kiss. Steven wipes his mouth as though she has kissed him.

"Yuck."

I bite my upper and lower lips together, so I don't laugh. I shrug my shoulders as if to say, what happens now? Steven sticks his tongue out towards the back kitchen as if he is mocking Grandpa like Mummy often does.

I try to understand how I'm supposed to feel about Grandpa and Grandma. He can be scary, yes, and Grandma can be strict, but it does not stop me loving being here, and sometimes Grandpa can be unexpectedly funny. He gets his 'w's and 'v's back-to-front, and I enjoy listening to his accent. In the car, he always gets us to sing and often tries to teach us to count in German. I can remember up to five so far. He's happy to tell us a story or two and kids us about things. When he smiles, his eyes become kind, and I love to see the two gold teeth he has in his mouth. Grandma has a gold tooth too. I don't know anyone else with a gold tooth. They are special people I think.

When I found out that Grandma is my mummy's mother, I thought it was a joke. I love Mummy so much; I do not understand how she could not love hers as much. I can tell by her voice that Mummy is sometimes angry with her. Sometimes she completely ignores her, and she always takes a deep breath in and out after we leave Grandma's house. I know it means something; I'm just not sure what. When Grandpa is around, she always seems to tell us off for play fighting with our plastic swords or tells us to be quiet and not make noise. She scowls behind his back or pulls out her tongue at him when he is not looking. Our visits during the day always end up with Grandpa driving us home after supper and Mummy never speaking to him at all.

As we would leave, Grandma would always kiss us goodbye, and I would see Mummy wipe her cheek like she was wiping off Grandma's kiss. No-one ever wiped away my kisses, so I never did it either. Steven always swiped grandma's kisses away. She caught him once and said,

"What's the matter, you don't like my kisses?"

He just looked down at the floor, and his cheeks went red. He shook his head and then nodded it. I just kept quiet. Later Steven told me he did not like her kisses because they felt wet. He was wiping the wet off. Neither of us asked Mummy why she wiped her kisses away, but I always wondered.

I once asked Mummy if Grandpa Krupp is her daddy. I won't ever do that again. She ranted about her daddy having more goodness in his little finger than Grandpa has in his whole body.

"Where is your daddy these days Mummy?" I dared to ask.

"He died Lizzie. I'll tell you when you get older. Now stop asking questions."

My daddy is never around, neither is Mummy's. Grandpa makes me feel that men can sometimes be bossy, grumpy people, who like it when we do what they say. But at other times he can be fun.

Grandpa Krupp comes into the front kitchen with two plates. Before he puts them down on the table in front of us, his voice booms,

"Is everybody happy?"

Steven and I know how this goes, so we say, "Yes."

"I can't hear you. Is everybody happy?"

"YES," we shout as loud as our voices will let us. We start to feel joyful. We know he's trying to be jolly.

"Good, then ve can all have breakfast. Eat up. No vaste, lick your plates then ve don't have to vash them. Just put them right back in the cupboard."

We laugh. We think Grandpa's kidding us. We don't know he'll fetch out a stool for us to stand on after breakfast and tell us to put our licked-clean plates in the cupboard while he roars laughing. Sometimes grown-ups are puzzling.

Grandpa beams. His gold teeth glint at us, and I hope we can stay here forever. It's such fun.

CHAPTER 6: BETH: THE FIRST DAY OF THE REST OF MY LIFE.

Genesis 1:5, God called the light "day," and the darkness he called "night." And there was evening, and there was morning—the first day.

Lunch at the hospital is a strange affair. Nurses carry in four fold up tables and assemble them down the center of the ward between all our beds. The mothers who have been here a couple of days help with the tablecloths and silverware. Everyone's chatting and happy. A nurse asks everyone to settle into chairs at the tables. I stir but don't feel hungry. A nurse calls out to me,

"We want you to stay in bed today for lunch. You can get up and sit in a chair at visiting-time this afternoon if you're feeling up to it."

She brings me a plateful of food on a tray, then returns with a cup of tea. I try to protest.

"I'm not very hungry. I don't want anything, thank you."

"I want you to try to eat a little," she insists, "you're weak and need to build up strength. You missed breakfast, and we did not wake you. So just try a few forkfuls, okay?"

I feel irritated and imagine shouting, 'How old am I? Two? I'm a grown woman. If I don't want to eat, I won't.' Instead I say,

"Okay, I'll try some."

I'm pathetic, unable to stand up for myself.

I pick at the food, and as I sip tea, I remember more about my time with Lonnie. I even remember my thoughts the day I was supposed to meet him for the dance.

I'd been anxious about my first date with him to the point where I was obsessing about how I would look and how on earth I would be able to get ready in time. I wanted to have all my ducks in a row.

I would be catching the five minutes past seven, bus to the Airbase, which meant I only had one and a half hours to get ready. For me, it was impossible. I wanted to wash my hair, wave it, take a bath, pluck my eyebrows and shave my legs again. Not to mention extra time for filing and polishing my fingernails.

My dress, a beautiful emerald green satin with embossed flowers, needed to hang in steam so the creases would drop out and refresh it. I needed to run my bath well before time. The only way I could get all this accomplished was if I took time off work in the afternoon. Another couple of hours would be enough. It was sunny so I could sit in the back garden, let the sun dry my hair and do my nail polish at the same time.

Marilyn was furious, but I didn't care. At two o'clock I told her my head throbbed so much I had thrown up and needed to go. I got on the quarter-past-two bus. I felt guilty for about a minute but then Diane and Judy got on the same bus. They just laughed when I told them what I'd done.

"A girl's gotta do what a girl's gotta do," Judy said.

Stolen hours are so satisfying, and getting ready held as much excitement as the actual date. I loved every minute of it. The landlady seemed a little perturbed that I took over the bathroom all afternoon, but by the time other people in the house needed it, I had left to get on the number three bus that stopped outside the gates of the Airbase. Diane and Judy told me they only arrive at the base by nine o'clock on a Saturday night because before then it's quiet. I didn't care, and I found out later that Lonnie had planned it that way so we could talk and he could show me some dances before it got crazy.

I remembered his prophetic words about me not wanting to be at any other place, on any Saturday night in the future. He was right. We had a fantastic evening.

My dress was a hit. It's pinched waist and flared skirt was the latest fashion, and Lonnie told me I looked gorgeous. He wore some snazzy light slacks with perfectly pressed seams and a shirt with some green splashes of color on it. He wore his shirt over his trousers, which was new to me. His shirt had a straight hem, not a shirt-tail curved hem like British shirts. He looked adorable. And of course, he got to see me in my new silk stockings. The back-seam was perfectly straight from the center of my high heels, all the way to the top.

I sipped on martinis and danced until I was dizzy. Lonnie twirled me all over that dance-floor. He showed me some intricate moves, and before the end of the night, we danced as though we were meant to be together. Swing dancing was the most fun I'd *ever* had. He could pick me up like I was an extension of him, literally whisking me off my feet and landing me right back down on terra firma without batting an eye. It was wonderful. No one had ever made me feel like he did. Any misgivings I may have had about his bragging, melted away like snow on water. He knew his dance steps like a pro. One of Lonnie's friends said,

"You're a great dancer Ma'am. How d'ya manage to dance in those high-heels?"

Before I could reply, Lonnie answered for me. He smirked and said,

"It's called class, something you know nothing about." I laughed.

"Why thank you, but next time I'm getting into a lower pair of heels. I'm afraid I might stick someone."

Lonnie grinned, "Next time huh?" I blushed.

"I mean if you ask me again."

"Sure," he said. "I'm just kidding you. I hope you'll come with me every Saturday." His friend retorted.

"Hey Miss Elizabeth. If this guy gives you any trouble, be sure to let me know." He held out his hand. "Would you like to dance with me now?"

Lonnie put his arm around my waist and guided me away.

"In your dreams buddy. This is my girl."

I looked at his profile and felt a flutter in my soul. He turned his face to me, smiled, then winked.

The noisy, exciting band was a far cry from the village dances in the Lake District. American men were such a contrast to the polite diffidence of the English variety. It was like I had been waiting for life to happen, and here it was. I felt as though my first date with Lonnie was the start of the rest of my life; like the flower buds of cautious love had exploded into massive blooms of huge colorful gardenias and nothing could turn back the clock or the season.

I never did get that last bus home. Of course, Mrs. Maxwell took the spare key off me, but I didn't care.

Diane and Judy were at the dance and greeted me as though we'd always known each other. Lonnie and their boyfriends got on like a house on fire, and we had such a fun time. From that night on, we all shared a cab to the girls' flat where we continued to party until dawn. Lonnie would walk me home on a Sunday morning just before lunch. We would kiss long and hard, on the doorstep. The front bay-window curtains twitched every time, but I was happier than I had ever been. How beautiful and captivating it all was.

I don't regret one moment of those first few months. Lonnie and I loved each other. I walked on air. He gave me wings. My every breathing moment had meaning and excitement. I basked in its fragrant heat. He was the most handsome man I had ever seen or dated. He was funny and charming, courteous and cheeky, all at the same time. He took care of me in ways I had never known, making me feel like the most adored woman in the world. He would light up two cigarettes at the same time and say corny little sentences as he gave me one of them.

"You can't have one without the other," or "From my lips to yours."

Sometimes when his favorite songs played, he looked into my eyes and sang. We connected like an electric wire to a switch. He seemed so totally at home with himself, confident, so alive. He told me all the time how beautiful I looked; how I had such style, how proud he was in my company. If I had a million pounds, I would gladly give it all away just to get those times back. I would go back in a second.

Diane and Judy were very modern in their attitude to boyfriends. They would give us a pillow, some sheets and a blanket for the sofa before they went to their separate bedrooms. We could hear their lovemaking, and for some reason it made me giggle. I think I was embarrassed.

We always ended up on the floor. I didn't let Lonnie go all the way for about four weeks, and at first, he never pushed me. Heavy-petting was awesome. He drove me crazy, but I was afraid to go further. Then one cold and rainy morning, we had all retired a little earlier than usual, and Lonnie whispered into my neck.

"I like you a lot, Beth. Matter of fact, you drive me crazy."

I kissed him.

"I like you a lot too, Lonnie. You're the first one I ever allowed to call me Beth."

"It suits you. 'Lonnie and Beth' just roll off the tongue."

"I guess so. I've got used to it."

"I'm crazy about you. I want to show you how much."

"You do show me how much Lonnie."

"Yes, but I can do so much more for you doll. I wanna go all the way with you."

There was a long silence. How could I tell him I didn't even know what 'all the way' meant?

"I'm scared of getting pregnant Lonnie."

"You won't," he said. "I promise you. I'll be super careful."

"How?" I asked, as green as the day is long. "What if you put a seed inside me and I get pregnant?"

He pushed himself up on one elbow. "Seed? I ain't never heard anything about seeds," he laughed. "But if you mean my sperm? I'll withdraw. My sperm never gets a chance to be inside you to get you pregnant." He sounded knowledgeable and sure of himself.

He was looking at me with a question in his expression. I suddenly felt foolish. No one had ever talked to me about such matters. My Gran had once said that we start out as a seed inside our mother's tummy. When I asked her how it got there, she said that my husband would one day put it there.

"That is why Elizabeth," she said, "You do not sleep in the same bed with any man until *after* you're married, or you'll get pregnant and be like Joanne Buttersley down the street. Her man ran off, joined the Merchant Navy and never came back."

Back then, Joanne Buttersley had caused quite a stir in the village. I had asked Gran, "So he put a seed in her tummy before they got married. How?"

"Ask me when you're older," she replied.

She refused to say another word, and I never did find out. My romance novels were not much help either. They were full of the kissing and rolling around kind of lovemaking, but never fully explained anything in minute detail. The birds and the bees had more idea than I had.

To add to the mystery, Judy had once shown me a rubber apparatus she had bought at the pharmacy on base. We were on the back of the bus whispering about it. She said after she sleeps with her boyfriend, she has to fill a bottle with vinegar and water, put the end of the tube in the bottle and use the round hand pump to squirt the liquid into her vagina at the other end of the tube. When I asked 'Why?' she and Diane sniggered.

"So you don't get pregnant idiot. The vinegar stops you getting pregnant, something to do with the acidity. It's easier than half a lemon."

I had nodded as if I of course, knew what she was talking about, and did not ask any more questions. But half a lemon? It boggled my mind.

Lonnie was still leaning his head on his hand above me. It was as though a cold blast of air had come between us. I repeated his statement.

"You withdraw, so I definitely can't get pregnant?"

"Of course Beth."

He said it as though I should be in total awareness of these facts. 'Withdraw' was a term I'd never heard before. Did he mean he'd get out of bed? I wanted to feel his warmth, for him to stroke my body. This coldness was unacceptable.

"Well, okay then," I said. "If you're sure you know what you're doing?

"I know what I'm doing sweetheart."

Softly, he kissed my neck. Goose bumps rose all over my body. He continued to kiss and touch me. He knew what I liked. When his fingers pushed inside me, I let out a soft moan. That is all it took. He got between my legs, pushing them apart; took his penis and pushed it into my vagina. It hurt. I knew that I could not easily accommodate something so large. That morning I found out what 'going all the way' meant. It meant he got very active and went up and down like a bloody yo-yo. The hurting was not just a great disappointment to me; it horrified me. The pain was torturous. I hated it. His body movements were an alien experience that did nothing to endear him to me. His face had no smile; his eyes looked dead, his sweat dripped onto my cheeks, and irritated, I wiped them away immediately. Then he screwed his face up, so I thought he was in pain too.

He quickly withdrew his penis, shooting wet stuff on the bed sheet between my legs and creating a big wet spot. Then he collapsed on top of me breathing like a marathon runner, and his sweat soaked my entire torso. He was like a dead weight, pinning me to the bed for many minutes. I couldn't speak. I wasn't shocked, just dumbfounded. This was it? *This* was making love, going all the way? What in the hell just happened?

Lonnie told me how special I made him feel giving my virginity up to him. When I told him he hurt me, I cried. I never realized what an emotional boundary I would cross. He held me and whispered soft endearments in my ear. He assured me it would get better every time we did it. That night, I felt if I never did it again, I couldn't care less.

We didn't do it again that night, but the next time we did it, he was gentleness itself. He was more concerned about pleasing me than himself, and he was right, it did get better. There were many more evenings and mornings of him teaching me all about lovemaking. As my mind and body relaxed and responded, I came to love everything about what we did and couldn't wait to be in his arms again every Saturday night and Sunday morning. All I wanted was to hear he loved me because I knew he was the love of my life. One Saturday, dancing to a slow love song, his breath on my hair, he said it.

"I've fallen for you, Beth. I love you."

I looked at his face; there was a tear in his eye. I smiled with pure joy.

"So, am I that bad? You're not looking too happy about it," I laughed.

"Well shucks Beth, you done made me cry. I ain't ever cried over a woman before."

"Well, I love you too Lonnie. But you already know that." To my surprise, a couple of tears welled up in my eyes. Lonnie pulled me closer, and as I pressed my cheek to his chest, I could hear the beat of his heart.

That night we got a cab to a local hotel. It was a beautiful clear night, cool and fresh. We walked up the front hotel steps; his arm, gently guiding me. We separated to go through the revolving door and resumed our embrace as we walked to the reception desk. He told the receptionist we were Mr. and Mrs. Caradine and that we would get our luggage later. The receptionist did not believe him, but she said we could have a room if we paid for it up-front. Lonnie paid cash. We had a couple of drinks at the bar and then went upstairs to our room with more drinks. We spent all night making love, talking, drinking, smoking, listening to music on the radio, and making love again.

Back then, I ate, slept and breathed in Lonnie Caradine. I couldn't get enough of him. He invaded all my dreams and all my thoughts. I was besotted. He showered me with flowers and expensive gifts. Silk stockings, a gold watch, Belgian chocolates and Chanel Number Five perfume. At Christmas, he gave me a gorgeous pearl necklace. It had a beautiful silver rhinestone catch, so ingenious in design. He said the pearls were cultured and 'only the best for my girl.'

As far as I was concerned, he was my first, my last and my world. Lonnie walked on water, and I floated somewhere between the stars and the earth; in among all the fluffy white clouds with the cherubs and Eros.

Then my period failed to show up. It was late by two days before I even noticed. I saw Judy and told her. She said she had missed two periods once, and freaked out. She said it was normal that every woman should not be bang on the clock with her periods. She said her sister wasn't. She eased my mind and said,

"Let's see what next month brings. I'm sure you'll be alright. You said he'd been careful right? In the meantime get one of those rubber douche tubes and use that before and after every time, okay, just to be on the safe side."

I got one the next day, but there was something about its black color and rubbery scent that put me off. I practiced with it once, so I could tell myself how thoroughly modern I had become; how wise and grown up. The reality was that by the time we'd become all steamed up, hot and hungry for each other, the last thing I wanted to do was mess around with tubes, vinegar, and water.

Lonnie said, "You worry too much. I've never slipped up once. You'll be fine."

And I honestly believed every word out of his gorgeous mouth. His word was his bond. He never gave me any reason to think otherwise, ever.

Then I noticed how firm my small breasts had become. 'Hey,' I thought. 'My breasts are growing a little, at last.' I felt pleased I could get out of my 'A' size cups into a 'B' size now. They felt perky and looked sexy. When I told Diane, she asked me if I was feeling okay. Did I ever feel sick, especially in the mornings? I said I'd never felt better, although I was going to bed earlier than usual and sleeping longer. She suggested that she would go with me to the doctor on the base; that I might be pregnant. I laughed.

"No. Judy told me she'd missed her periods before too. She says her sister is never on time." But Diane insisted anyway.

I made an appointment. Diane came with me.

The male doctor asked me lots of intimate questions about how many times we had sex, what was the method of contraception if any, and how was I feeling? I was glad Diane was with me, his questions mortified me. Then he took a blood sample and asked me to urinate in a glass cup. What a performance that was. He said I had to get a *mid-flow sample.*

"Come with me," I mouthed to Diane, as I fled from his room. In the bathroom I asked her, "What does he mean?"

"Start to wee and let the first part go into the toilet bowl. Then, wee in the cup but don't let any of your last bit of wee get into the cup, just the middle part."

"You've done this before, Diane," I said. She nodded. "Is it because I might overflow the cup?"

"I have no clue," said Diane. "Just do what he says."

So I did and managed to splash everywhere. Unlike a man who has precise aim because he holds a ready-made projecting faucet in his hands, mine was not that good. Even my undies got wet.

"Drat," I said.

I could hear Diane laughing outside the door. I gave the full cup to the nurse who was waiting outside in the small corridor.

"We just need a sample, Ma'am," she said. "Let me pour most of this away. We don't need all this."

I felt my cheeks burn while she emptied some it down the bowl. Diane mimicked her. "We don't need all this," she said, then lifted the pretend cup in her hand and made as if she was drinking the excess. We doubled up laughing.

The doctor came out of his office.

"You girls are having far too much fun," he said. He was telling us off. We both stopped laughing. "Come back in a week," he said.

We filed past him quietly.

A week later, I returned for the results. It had been the longest week of my life, wondering and worrying. Diane could not come with me, but I promised I would walk over to her flat that same night and let her and Judy know what the results were.

"Get the wine ready," I told her. "I won't be pregnant. Lonnie's always careful."

Huh! Famous last words.

"You are pregnant Miss Borge," said the doctor, as if he was saying I just had a cold. "You need to make an appointment to come to our pre-natal clinic next week. In the meantime, I suggest you tell the father of your child and see what he intends to do for your future."

I dropped into the chair behind me, faint. I could not be more shocked if someone said I had a terminal illness. The nurse got me water. He took my blood pressure and told me to sit in the waiting room until I felt able to leave.

"Eat lots of lean meat, fruits, and vegetables, drink plenty of milk and water, cut out headache pills, cigarettes and alcohol and come back to the clinic in a week."

"But how did this happen? We were always so careful. Lonnie withdrew every time."

"Withdrawing is not a guarantee you won't get pregnant Miss Borge. In fact, it's like playing Russian roulette. Do it enough times, and your luck runs out. It's as simple as that. You're a healthy young woman, and there's no reason on earth why you shouldn't get pregnant if you're having regular sex. Did they not teach you the facts of life at school?"

"Never," I said. "Who gets taught this stuff at school?"

"We're having sex education in many of our schools in the USA now."

"Not in England Doctor. You're told to be careful and get married before you sleep in the same bed as any man. That's it."

"Ignorance is not bliss. You must remember what I told you. Withdrawal is not the answer. There is no one-hundred percent guarantee unless you count abstinence. Or you could use condoms, as well as douching before and after with vinegar solution, in case the condom leaks"

I sat for a good ten minutes in the waiting room and left his office with such a mixture of sensations. At first, I was numb, in denial. Then I felt dumb. How ignorant I was. Finally, I had butterflies; I was excited and hardly able to contain my pleasure once I was over the shock. I decided I would tell Lonnie the very next day, which was a Saturday. I didn't visit Diane and Judy. I wanted Lonnie to be the first to know.

I hardly slept that night, rehearsing over and over what I would say, how I would say it; imagining his surprised reaction. We had talked about him taking me with him whenever it was time he posted back home. He seemed excited by the prospect of me meeting his family in Florida. All his stories about the United States of America fueled my imagination. He said Florida had palm trees and beautiful sandy beaches with a blue, azure sea. When I found out I was pregnant, it filled me with such a surge of hope. I wanted so much to be with Lonnie, to marry him and wake up with him every morning. We would make a home together. I longed to be his wife, cooking, cleaning and doing all the things I loved, just for him and now for our baby too. It was like a dream come true. I danced around my room with ecstasy welling in my heart. I had never, ever, felt such joy.

CHAPTER 7: BETH: FACING THE MUSIC IS NOT DANCING TO IT.

Job 30:15, Terrors overwhelm me; my dignity is driven away as by the wind, my safety vanishes like a cloud.

Yesterday, my mother had called the hospital, and they had told her I needed to rest and not to visit me on my first day, thank heavens. She was the last person I needed to see. Sitting here at the lunch table today I contemplate how some people say hospital food is atrocious, and sometimes they may be right, but this mashed potato and carrots with a pork chop, gravy, and even some apple sauce, tastes bloody good to me. I look up and notice someone from the corner of my eye, going into the Sister's Office. I jolt. It's my Mother. A male voice mentions my name. I look back at my food and feel a knot slowly twist inside me. This may be the moment I've been dreading. I take a deep breath and swallow some water and whisper to myself,

"Oh, to hell with them. They can only shoot me."

Minutes later, after losing my appetite, I take my plate to scrape it off and I hear my mother's voice, loud and clear.

"She and her two kids will be staying with my husband and I. We have plenty of room with four bedrooms."

I feel bilious. Not only do I not want to see my mother, but I also have no desire to see her brutish peasant husband from Poland. She is fully expecting me to move in with them, under the same blasted roof. I know I should stay calm and not get worked up again, but I'm a grown woman, and I can hear plans, without anyone asking for my opinion. My mother just makes my blood boil.

I walk over the pristine shiny floor and remind myself I no longer need to waddle. The office door is semi-closed, I rap on it before pushing it open. All heads twitch and four pairs of eyes stare in my direction. I'm seething. The Matron takes charge before I have time to speak.

"Ah. Good afternoon, Mrs. Caradine. We were just discussing your predicament with the Sergeant here, and I was about to come and get you."

"And who might you be?" I ask with one eyebrow arched.

"You know who I am, Mrs. Caradine, so let's stop this pretense shall we? I'll show you, your mother, the Sergeant and your social worker to another office just across the hall. Please follow me."

She marches past me, nose in the air. And that's what we all do. We all follow her. My goodness, it's amazing what a bloody uniform and a bit of authority can do for a person. Was Florence Nightingale ever this arrogant? Even the police Sergeant looks at me and raises his eyes to the ceiling. He pulls the corners of his mouth down as if emulating her expression. I think he is trying to sympathize with me. She holds a door open and allows us all to enter the room. I feel like a naughty school-girl filing into the headmistress's office. Even my mother looks diminutive compared to her. Then without another word, she closes the door, and we hear her footsteps fade down the hallway.

We are in a larger office with a table and six chairs around it. The police Sergeant removes his hat and gestures to the chairs.

"Let's all sit down. Mrs. Caradine, Mrs. Krupp, Miss Jones." We all move forward and pull out a chair each. He chooses the seat next to me. I feel uncomfortable and pull my dressing gown tighter over my chest, then pull it over my knees and hold it there.

"Hello," says my mother. We stare at each other. My jaw tightens. I don't answer.

"What on earth were you thinking?"
It's not a new question. Someone already asked me that. I ignore her and look at the social worker.

"Who are you?" I ask.

"My name is Susan Jones. I'll be your social worker for the foreseeable future. How do you do, Elizabeth?" She holds out her right hand and smiles. Her voice sounds warm, and her smile seems genuine. "I'm pleased to meet you."

"I go by Beth," I say, barely touching her fingers. "Why do I need a social worker?"

"Sergeant Thomas will explain, and then you can ask me any questions you may have."

The Sergeant is seated sideways on his chair, one foot under the table and the other out, almost touching my seat. Before he speaks, he nods and puts his hat on the table.

"Hello, I'm Sergeant Tony Thomas."

He doesn't smile but stretches his closed mouth like people do when they want to look earnest.

"Hello, Beth. I met your mother the day before yesterday; I brought her to the hospital. We took your lovely children to her house that night." He looks over at my mother. She nods and manages a small smile. It seems like he's starting a speech.

"First of all, I want to say how glad I am to meet you today, Beth. I wasn't sure you were going to make it two days ago. Your mother was very concerned about you, and she did a sterling job getting your children from your neighbor's house. They're very well behaved; they are a credit to you." I swallow the lump in my throat.

"Secondly, I want to say congratulations on the safe birth of your baby. I understand she's doing as well as can be expected and her prognosis looks positive. We are not out of the woods yet though. These next few days are crucial in seeing her improve and get stronger." He clears his throat.

"Thirdly, it is my duty to tell you, Elizabeth Caradine, that I'm charging you with the following: The attempted murder of yourself and your child; Aggravated battery of yourself and your child with intent to endanger life. Abandonment and neglect for the safety of your other two children, Steven and Elizabeth Caradine. You do not have to say anything, but if you do say something, what you say will be written down and may be used in evidence against you."

Tears fill my eyes immediately, and my chin starts to wobble as I struggle to control my emotions. He pauses slightly then continues.

"Child Services and the court agree that you must stay in the hospital until a doctor deems that you and your baby are well enough to be discharged. At that time the court will take into consideration your doctor's opinion on whether or not you are still considered a danger to yourself or your children. Miss Jones here will be giving the court a report on your condition of mind as decided by a psychiatrist. She'll also make recommendations to the court as to the continued welfare of all your children. There is a chance they could be taken into the care of the local County Welfare Department and placed with a family or families as foster children."

Panic rises in my chest. I feel naked, exposed. I clutch my gown at my throat and look at my mother. She looks at the policeman, and I know she's about to speak. I'm willing her to speak. Do something. Do anything. He interrupts the silence.

"Do you understand these charges against you Elizabeth Caradine?"

My world slows down as I turn my head to look at him. Like a slow motion nightmare when everything gets terrifying, and you just know this is the moment when you meet your fate head on. Some tiny mechanism in my mind, finer than a human hair, stretches and snaps. I scream as though I've just been set alight. At the same moment I bang my fists down on the table and rocket from my seat so suddenly, my chair flies backward and falls over. I'm leaning over him, his eyes wide.

"No. I don't understand these charges against me, you bloody idiot. I do not understand any of this." Spittle flies everywhere.

"Calm down Mrs. Caradine." He tries to get up, and I scream in his face louder.

"Calm down? You're going to take my children off me, and you ask me to calm down?"

My eyes sting with tears. I can no longer hold them, and I cover my face ashamed of the sounds in my throat. I hear myself wailing like a banshee but can't stop it. The dam that had been leaking ignored the fact, that I had every finger in every hole and eventually exploded through my chest, taking my heart with it.

No one speaks. A hand holds my right shoulder. I hear my mother's chair scrape to my left. She's up and at me. I feel a seat behind my knees and her hands holding my upper arms tightly. She squeezes both my arms and pushes me down onto the seat and talks to me.

"Beth, Beth. Don't take on so. I'm going to see a Solicitor this afternoon. Don't worry. No one is going to take Steven and Lizzie. Let them try. It will be over my dead body. Don't you fret girl? It will all work out okay. Come on now girl."

A voice behind me, maybe it's the Matron coming into the room, I don't know.

"We'll take her to Ward 10."

Then there are mumblings, hushed whispers, I hear 'not well,' then 'sleep for three days.'

I'm running snot, and a soft female voice says, "Here's a tissue." I can barely lift my head; my vocal chords ache with all the wailing like there's some primeval, guttural creature inside me. The world has tilted in some immeasurable way. I must have slid off its edge. There's an incessant buzzing in my head. I take the hanky, blow my nose and screw it into a little ball. She gives me another. I wipe my face and eyes. My stomach and chest keep catching as I strain to end my crying. But it just envelops me. My whole body is just one exhausted, helpless, mess of heartbreak.

I detach from them all. My mother's voice has that far away sound. The policeman and the social worker continue a conversation with her, but their words have no impact on me. My body sits lifeless on the chair, my connection with them all, non-existent. I'm in my bomb-free bubble, floating somewhere in mid-heaven.

I can hear my voice as though I'm a child again.

"They can't touch you here. No one can. They will never be able to touch you here."

Then I hear a familiar sound; the whistling kettle. I can smell bacon. My heart soars over the mountains through the lilac mists, past the dogs herding sheep, swoops low over the rushing force of downward fleeing streams, across the field of Jersey cows and over the kissing gates. I'm at Gran's breakfast table. We are laughing together.

She's reciting the same story she always did when she wanted to get a laugh out of me. I never tired of this story in her Geordie brogue.

"What time o'cock is it by yur cock? Wo Jodi's cock's stanin'. Tell me what time o'cock it is by yur cock; an I'll get wo Jodi's cock gannin."

She was emulating her old neighbor, Sally, in South Shields. Gran said, Sally, would walk into her house almost every day and chant these words. Her son's clock was a daily wind up one. Gran would say,

"You would think by now, they'd know to wind up their bloody clock, but no, they always have to go through this daily rigmarole. I think she just wants to smell what I'm having for breakfast."

That would always set me off laughing again. It was like Gran could set *her* clock by the neighbor each day. Around 8 o'clock to quarter past, every morning, Sally would lift the kitchen door latch and almost sing her sentence throughout Gran's house. Gran said it was such a habit that she would mouth the words along with her, and then tell her the time from the clock on the mantel.

"What time o'cock is it by yur cock? Wo Jodi's cock stanin'. Tell me what time o'cock it is by yur cock an I'll get wo Jodi's cock gannin."

Gran said one day the latch never lifted. Sally stopped coming. She'd passed away. Gran swears up and down that Jodi showed Gran, Sally's wind up clock. I always got chills whenever she told me the story, her eyes wide, pretending horror.

"Her bloody clock stopped at five minutes past eight that morning, and it never worked again."
Then Gran would cross her heart like a Catholic and swear it was true.

My picture fades, and I'm back in some god-forsaken hospital office. I can hear my mother calling my name.

"Beth. Come on now. Everything's going to be alright. You'll see. Now come on girl look at me."
But it's never going to be alright. I have nothing to say. Next thing I know, I'm in a wheelchair, being propelled down a hospital corridor by a nurse. Somewhere, I hear Gran's voice again, telling me Sally's clock

has stopped forever. I laugh out loud and can't stop giggling. My mother asks me what's so funny. I tell her.

"Sally's dead Mother. Her bloody clock stopped forever. She doesn't have to look at the bloody stupid time anymore. There are far worse things than dying you know."

Then we are outside. My world keeps changing. Am I here or over there? We are going down a ramp, around some grass. The wind catches my hair; it blows everywhere. Strands stick to my wet cheeks. I'm not laughing anymore. I look up at the blue sky with the ever changing clouds and take a long deep breath. It's what Gran would call a nor-easterly wind; she taught me that the mackerel clouds, the ones that look like the bare bones of the spine of a fish, always portend rain, no matter how blue the sky may look right now. I speak out.

"Dead fish bones know more about the weather than the stupid weather man on the radio." No one responds.

There is a ramp ahead. We are going to another building in the hospital grounds. The door seems to grow in size. I don't even ask where we are going. It feels like it's a bomb shelter of some kind, it has that ominous look of austerity and a metal door that someone painted a long time ago and forgot existed. It swings open. A tall, fat-bellied man with a bald patch in his brown hair is holding it. He's wearing a short sleeved white jacket. We're in Alice's Wonderland, and he's Tweedledum. I know that Tweedledee is never far away. It wouldn't surprise me if the Mad Hatter were to appear, with the Queen of Hearts shouting; 'Off with her head, off with her head.'

The interminably long, rabbit-hole corridor ahead is dark. There are doors on each side of it, all of them closed. The only light is from glowing white globes, hanging in line, two by two. They send next to no light to the floor. At the end of the corridor is a sign I can't make out with two arrows pointing left and right. Tweedledum passes us and obscures the sign. He turns around to wait for us. He doesn't even look at me, just points to his left and we turn to go down another corridor. He asks for my mother to come to the office in the other direction. I'm not even curious where I'm going. All I can see are memories swirling in my mind.

It wasn't long after that wonderful Christmas of 1954 when Steven was three and Lizzie was two, and I shared my bed with Lonnie that he was sent back to America. We were both sad, but we'd talked ourselves into exciting things ahead.

I'd been waiting for a letter from Lonnie, outlining our plans to get married, when he was returning to England and what I needed to apply for a visa. He said he wanted to save up so we could live off-base in a nicer house. I had written to him every day for three weeks. I watched the letterbox and checked the time every morning for when the postman would arrive.

His next letter to me was cooler than I expected. He wrote I was the love of his life but to be patient. He said red-tape is always a long haul. I didn't hear from him again for another three weeks. It was that same waiting, checking the time, watching for the postman. His next letter, written in the same tone, had almost the same words. I felt like sending out a posse; 'Find my Lonnie and bring him back.'

Four weeks later, and eight more letters from me, I got another letter from him. I remember the moment so clearly. It was a fairly nice day, and I had given Steven and Lizzie their breakfast. Steven was out playing with his guns and holster, shooting at imaginary Apache Indians, his red and cream cowboy hat and shiny sheriff badge showing all the world his authority. His chaps were red and cream too with red fringing down the side, and his shiny silver spurs finished the look. He would be out there for hours. His posture and demeanor transformed when he put on that outfit. Joy shone out of his face like a sunbeam.

Lizzie was sitting in an armchair, content to be with me. Wherever I was, she wanted to be. I'd told her I would take her and Steven to the park after I'd finished some laundry.

"You can take dolly out for a walk in her pram," I told her. She just nodded and smiled. Then the letter box flapped open with its flat, tinny sound and a letter fell onto the mat behind the front door. Lizzie jumped off her chair and picked it up before I could move. I knew by its stamp and its lettering in the top left corner; it was from Lonnie.

"Here you are, Mummy. Is it from Daddy?" she said. Lizzie's so intelligent. A 'canny little bairn,' my mother calls her. She's a thinker. I can almost see the wheels turning in her mind when she's working out the world around her.

"I hope it's from Daddy," I said, "and about time too. He's not very good at writing letters is he?"

I had the letter opener under the envelope flap, faster than a shepherd could whistle his dog. Lizzie was looking up into my face and dancing on her toes. I opened it, and something about the paper made my hands shake. It wasn't the usual thin blue airmail paper. It was a plain white envelope with his same PO Box number on the upper left corner. Inside there was a single sheet of lined paper still showing tiny jagged edges down one side where it had been carefully torn out of a notebook. Written on both sides, I thought it must be official information about us getting together. Each sentence was supported by a thick blue line as if carrying the weight of the words.

Words I would never forget. Those words were a shrieking bomb that hit my corrugated-iron shelter of a heart, dead-on. I fell to my knees.

But today, I'm not on my knees. Today I'm in a wheelchair wishing again I could be in my coffin, where sleep is sweet and empty of dreams; and where nothing and no-one can reach me.

CHAPTER 8: MARY: SHELLING PEAS.

1Kings 21:5-7, His wife Jezebel came in and asked him, "Why are you so sullen? Why won't you eat?" Jezebel, his wife, said, "Is this how you act as king over Israel? Get up and eat! Cheer up. I'll get you the vineyard of Naboth the Jezreelite."

Lord, what a day. The children are asleep, thank goodness. John is finishing up his lambs' fries and wiping his plate clean with the last of his four slices of toast. For a grumbling old sod, he sure looks handsome. It's true. The way to a man's heart is definitely through his stomach. He grins at me. He has such gorgeous eyes. He wipes his mouth with his serviette before speaking his clipped English with his V's where his W's should be.

"Vell Mary, you outdid you-self darling. That vos delicious."

"Nothing like fried balls on toast to satisfy an appetite," I say. He roars laughing.

"Glad they're not mine, huh?"

"Huh! Yours wouldn't fit on the plate, John. Why do you think I got lambs?"

His gold teeth glint, enjoying the joke. His grey-blue eyes follow suit. I can see the mischief in them and know his mind is where I'm precisely leading it.

Sex is ok I suppose. Well, I can take it or leave it actually, but whenever I want to ask something of him, and I want to get whatever it is, well let's just say; food first, fun next, frolicking later. Bob's your uncle and Fanny's your aunt. Done and dusted, which in Queen's good English means; 'If I want it, I know how to get it.'

"So how's your daughter doing today?" He asks with his usual chin lift.

He picks up a toothpick and starts his nightly teeth routine, which I want to say, is better done in private in the bathroom; but I don't say anything. Why spoil a good mood.

“She’s very sick actually. They had to take her to the psychiatric ward today. She’s just not coping John.”

“She never is coping. Vot’s going on?”

"They're giving her sleeping pills for a full three days, keeping her under heavy sedation. It's supposed to give her mind a rest. They've to be careful of the dose though because she already had a bellyful when she overdosed."

He pulls his mouth down like he always does when weighing things up. His head tilts one way then another before he speaks. He sighs.

“Vot can vee do? How long is she in there?”

He tilts his chin up at me, demanding an answer.

“At least a week, if not two, it depends on how she does.”

“So vee have the children for another two veeks?”

"I was going to ask you about that." I try a small smile. "What would you say if I told you I could take the children up to the Lake District for a week or two?"

“Huh? I don’t care,” he shrugs. I can feel one of his pouts coming on fast.

"Well, I could take them up there and maybe stay a couple of days, to settle them in. Then leave them up there with Mother and Maureen. She's almost eighteen now. She can help look after them. Then I'll come back. That way they're out of our way for a while, and I can get some business seen to."

“Vot business?”

“Beth’s.”

“Vot does she need?"

“A Barrister.”

“A Barrister? Vot is that?”

“He’s extra good at his job. Wins more cases than Solicitors.”

“So the police charge her already? Vot happened?”

“Yes, today. I was there. If we don't help her, the courts may send her to prison. Then, they'll put Steven, Lizzie, and the new baby into care. She might never get them back."

"Maybe that's not a bad thing."

He shrugs, nonchalant and uncaring. Steam is rising inside me. I can feel it in the warmth of my cheeks and ears. I keep calm.

"She loves Steven and Lizzie, John. What would she do without them? They're her world."

"Huh. Now she has another von. Vot good is that? How many more children will she have?"

An alarm goes off in my head. I know this conversation is going west. I start to get off my chair, slowly, casually, as though he's not rattled me.

"Well, we can cross that bridge later John. Right now she's asleep for three days."

I start a gentle massage of his neck and shoulders. He relaxes and closes his eyes. I wait a couple of minutes before speaking again. My voice is soft.

"Let me take the children to my mother's. They'll love it. They need some fresh air. It'll give us time to think about what's happening." I know he'll not answer me straight away. He keeps his eyes closed.

John's not very astute when it comes to our legal system. He never even met a Solicitor before we bought both houses. He's never heard of a Barrister. I could kick myself for mentioning one. If I have my way, he'll not hear it again. Barristers are expensive. It's a good thing I have money put away that John is ignorant of. I knead his shoulders for about five or six minutes before he speaks.

"Ok, tomorrow, you take the childer to your mother. I vill come home sooner tomorrow, so Mama's not alone for a long time. You can come back Sunday, maybe Monday is ok."

I feel relief wash over me. I do like the children, but patience isn't my strong suit. I was brought up to believe children should be seen and not heard. Unfortunately Beth's two kids aren't used to that. They're always asking questions, why this and why that. I like them alright, but in small doses. And the legal aspects for Beth need sorting out too. The welfare is not going to get her children, not as long as I have a breath in my body. We women have always coped with our problems. No government department is going to interfere with our family. They can go to hell.

"I'm glad you don't mind John. I'm only thinking of you and Mama. You've enough to cope with right now. Would you like me to run you a bath darling? Nothing like a good soak to relax you."

He roars laughing. Sometimes I wonder what he finds funny. When I ask him, he always says, 'You Mary.' It's like he can see straight through me.

"A bath is just the ticket Mary," he says, still grinning.

I don't bother asking him what it's a ticket for. We both know the answer to that one.

He gets up and holding my hand, takes me through the kitchen door. Men are predictable. Still, I got what I want, so I won't have to try too hard, just lie back and think of England.

As I run his bath, I tell myself,

"It's like shelling peas, Mary, my girl."

Okay, maybe shelling peas in the dark. I always keep my eyes closed. He's given up asking me why I shut my eyes. I always tell him the same thing.

"The same reason you close your eyes when I massage you. I'm in seventh heaven, John. You're such a wonderful husband."

He'll fall asleep after and snore like a herd of boars. I'll get up and see to his mother; then she'll do the same. I ask myself,

"So what do I have to complain about Mary? Life's good on the farm. Pork and peas. Mm, just the ticket."

Oh, my goodness.

CHAPTER 9: MARY: THE LAKE DISTRICT.

Proverbs 31:10,14,15, A capable wife who can find? She is like the merchant ships, bringing her food from afar. She gets up while it is still night; she provides food for her family.

Mrs. Wheedler, next door, was very accommodating last night when I asked her if she'd give me a hand with the children this morning. I told her I intended to take a taxi to Beth's house to get more clothes and toys.

I got up early, attended to Mama, made John a bacon buttie for breakfast and two for his lunch. Then I fed, washed and dressed my grandchildren and they were next door with Fannie Wheedler by quarter past eight.

When I got back from Beth's house at ten o'clock, I'd already discussed with the taxi driver about him taking us all to the Lake District. We'd come to an amicable compromise on price, and I had him stop at the post office to withdraw some of my secret savings. I lied to Mrs. Wheedler and told her the taxi would come back to take us the railway station and we would catch the one o'clock train to Penrith. John would have a fit if he knew we went all the way to my mother's house in a taxi. He's all about saving pennies. I just want to get there with the least fuss.

I wish I could be honest with him, but some things are best left alone. John was brought up in Poland where food and many other commodities were either scarce or non-existent. I'll never forget the day I discovered how tight he is. I'd been peeling potatoes for dinner, and he came up behind me and told me he wanted to do it; so I gave him the knife. The first thing he did was peel my peelings. I was flabbergasted. I thought he was joking. His peelings were so thin; you could almost see through them. He told me I was wasting food. With some things so ingrained like that, well, as Mother would say, 'You can't teach an old dog new tricks.' So if I need to spend money on something and I want peace in the house, there's another saying that's authentically useful. 'What the eyes don't see, the heart won't grieve over.' It's my motto now.

I pack pillows, bedding, toys, and clothes for the children. To be honest, they don't have much in the way of anything, and they fit in two suitcases. I have ready cash for my mother to soften the blow. I'd sent her a telegram from the post office.

'Bringing Beth's children today for two weeks STOP. She's sick STOP. Bringing cash STOP.'

I'd explain the rest when I got there. I'd also get to see how Maureen's doing. I haven't seen her in nine months, not since John and I went to Blackpool for a few days, and she came down to look after Mama. She's grown into a sensible, level-headed girl, thank goodness. Why couldn't Beth have been a boy? So much less of a worry. But then Mother's true saying puts life into perspective. She always says,

"If men got pregnant and had the bairns, births would come to a standstill."

The drive is comfortable at first as Steven and Lizzie sleep for a good hour in the taxi, but I have to put up with another two hours of their constant inquiries. 'What's that?' 'Why is it?' I use John's method of control, singing 'Old McDonald had a farm' and 'Ten green bottles hanging on a wall.' It keeps them occupied as well as having fun, but I'll be exhausted by the time we reach our destination. All I'll want to do is lie down for an hour or two, but fat chance of that with these two, and my mother asking a million and one questions.

"Grandma?" says Lizzie for the hundred and third time. She's the only child I know who can make the word Grandma into a question, over and over again.

"Yes, Hinny. What is it?" I reply for the hundred and fourth time.

She has her nose pressed up to the window and is taking in everything she sees, every blade of grass.

“Why are there so many walls built over the mountains?” This is the second time she has asked this question in the last ten minutes.

“I told you the answer already Hinny. It’s to keep the sheep inside so they don’t go wandering off.”

“We-e-e-ell,” she replies with a dozen letters in the word instead of just four. Whenever she says ‘well’ like that and extends it out for a couple of seconds, I know her next remark is going to be a hoot. I imitate her.

“We-e-e-ell what? Let’s hear it Hinny.”

“We-e-e-e-ll. They are not doing such a great job of it are they?"

“Why not?” I ask.

“Well, I don’t see any sheep in the fields. Can sheep jump high Grandma? It looks like they all jumped over the walls and ran away.” I stare out the window, and she's right. There aren't any darn sheep out there.

“You know what Lizzie, you’re exactly right. They’re not doing such a good job at all are they?”

“No Grandma. They’re useless.” I burst out laughing.

“Bloody useless. I agree.”

“Buddy useless Grandma,” she mimics.

“Ok, Lizzie. Don't ever say that word, ‘bloody.' It's not nice." I tap the back of my hand in self-reproach. "Naughty Grandma for speaking that nasty word. I'm sorry Hinny."

"Alright, Grandma. We won't speak it again."
I know my mother will have a fit if she hears Lizzie swearing.

Steven is coloring his book, and Lizzie continues to watch the world. I manage to doze a little, and before I know it, Steven and Lizzie are leaping about over me trying to get out of the car. We've arrived. The children jump up and down and hug their Nana then grab some toys and books out of the car. I follow the driver as he unloads the cases and takes them through the gate, up the path and parks them at the front doorstep. I pay him our agreed rate, and he leaves. Every curtain in the row twitches. Connie Clarkson, who likes to be the first to know everything, comes out of her house, followed by her two children. They come to greet me.

“How are you Mary?” she asks.

Before I can answer, she looks at Steven and Lizzie and says,

“Goodness me, no. This can’t be Beth’s two children, can it? Look how they’ve grown. How is Beth? She’s not with you?”

I try to be nice. I’m a private person but arriving suddenly in the car like this, is big news here in this tiny village of thirty houses and a shop.

“She’s a little under the weather Connie, so I thought I’d bring the bairns up here to give her a break an’ all.”

"Oh, nothing serious I hope?"

“No just a little under the weather like I said. How are you all?”

“We’re doing well Mary. Ben still works in the mine.” She turns to her two daughters, “Say hello to Mrs. Borge now.”

I don’t even correct her with my new married name. That would spark a good half an hour’s worth of questions. I look at her two girls, all ruddy faced and sparkly eyes.

"You two have grown so big since I last saw you," I say. "You have such lovely girls Connie. If you'll excuse me, I must get inside; the bairns will need the toilet after our long drive. We'll catch up with you later if you don't mind."

“Aye, alright then, Mary. You’ll all be needing a cup o’ tea an’ something to eat too. I’ll let you go. See you later. Say goodbye girls.”

They say goodbye and turn to walk back to their house. My mother and I exchange looks. We don’t say anything until we are all inside.

My mother speaks first. "Well, you’re certainly giving everyone something to gossip about our Mary. It’ll be all round the village within the half-hour. She’s a nosy one that Connie, I tell you.”

"Oh, they'll get nothing from me Mother. So, what do you want to know first?"

"I don't want to know anything right now. Let's all have something to eat and a cup o' tea; then the bairns can go outside with Maureen. Then we’ll talk. Here give me your coat and let’s get sat down at the table. Maureen, get a washcloth and wipe the bairns' hands and faces. Then we'll eat."

"Hello Mother," says Maureen. She comes over and kisses my cheek. "What a surprise."

"How are you, Maureen? You're looking well. You still helping out at the Red Lion?"

"Only a couple of hours in the morning. No weekends. I help with breakfast, that's all."

"Good girl. It's better than not having a job at all."

"It is. I'm so glad you're all here. I'll get the children washed for dinner." She turns and goes about her task. The children take to her immediately.

My mother deserves a medal. She's already cooked us all beef stew. It's delicious as always. Then she asks Maureen to take the children out back to play. She puts the kettle on again for our second pot of tea, and we soon settle into two armchairs to talk. I know to let her go first. She's dying to know everything. She nods in the direction of the back window where we can see the children playing and running around in the field.

"Little pigs have big ears," she says, "Maureen included. I told Maureen she'd have to get them outside after we ate so we could talk in private. Maureen's been driving me mad asking me questions I can't answer about Elizabeth. So what's going on? What's up with her? Is it her pregnancy?"

I struggle with how to say it but realize there's no easy way.

"Our Beth, I'm sorry to say, took an overdose of pills on Wednesday. Now from what I can glean, they…" She cuts me off.

"An overdose? Oh, my godfathers. Is she ok? What happened? Did she lose the baby?"

"She's going to be alright Mother. They think the baby will be ok too. It was born on Wednesday night, that's all I can tell you about it for now."

"But why did she do it, Mary? I thought she was doing alright?"

"Well, obviously she's not okay. She's not coping at all. I wish to the high heavens she'd never got pregnant again."

"Don't we all. Can't she see that sterilization is the best thing? It would be a godsend."

"I tried telling her that. It didn't sit too well with her."

"Is it a boy or a girl?"

"Girl. Natalie. Four pounds eleven ounces. She's doing nicely for seven months. We have to pray she lives."

"Is she still in the hospital?"

"Yes."

"When's she out?"

I'm already telling a hellish enough story; now I've got to say to Mother, it gets worse. I take a deep breath, almost a sigh. Mother reads me like a book.

"Well go on Mary. The cat got your tongue?"

"I'm not stopping for long Mother. Can I leave the bairns with you? I have to get back in a day or two and meet with my Solicitor."

"What the hell for?"

"For Beth. They've thrown the book at her. She's charged with attempted murder of herself and the baby. The Welfare is coming to see me next week to look at where we live. Make sure we're clean and all."

"Attempted murder? Clean? What do you mean clean? Clean for what?"

I sit up straight and lean forward slightly. I want my mother to stop bombarding me with questions.

"Let me explain Mother, start from the beginning. This story has a lot of parts to it. So just let me tell you the story. Then you can ask me as many questions as you want when I get to the end. If you keep asking me a question every third word, I'll never get it told right."

"Well hurry up then our Mary. I'm getting cobwebs sitting here."

So I tell her from when the policeman arrived on my doorstep, the children unable to wake her, the neighbor, the pious Matron, John, his mother, the kids at our house, John being kind to them, my second visit, the social worker, the murder charge and other charges. Worse still, the threat of her children going to Foster Parents. Then, finally, the piteous demise of her mind. Her heartbreaking howls, like a starve-crazed wolf, mad at the moon. Beth's in the loony ward in the hospital. Only I don't use the word 'loony,' out loud. I use the proper term, 'psychiatric ward.' I don't want to upset my mother unduly.

She's on her third cigarette by the time the tale's told, and she's finished asking questions.

"Well I'll be blown, our Mary. I'm shocked. I really am. She'd been workin' and gettin' on her feet again. Now you're telling me she's in the loony bin. I can't believe it."

I try not to smile. Mother is on me like a bluebottle on manure.

"What *you* smirkin' at?"

"Sorry Mother. It's just when you said loony bin. I never heard you say that before."

"That's because no-one in our family ever got put in there before. Mind you; she always was a bit highly strung. Those bombing raids are what did it. I swear it was those that started her off being nervy. I'm sad for poor Beth. What're we gonna do with her, I don't know."

She sighs and finishes off her tea before resuming.

"And I could strangle that Yank, Lonnie. The bugger broke her heart. I'd just started to get to like him a bit even though he was a cheeky bugger; too big for his boots in my opinion. I wish she'd ha' never gone down South for work. She should ha' stayed here with me and continued helping out in the Red Lion Hotel, but no, she wouldn't listen to me."

"Beth has a mind of her own Mother. When did she ever listen to anyone?"

She ignores me and carries on, plowing through her thoughts. I can tell she's awful upset. I think she's talking instead of crying. I've never seen my mother cry.

"I should ha' moved from the Shields when they first wanted to evacuate us. I never thought the bombing would get that bad up there. It's probably my fault, all this."

I clink my cup down on its saucer, harder than I intend.

"Now, now, Mother. We were all in a black spot back then. I worked away. You had the girls. The Jerries were bombing. Life wasn't easy, so don't go around blaming yourself for anything. We all did our best. Beth has a mind of her own. You know she can be bloody-minded and stubborn when she wants to be."

"Well, she's not here to defend herself, so let's not talk about the girl behind her back."

I get up and take the tray from where I'd leaned it against my chair. I clear away the china, leave the room and start to wash everything in the kitchen sink. I'm feeling irritated. It didn't take long, it never does. My mother never says a bad word about Beth. It's as though someone studded her nose in diamonds or something. I can point out all her flaws until I'm blue in the face. It just hits a brick wall as far as my mother's concerned. I scrub the inside of the teapot with scouring powder to get rid of the stains. I don't remember Mum ever being so protective of me when I did things wrong. A sharp clip 'round the ear was all I remember, then no supper and straight to bed. I never got away with anything. She calls into the kitchen.

"Don't you be taking out your peevishness on my teapot our Mary. You know I don't scrub it out. The browner it is, the better the tea next time."

My mother has eyes in the back of her head, I swear.

I stop. Most of the stain's disappeared, and she'll not let me forget it while I'm here. Maybe I'll go right back home tomorrow. Beth's always been a bone of contention between us. It gets on my nerves.

Suddenly the back door flies open. Maureen and her new charges are in the kitchen. They look bright eyed, their cheeks glowing. The fresh air is doing them good already. Mother calls out,

"Wipe your feet at the back door please."

"Aunty Maureen is taking us to the stream," shouts Lizzie, jumping up and down.

"I'm going to float my stick on the water," Steven joins in. He's as happy as I've ever seen him.

Maureen shushes them. "Whisht Hinnies. Sit down and calm down for a few minutes. Get your breath. Can we have a cup of tea Gran? Then I'll take them for a paddle in the stream."

My mother laughs and beckons Lizzie.

"Come here Hinny and sit on Nana's knee for a few minutes. Steven, sit on the pouf and put down that stick before you break something. Mary, you can make another pot o' tea for us all, then, we can all go out for a walk to the stream. Blow some cobwebs away. Maureen, help your mother with the cups and saucers and put two sugars in each cup. It'll help sweeten us up."

As usual, my mother is organizing us all, and she sets our afternoon in stone. She always bounces back. I'm glad for it because I don't really want to argue with her. Goodness knows I need her cooperation with everything that's going on. Maybe it'll do me good to take off my shoes and socks too. I can't remember the last time I paddled. I start to cheer up a bit, stop my sulking. I have an idea.

"I'll make a flask of tea to take with us if you like. And some custard cream biscuits for a little picnic."

"Good idea Mary," says Mother. "I've some slab cake and some soda-water. We'll pack the basket. It's only down the street. We can always come back to get more tea if we need it."

Then Maureen catches our uplift and chimes-in.

"Tell you what. We can just have a drink of milk before going out, that way we'll get more time at the stream before the sun goes down. We can still take a flask of tea with us though, for you and Mother."

"Yes, let's do that," I say. "I'll make the basket up while you all get your breath back. We should get a couple of hours outside."

"Okay," says Maureen. "Come on Lizzie and Steven. We have to sit up to the table in the kitchen to drink our milk."

They obey instantly; no if's, and's or but's, and sit without making a peep. Lizzie is first to finish her milk.

"Thanks, Auntie Maureen. Please, may I get down from the table?"

"No, wait until we've all finished and everyone's ready to go. Then you can get down," says Maureen, like an old mother hen. It makes me smile, how sensible she is.

Twenty minutes later, Mother and I are sitting on her 'faithful tartan' as she calls her picnic blanket. We are watching Maureen in the stream, bossing the children around, trying to get them to stay close to her. They ignore her completely, lost in their own little world of staring at a frog on a stone. Steven's blond hair is touching Lizzie's brunette hair. They are whispering in wonder at this strange thing. Steven pokes his stick at it. It leaps three feet onto another rock. Startled, they squeal with delight.

"Grandma," Steven calls to me. "Did you see it jump? It has big, long, legs." I nod and call back,

"What is it?"

Maureen chimes.

"It's a frog, Mother."

"I know that Maureen, I just wanted to see if Steven knows what it is."

"It's a frog, Grandma," he calls, very pleased with himself.

"It's a toad Grandma," calls Lizzie. "It's like the toad in my book. I've seen it before."

"No it's not, it's a frog," says Steven.

"It's a toad."

"It's a frog," he shouts at her.

"Hey you two," says Maureen. "I don't care if it's a frog or a toad. What matters is that he's swimming away from us. Let's catch him."

Then there is such squealing, shouting, splashing and slipping as they, all three try to corner it again. Naturally, it gets away. It knows more about the currents and swirls of its stream than they do, and all the hiding places.

Steven looks in earnest for another one. Lizzie loses interest in the hunt and starts to build stepping stones with Maureen across the stream. Steven soon joins them to help. I find myself enjoying watching them together. How they negotiate which size stone, what shape, exactly where it fits best in the stream. I laugh as they practice stepping on each stone and then move one if it doesn't seem in the right place.

The saying, 'There's a first time for everything,' is so true. Here it is, right here and now. I'm sitting on a picnic rug with my mother; my youngest daughter is enjoying the attention of her little nephew and niece, who seem to adore her. We all got so excited about our little outing. We only had to walk a hundred feet or so to the stream on the other side of the road. Who do I know who lives in a valley, surrounded by mountains and fells, so close to a beautiful bubbling stream? You know, for the first time in a long time, I feel a stirring in my heart. I say a silent prayer to God for small but happy blessings. I never planned any of this, but here we are, together as a family for a few happy, precious moments. Four generations. We span from the last quarter of the eighteen hundreds, when horses and carts got us all around, to the middle of this century where we have motor cars, buses, planes and goodness knows what else. We've been through two World Wars, terrible shortages, the Depression, and here we are, all together. We survived.

Ok, so we all got a bit banged up and bruised on the way. Churchill said we might lose a few battles, but we won the War. I have a sudden swelling of pride for my family. We each have a place and a part to play. Even if we don't feel positive all the time about each other, I know at this moment in time, I feel fabulous about my family. I'm confident that as the mother of Beth and Maureen, as a daughter of their grandma, and as the grandmother of Lizzie and Steven, I'll do everything in my power to help my family stay together; who knows, maybe we'll survive another century at least.

I say a silent Hail Mary. Then I remember I'm not even Catholic. I learned that from my best friend in the bomb factory. She was always saying them under her breath. I have to smile at myself sometimes; it's good that I can laugh at my own idiosyncrasies.

For a couple of sunny, lazy hours, we are happy. I stare at the mountain top just a mile away and see far below, a sheep-dog working the sheep down the slopes. It must be shearing time. No wonder they're off the slopes. I smile as I remember Lizzie looking for them. I'll explain it to her later. I rub the wool texture of the tartan and feel love for my country, so glad the Germans suffered defeat in their madness; thankful for what my Bertie did for his country, along with thousands of others. I join in the paddling and splashing with the three youngsters. We eat delicious slab cake, drink tea and soda water. All the custard creams have gone. I sit chatting with my mother until she relaxes and falls gently asleep. I notice her wrinkles or her 'laughter lines' as she calls them, on her soft downy face.

The gushing stream has its own unique chatter as the water swirls around its beautifully rounded rocks. The sound creates a soothing backdrop to the laughing and giggling of Maureen and the children. I think one day, when we get older, John and I can maybe retire to the Lake District and have what my mother has now. Peace, tranquility, and frogs in a stream.

Then the sun disappears in a pink and lilac haze behind the fells to the west. A sudden chill wakes up my mother.

"Come on everyone she calls," still herding her sheep. "Let's go home and have some supper."

CHAPTER 10: LIZZIE: ABLUTIONS AND EYE COLOR.

Numbers 14:18, The Lord is slow to anger, abounding in love and forgiving sin and rebellion. Yet He does not leave the guilty unpunished; He punishes the children for the sin of the parents to the third and fourth generation.

Steven is pushing my arm back and forth as I lie on my side. I'm kidding him that I'm asleep. According to my mummy, he's not to awaken me in the mornings. Usually, he plays quietly by himself, but I think he wants to go back to the stream on a frog hunt.

“Lizzie, time to get up,” he says.

I open my eyes. Steven's blue eyes look like my daddy's eyes. I can remember Daddy and so can Steven. We talk about him sometimes. We always say how tall he is. I always say he's bigger than a door because he has to duck his head going through some doors. Steven always says that when he grows up he’ll be taller than Daddy, up to the ceiling.

Steven is smiling at me. It feels nice. He doesn’t smile at me a whole lot.

“You look like Daddy Steven. He has blue eyes.”

“Well. You look like Mummy. You have brown eyes.”

Then Aunty Maureen bounces into the room with her eyes tightly shut.

“What color are my eyes you two?”

We both laugh.

“Open your eyes Auntie Maureen, so we can see what color they are,” says Steven.

"No," I shout. "Don't open your eyes, keep them closed and we have to guess."

Steven calls,

"They're blue."

I respond,

"No they're not, they're brown."

Maureen shushes us.

"Mother's asleep, whisper. You're both wrong. They're green."

She grins and opens her eyes, and we see that they're green.

"I have the same green color eyes as my daddy according to Gran."

"Mummy has the same color eyes like her daddy too," Steven pipes up. "They're brown."

Auntie Maureen laughs.

"No you got that wrong Hinny. We can't both have the same color eyes as our daddy. He has green eyes. So your mum has the same color eyes as our mum, your grandma. They're brown."

Steven shakes his head.

"No. My mummy told me, she has the same color as her daddy."

"Well, let's ask my mother all about it after breakfast. She's having a lie-in this morning. She's fatigued. So, walk on tiptoes to the bathroom, do your ablutions and don't forget to pull the chain after using the toilet. No running or jumping down the stairs. Nana's making pancakes for breakfast."

"Ablutions? What's that?" I ask.

"It's a way of saying attend to your 'toilet.' Wash yourselves, brush your teeth and hair. You know, like you do every morning."

"Ablutions," I say.

I like the word. It has a 'sh' sound in it. I like learning new words.

Steven nods his head and says,

"Never mind about ablutions, I can smell pancakes. I love pancakes. They are my favorite in all the world."

"Mine too." I chime in. "With brown sugar and lemon juice. Mm, scrumptious."

We walk very quietly but very quickly to the bathroom, which makes my auntie Maureen laugh.

"You're walking funny," she whispers. "Slow down."

But we don't. I sit on the toilet seat before Steven has a chance. He comes up to my side and pees behind me into the bowl.

"Steven. Don't wet me," I say as quietly as I can while Aunty Maureen giggles.

"I won't. I can get my wee in the space behind you."

"It's not fair," I say. "You have a pee-pee, I don't."

Aunty Maureen corrects me.

"It's called a 'Thomas' Lizzie, not a pee-pee."

Steven, still weeing behind me, says,

"Daddy told me it's a pee-pee."

I say, "A Thomas? Like Thomas the tank engine? That's funny."

Steven and I snort as we laugh. Aunty Maureen shushes us again.

Steven mocks me about being a girl.

"You're a girl. Mummy says girls don't have them, only boys."

"Auntie Maureen? Why does Steven have a Thomas and I don't?"

"I'll tell you when you're older," she says. "You wouldn't understand right now."

"Yes, I would. Tell me."

"All I know is boys have them and girls don't. Whenever I ask Gran she always says, 'I'll tell you when you're older. You wouldn't understand right now.' "

"How old do you have to be?"

Auntie Maureen shrugs.

"I don't know. Twenty-one? I think it has something to do with where babies come from. Ladies can have babies, but men can't."

Steven is washing his hands and face. I say to him,

"Well I may not have a Thomas, but I can have a baby. You can't. You're a boy."

"Who wants a baby anyway," he says, "all they do is cry all the time, like you."

He's always calling me a cry-baby. Mummy told me to ignore him and pretend I don't hear him. 'That way he'll get fed up and stop calling you names,' she said. I get off the toilet, pull the chain and go to wash my hands and face.

"Where do babies come from Aunty Maureen?"

"From inside your tummy. Gran says they grow from a seed in your tummy; like a plant grows."

I imagine me as a green leafy plant, inside my mummy's tummy. Maureen interrupts my plant thoughts.

"Stop asking questions. Finish up your ablutions and let's get downstairs before Gran has a fit."

So quickly and quietly, we finish up and tiptoe downstairs. I can smell pancakes, a delicious warm sugary smell.

"Mm," I whisper. "Smells good. I want three pancakes."

"I want ten," says Steven.

He's always trying to be better than me.

"I wish Mummy was here," I say. "She loves pancakes. I bet she would eat ten."

Auntie Maureen agrees.

"I wish your mummy was here too. I miss her. Gran says when she gets better, she can come stay for a while, get back on her feet a bit."

We reach the kitchen and are immediately silent. We sit at the table, waiting for our pancakes.

"Well good morning you three," says Nana, as she puts a huge plate of rolled up pancakes on the table. "Eat up, shut up and enjoy."

I put my hand over my mouth and giggle. I copy the words.

"Eat up. Shut up," I say.

"That's right," she says. "I've already sprinkled the brown sugar and lemon, so tuck in."

So we do. Our mummy doesn't let us speak at the table when we're eating, neither does Grandma and Nana. Even Aunty Maureen's quiet. I'm chewing on my thin pancakes with their yummy sweet and sour taste, remembering to eat with my lips closed. Lemon juice and brown sugar drip on to my fingers and plate. I lick my fingers and Nana passes me a serviette. She looks at me in that severe way she sometimes has, but she has a little smile too. When I've finished three pancakes and drunk my glass of milk, I'm quite happy to sit and think about what we might do today.

Then I remember about our different eye colors. Nana stops chewing on her third pancake and sips her tea.

"Nana? Please, may I ask you something? I've finished eating."

"Go on Hinny, What is it?"

"Does my mummy have the same color eyes like her daddy?" Nana nods.

"She does that; big brown eyes."

Just then, Grandma enters the kitchen looking very sleepy and yawns as she mumbles.

"Good morning everyone. Those pancakes smell scrumptious. I hope you've left me some."

"Oh no, Grandma." I gasp, "we've eaten them all up." I look at Nana quickly. She grins at me.

"Yes, there's four in the stove keeping warm," Nana tells Grandma, "I've not long made them."

Suddenly, Aunty Maureen speaks up.

"Mother, what color eyes did daddy have? Were they the same color as mine, green?"

Grandma looks at her and gets big lines across her forehead. Then she nods at the teapot.

"Is there enough tea in that pot?"

Nana picks up the teapot and starts to pour tea into a clean cup for Grandma. Nana answers Aunty Maureen.

"Yes. Both you and your sister have the same color eyes as your fathers. One had brown eyes, and one had green eyes."

Grandma starts coughing and spluttering like she's choking. She can't seem to get her breath. I think there's something stuck in her throat. She hacks louder and hits her chest, then bends forward. Nana leaps up and pats her back repetitively.

"Bloody hell Mary. Your eyes are popping' out o' your head. You need a drink of water or something?"

As if there's not enough commotion already, Aunty Maureen bursts into tears, stands up and starts shouting as loud as can be.

"What, we have two different dads? One with brown eyes and one with green eyes? So my sister Beth, is not really my sister, just my half-sister?"

I glance at Steven. He's stopped eating and is staring at Aunty Maureen. He looks a bit scared. Nana looks shocked and stops banging Grandma on her back. Big lines crease her forehead too. She speaks to Maureen quickly. By the tone of her voice, I can tell she's trying to be a little bit kind to poor Aunty Maureen.

"Calm down Maureen. Let's not get hysterical Hinny. Get your mother a drink o' water before she falls over."

She turns to Steven,

"Steven and Lizzie, run upstairs now and get your clothes on and clean your teeth. I'll shout you when I'm ready for you to come down the stairs again. Go on now, quickly. Shoo."

We jump off our chairs, and Steven beats me up the stairs, our minds ablaze, trying to understand how a simple question about eye color, could have got so out of hand. Steven speaks first.

"What's the matter with them all?"

I think a while before I say anything. It all seems like a big argument to me, but I feel baffled like Steven.

"I think Maureen's upset because she's only half a sister. Which half though?"

Steven shrugs.

"Well it's a bit funny, no-one can be only half? Nana said they have two daddies, one with green eyes and one with brown eyes."

I shrug. Then we hear Maureen's shrill voice again.

"I hate you, Mother. Why didn't you tell us we have two different daddies? How come we don't know that?"

I look at Steven and say,

"What's wrong with having two daddies?"

We hear the taps go on and off. Grandma's spluttering stops. She must be drinking water. Finally, she says something.

"Maureen, *your* daddy, my Bertie, died in the war. You never met him. He died before ever you were born. I kept yours and Beth's last name the same. It was just simpler that way. I didn't want people asking why you both had two different surnames. It's no-one else's business. I thought I might tell you when you got older, but it never seemed the right time. I never wanted to upset you."

"Upset me? Not only am I not Beth's full sister, now you're telling me you lied because you wanted your life to be simpler? Beth and I knew our dad had died, except it's now, *both* dads died. You just lumped us both together to make it easier?"

There's no answer from Grandma, but Maureen carries on.

"Cat got your tongue Mother? Did you ever think I'd always wonder why Beth and I look nothing alike? Did it ever occur to you that I would have had fewer unanswered questions if you'd just told me the truth from the beginning? Does Beth know about this? She was seven when I was born. Did you tell her to lie to me too?"

Nana's voice is still trying to be soothing.

"That's enough now, Maureen. You're going a bit too far now. Simmer down Hinny."

"Too far? The Outer Hebrides is not far enough for me to get away from her."

She starts crying as she speaks."I'm shocked Gran and disgusted. You could have told me."

We hear a chair push back.

"I hate you, Mother."

Maureen runs out of the kitchen through the sitting room, and we see her open the front door and disappear, leaving it wide open. Nana calls after her.

"Maureen, come back here now. Let's talk about this."

"Oh let her go, Mother," says Grandma. "She'll run up and down a couple of fells before she's finished. That'll take the wind out of her sails. She'll be back then."

"Good grief Mary. I thought she knew. You said you told her."

"Well I didn't, she knew nothing, and I thought, let's keep it that way."

Nana says, "He never came up in conversation ever, except when Maureen asked me why she was the only one in the family with green eyes. I just told her; You've got your dad's green eyes. End of conversation."

"Well, hell's teeth Mother. How was I to know? When I told Beth *her* dad died she cried for days. Then I reminded her how much she looked like him, had the same brown eyes as him. That seemed to comfort her."

"When did all this happen Mary? She never told me."

"Remember when I had to take her to Newcastle to see that lawyer about the money he left us."

"Left you, you mean. Beth didn't see a penny of that money."

"I know, but I took her with me in case there was something for Beth too. Good grief Mother, it's not like it was a fortune and I kept it all to myself. I gave you money to get this bigger house. You said you wanted to get out of that tiny cottage."

"I did. You couldn't swing a cat round in it. But it would have been nice if Elizabeth's father had left her something for when she got to twenty-one. Maybe she wouldn't be in a mess if he'd looked after her financially."

"Well, maybe not Mother. Who knows? The cat's out of the bag now, good and proper. I wish I could have had boys." She turns to pick up the kettle. "I'm putting on the kettle. Do you want another cup of tea?"

"Of course I do. Where are my cigarettes? I need to calm my nerves. I'll shut the front door. Let's stop talking about this now and call the children down. You know little pigs have big ears." Nana raises her voice and calls us as she walks to the bottom of the stairs and looks up.

"Steven, Lizzie, come downstairs now, Have you brushed your teeth?"

She spots us as we run into the bathroom from the landing. She bangs the front door shut and goes back into the kitchen. I hear her speak sharply again.

"Too late. They were listening on the landing." Then I hear Grandma's voice.

"Well, they'll hear worse things about life before they're much older. They won't understand half of it, and they'll certainly not remember any of it. I can't remember back before I was about seven. They'll have forgotten it by lunchtime."

"Yes, thank our godfathers. It's a good job we don't remember everything. Our brains would burst."

As I clean my teeth over the sink, I wonder what a brain is and what it looks like when it bursts. I remember when a big watermelon once fell off our kitchen table. Seeds and water exploded everywhere and reddish-pink all opened up inside. Mummy said some loud words like she was angry, then she said,

"And that's swearing."

I'd heard her say words like that before when our daddy was with us in the front room, and she was peeling potatoes in the back kitchen. I was crying and trying to get into the kitchen, and Daddy held me back and said to leave her alone for a while. She came out of the back kitchen shouting words at me to stop making a noise. Then she said,

"And that's swearing."

Then no one said anything after that for a while.

I can still feel Daddy's strong arm around me. I couldn't get past him. He was usually nice to us when we saw him. He bought us some nice toys, and he talked to us. I miss him. I wish he would come back. One day, I asked Mummy,

"When will we see Daddy again?"

"We'll never see him again; he lives far away in America. He isn't coming back."

I was sitting on a chair in front of the fireplace when she told me that. It was all sooty-black and empty. It was black for a long time sometimes. I remember staring at it and feeling sad. I wanted to see my daddy again.

Steven and I race to finish our teeth, brush our hair, get dressed and see who can win the race downstairs. I always seem to be winning, but then Steven always gets ahead of me because I've buttons to fasten or shoe buckles to do up properly. One of these days I'm going to win him and get downstairs first. I know I will.

CHAPTER 11: MARY: WHEELS IN MOTION.

Luke 18:3-5, A widow of that city came to him repeatedly, saying, 'Give me justice in this dispute with my enemy.' The judge ignored her for a while, but finally, he said to himself, 'I don't fear God or care about people, but this woman is driving me crazy. I'm going to see that she gets justice because she is wearing me out with her constant requests!

Today I visited Ingham Wilkins and Co., Solicitors and started some provocative but needed, 'wheels in motion.' Last year I wrote to the President of the United States and received a letter back signed by Eisenhower, telling me an inquiry was in progress about my allegations that Lonnie Caradine is the father of my two grandchildren. Yesterday I received a letter from the Department of the Air Force in Washington, dated Jan 31st, 1957. It reads;

'Dear Mrs. Krupp:

I refer further to your letter to The President of the United States concerning the support of the alleged children of Technical Sergeant Lonnie K. Caradine.

A report received from Sergeant Caradine's unit of assignment indicates that he has acknowledged parentage of your daughter's two children. He has expressed a willingness to contribute toward their support and has stated that he will forward payments of $10 on the 15th of each month and $15 on the 30th of each month.

Sincerely yours,
Joe W. Kelly
JOE W. KELLY
Major General, USAF
Director, Legislative Liaison'

I'm thrilled that at last, something is being done to get that irresponsible Yank, Lonnie, to pay up for his children. He probably thought he could get away with it, living so far away. But he didn't reckon on my tenacity. Beth gives up, accepts the hand that's dealt her. Not me. Not now, not ever. Mess with my family, and you're messing with the wrong woman.

My Solicitor could not believe it when I told him I'd written to The President of the United States. He was even more astounded that I got a personal reply and a signature from The President himself.

"Mr. Wilkins", I said, "America came in and helped us drive back the bloody Germans, and for that I'm grateful. I don't suppose the President thought much about how his soldiers would behave in the meantime, that was probably the last thing on his mind. However, they came over here, dated our girls, and most of them went back to America with not a thought in their heads about how our pregnant women would cope with a life without a husband. I know some women did get to go over to America to be with their intended. The lucky ones got married. But do *not* suppose that as the grandmother of these children, I'll not go to 'The Top' to trace that SOB and get justice for his dirty deeds."

I had convinced Beth that she needed to change her name by Deed Poll when she was pregnant with Steven. That was very sage as it showed her connection to Lonnie back then, got the children his last name and is a legal document. I put the Deed Poll down sharply on Mr. Wilkins' desk. He jumped.

"Sorry Mr. Wilkens, I didn't mean to startle you. Here is the Deed Poll change of name for my daughter. As you know I can get a bit passionate about all of this at times."

"Yes, I know you can. You are a very determined woman Mrs. Krupp. You have done a sterling job of tracing this fellow. You would make a formidable Solicitor yourself."

There it is, another man who feels threatened by my efforts. He is taking superior credit for his station in life. I bet he could not have done half as good a job as me in finding Lonnie Caradine, even if he is a bloody Solicitor. Men. They irritate the life out of me at times.

"In that package are Photostat copies of the original Deed Poll, Steven and Lizzie's certified copies of their Birth Certificates, and the response I received yesterday from the USAF with Lonnie's acceptance of his parentage of them both. How quickly can we get this thing moving, so we get regular checks from Lonnie Caradine? I need something to give the Judge when Beth has to appear in court. I want to get the Children's Department off our backs."

"I'll start on it today Mrs. Krupp. Do not worry about the Judge. Once a Solicitor gets involved and shows proof of ongoing litigation to get the children some monetary relief, I think your daughter will be safe. It's obvious this American fellow is admitting having fathered both your grandchildren. We'll use a copy of the reply from the United States President himself, as well as your recent notification and these will go a long way in determining your daughter's ability to look after her children once the money starts coming in. In the meantime, your circumstances show adequate care for your family. There is no need for the Children's Department to recommend any other care than what they are receiving now." He pauses. "You say your daughter is doing well now, back home with her new baby, no harm done thank goodness." It felt like a question.

"Yes, everything's fine. John and I have plans to eventually move out to another house and rent out to Beth, the house we are in now. She can run it as a boarding house and make some money herself, as well as get something off the children's father. I think she'll be fine."

"You're certainly a good business woman Mrs. Krupp."

"I have to be, really don't I? There's no point crying over spilled milk. Just mop it up and get on with life."

Mr. Wilkins gets up.

"Well, I'll be in touch Mrs. Krupp, as soon as we hear something back. Once again, thank you for all your hard work in getting what was needed to us today." I rise and shake hands,

"Until we meet again then."

He comes around his desk and opens the door for me. We say our goodbye's and I step out into the plush carpeted hallway. His secretary bids me goodbye, and I step into the sunshine outside, on the lovely

Victorian Square surrounded by beautiful Victorian homes of the 'well to do.' Like the houses in my street, these are mainly owned by Doctors and Solicitors.

I feel very proud that I have managed to purchase a larger home. I have worked my way up the social ladder, and while I'm not yet in a position to call myself anything other than 'working class,' at least my circumstances are more akin to the middle class. I am proud of our address, and we have escaped the regular 'two up, two down' houses that most people, like Beth, inhabit.

On my way to Booth's Café, I start to think about our large house. We had intended for me to run it as a boarding house at some point. Since Mama was with us and she needed some care, it was a perfect solution for us. To be honest, I really did not like the idea of cooking and cleaning for strangers in our home, but it was a viable option for us in our circumstances. Now, I can see that Beth's situation has presented us with another option.

Beth needs a home and needs to bring in some money. John and I need to get another house and move out. All the noise and tension is getting on my nerves. She can live downstairs and run a four bedroom boarding house and also pay us enough rent to ensure adequate cover for our mortgage. The house will gain equity, just as our other house has done over a period of years. I like the feeling I get when I tell myself, 'We'll own three houses.' I'm proud of myself for working hard and getting somewhere in life.

I suddenly feel lighter and have a bit of a spring in my step. We never know how and when life hands us seemingly big problems, but in this case, Beth's problems have given John and me a further opportunity to make more money. I smile with happiness and enter Booths Café. I think I'll treat myself to fresh cream, chocolate éclairs with my pot of tea today. I deserve it.

As I enter the main café area, who should be leaving but Ellen who lives in the house next to ours in Edward St. She smiles when she sees me and asks after Beth. She was over visiting Beth about a month ago. She has been about three times to see her in the past four months.

"Hi Ellen; how lovely to bump into you. Beth is doing fine, and her baby girl is putting weight on nicely. How are you?"

"I'm doing well thanks, Mrs. Krupp. It's funny I should bump into you today. I wanted to ask you if you'll be renting out her house to someone else now that Mr. Braithwaite has moved out. Or will Beth be coming back to her house soon."

"No Ellen, I'm not renting it back to Beth. With three children, she needs more room now. I'll be getting it ready next week to rent out again to someone else."

"I know someone who has a friend who is looking for a house to rent. May I give her a possible date and time when you'll be at the house, so she can come by and see you?"

"I know I'll be there on Tuesday all day. What's this person's name and circumstances? Is she married? Does she have children?"

Ellen responds quickly, "She's married Mrs. Krupp and her husband works on the docks. She only has one child. I believe her married name is Deborah Milligan."

"All I care about is that they are decent, hardworking people and will not be late with their rent, and no pets. If I'd known Mr. Braithwaite had a dog, we would not have rented to him. The back yard was a disgrace with all its dog-dirt."

"I know and the bloody thing barked day and night out there. I'm glad to see the back of them. Shall I tell my friend to pass onto Deborah, that you'll be there on Tuesday and to come to see you?"

"Yes, you can Ellen. I'm so glad I bumped into you today. I'll be pleased to discuss arrangements with your acquaintance."

"Thank you, Mrs. Krupp. Well, goodbye, I'll probably see you on Tuesday too, I think she'll be a good tenant."

"Thank you very much, Ellen. See you Tuesday."

As I sit and wait for the waitress to come over, I realize how everything seems to be falling into place. 'Someone up there must like me;' I think to myself. I don't know why. I haven't prayed in donkey's years. I never go to church either, unless someone dies or gets married. The last time I was in church was when we took Mama to confession. Apart from the magnificent arches, it gave me the willies. All around were pictures of Jesus carrying his cross, bleeding and bent double, with that crown of thorns sticking into his head. The stained-glass windows were beautiful, but all those halos, wings and sad faces did nothing to cheer me up as I sat and waited for Mama to come out of her confessional cupboard. I don't know what she needs to confess; she never goes anywhere further than the front door. John never goes to church, and he says he'll take his chances at the pearly gates. I like my rosary beads though, and some of my best friends are Catholic, but I can't ever imagine telling any priest my darkest secrets. I'd be too embarrassed. Who wants to tell someone all the bad things they've done? In *my* eyes, I'm not as good as some and not as bad as most.

I start to think about heaven and hell and what I would say to Saint Peter when he asks me why he should let me in the pearly gates. I would say,

"I've been a pillar of support to my children, to my mother, to my husband and his mother. I have put myself last and sacrificed my life to hard work, to help keep us all in clothes, food and a roof over our heads." Yes, who wouldn't let me into heaven after all that?

"Good afternoon Madam," says a soft voice. "What can I do for you today?"
The waitress looks smart in her black dress and frilly white pinafore.

"Please, may I have a pot of Earl Grey Tea and two fresh cream, chocolate éclairs?"

"Yes, of course, Madam," she says as she scribbles on her pad. "Will that be all?" I feel in a jolly mood. "Well a new Rolls Royce if you have it on the menu." She laughs, "Sorry we seem to be all out of those today."

"Yes, thank you." I say and she turns to leave.

I look at her shoes; shiny, yes, but a little more worn on the heel than I would like. I smile to myself and think about those pearly gates again and Mama's church visit. On reflection, it's a wonder the spire did not collapse on me when I walked in that church, sinner that I am. What is a sin anyway? I'm not a murderer, except in thought when John or other men do something that upsets me greatly. And it doesn't take much. Take that bloody Solicitor today. I did most of the hard work; all he has to do is follow through. Then he has the nerve to tell me I *could be* an excellent Solicitor. How about, I *am* a great mother, daughter, grandmother, provider, cleaner, cook, nurse, housemaid, landlady, painter and business woman? I was a pretty smart bomb assembler too. I'd sure like to see Mr. Wilkins achieve half of that. All he knows to do is be a great extortionist of my money. I could have gone to college if we'd had the money, but my life was mapped out for me before I was ever born. Still, I think I have done splendidly. I helped make the bombs that were a response to those Nazi blitzes. My war effort counts for my country, my family, and my Bertie. Most of all, it counts for the thousands of women who can now enter the workforce as something other than a nurse or a secretary. I helped carry the banner for equal rights for women, and no one can ever take that away from me.

My Earl Grey tea and éclairs arrive. I have extra hot water, in case I need more than two cups. I'm going to relish every bite and every sip of my treat. I'll probably tip the waitress like they do in the pictures. That'll surprise her. I'm feeling generous today. I'll leave her a shiny three-penny bit.

CHAPTER 12: BETH: PECKING ORDER

Amos 8:11, The days are coming, declares the Sovereign LORD, when I will send a famine through the land. Not a famine of food or a thirst for water, But a famine of hearing the words of the LORD.

My mother is up to something. I don't know what it is yet. She's too chirpy these days for my liking. She's been in and out of this house for a couple of weeks now. When I ask her where she's going, she still talks to me like I'm a two-year-old.

"Over the hills to see the men mowing," she said to me this morning.

"You sure like those men, Mother," I replied.

She slammed the door behind her. She's a sneaky one. You never know what she's planning.

Being here with her and John is exhausting. I'm on tenterhooks all the time and feel beholding to them. Just when I seem to get a couple of minutes on my own, she asks me to do something for her.

"Would you mind brushing out the bedrooms, Beth? Don't forget under the beds. You can sweeper the rugs. Then can you change Mama's bed for me? There are clean sheets in the airing cupboard."

I know where the clean sheets are. I washed them all Monday and ironed them all Tuesday. Let's see now, what was I doing Wednesday? Ah, that was it, brasses and polishing. Yesterday she rang a chicken's neck and showed me how to pluck all its feather's off and clean it out. The smell was appalling enough to puke.

"Just don't burst the gall bladder, Beth," she said, "Or you've ruined the whole chicken."

Then when we ate it for dinner last night, she told John I knew how to prepare it, and could prepare another next weekend for Sunday lunch.

"I'm ecstatic, looking forward to it Mother. Gotta love those innards," I quipped.

Steven piped up, "What are innards Mummy?" My mother laughed and said,

"That's for grown-ups to know and for children to find out when they're older."

"I know what they are," said little Miss know-it-all, Lizzie,

"They're what it wins when feeding. The hen that runs there first has the biggest kernels of corn. It gets its winners. That's right isn't it Grannie?"

"It's winners?" asked Mother. "Oh, you mean it's winnings."

"Yes, that's what you told me when we fed them last time. You said the red hen and the white hen, Sally, always get their winnings first. So is that what you have to pull out, their winnings?"

Mother laughed fit to burst. "Yes, I guess they do have their winnings pulled out when we can catch them."

I felt irritated by the whole conversation.

"Stop talking Lizzie and eat up. No talking at the table." I said. My mother always indulges Lizzie. Answers her questions, tells her how clever she is. She's not as patient with Steven, which irritates me, but most of all, I get annoyed because I was never allowed to talk at the table. Not ever. So is she annoying me on purpose or what? Lizzie had looked at my mother, who nodded at her and said,

"We can talk about it another time ok?"

Then she smiled at Lizzie, who smiled back and carried on eating. I think my mother enjoys pulling out *my* innards.

John was silent, enjoying his own game of hand-up-my-behind. Whenever I speak, he ignores me, never responds. He may hear me say, 'Please pass me the gravy, John,' at dinner, and he does, but without looking at me. That's probably the most interaction we ever have. I can't stand him. He wouldn't be anything if he'd stayed in his own country. He's a peasant, like the rest of the 'Poles' who come over here. My mother would never have thought to get all those hens in the back yard if it wasn't for him. Who keeps poultry? We're not farmers.

When he smiles, I want to rip the gold out of his teeth. Both he and my mother never smiled before they got gold teeth. Now she even looks like him when they smile. They're a good match; bloody gypsies, the pair of them. Not a genuine kind bone in their body. All they care about is money and that ridiculous mother of his. He talks about her all the time. Mama says this and Mama said that. He keeps inviting the children to go into her room and meet her. Why? She can't speak a word of English. She only speaks German. That grates me as well. We just went through a Second World War against the Germans, who I hate, and Mother brings two German speaking peasants into her life and ours.

I've tried to like my Mother. I even went to live with them for a while when I was fourteen. She was the one who invited me to stay with her. So, I gave it a try. Goodness only knows why I bothered. She was always advising me. Telling me what her opinion of everything was. She did help me find a job, but she only wanted the money I brought in. Her invitation was only ever self-seeking. I think I've got the most selfish mother in the whole world. Gran agrees with me and told me that we were too much responsibility for my mother, so she buggered-off all the time. Gran said she liked money, not motherhood.

When Dad died, Mother didn't even seem bothered. I never saw her cry. She just bustled around for a while after he'd gone, took me up to Newcastle with her to see a Solicitor about something to do with his death. She left me sitting in a cold corridor outside the office for a good hour while she talked to him. Then, they shook hands, and we left the building. She took me for lunch in a café near the railway station. I asked her why she brought me to Newcastle. She told me she wanted some company and it would be a 'nice treat' for me. She lied. I know her better than that and she never gives out treats.

I wish I could have been a fly on the wall of that office. I know something shady was going on. I wouldn't be surprised if my Dad left me some money. She obviously didn't want me to hear what she said.

My father, a Merchant Seaman was always away on dangerous journeys. The Germans targeted Merchant vessels and sank many with U-Boat missiles.

A couple of years ago, I asked Gran about how he died. No one had ever discussed his death, and it wasn't until I had grown up myself that I began to wonder about him. But Gran told me something I wish she had kept a secret. She said he committed suicide. He hung himself in the hold of the ship.

I keep seeing his feet off the ground, swaying with the movement of the ship, wondering what could have caused such sadness in his life that he would want to die. I feel so shocked by the truth of his death. It upsets me deeply.

Going over my memories back then, brought me to speculating about Maureen. How she and I look nothing alike. We are so different in every way. I started to put two and two together. I suspect that Maureen is not my full sister. If my dad knew this, maybe that's why he killed himself. I've never told anyone about my suspicions, but my heart harbors bitterness now towards my mother.

I also grieve the loss of my freedom as a child because I took on so much responsibility for Maureen. It was like I was expected to be a surrogate mother to her. I'm not over that either. I can barely sit in the same room as Maureen; she gets on my last nerve.

The last vestiges I ever had that I have a mother who cares for me, are gone. Once I realized the truth, there was nothing she had then, or has now, that I want. This woman I share a house with is little more than a stranger to me. I act the part she directs in her play to keep the peace.

I don't know why Gran told me such awful details. Gran is Gran. She's not someone who tells lies.

Anyway, who am I to talk? If I love my children, why did I allow them to be the ones to find me unconscious after taking the overdose? The whole motherhood subject seems to have too many twists and turns for me to fathom it. Aren't mothers supposed to be loving and kind? That's a cruel joke God played on all of us.

I have no idea why we are here. If all we have to look forward to, is mothers and fathers who abandon us, other countries waging war on us, wives who betray their husbands, husbands who betray their wives, lovers who lie to us, get us pregnant and leave; what is this bloody awful life's purpose for our children anyway?

They grow up to be fodder for the guns or harlots for the soldiers. Are they a blessing or a curse? Why on earth was I even born? It's all too much.

It's all about the pecking order. The strongest most aggressive hens plump up quicker. Ha! They also get their necks wrung first. My mother and her husband are pretty aggressive and seem to be getting fatter and richer. Is this why I want to wring both their necks? All I know is; I can't carry on living like this. I'm at the bottom of the pecking order in this house. My feathers get pulled out one-by-one, and my head hurts so bad I want to run away forever. Kill me! Eat me!

And I still don't know what my sneaky mother's up to.

CHAPTER 13: BETH: APPEARING IN COURT.

I Corinthians 13:4-7, Love is patient, love is kind. It does not envy; it does not boast, it is not proud. It does not dishonor others; it is not self-seeking, it is not easily angered, it keeps no record of wrongs. Love does not delight in evil but rejoices with the truth. It always protects, always trusts, always hopes, always perseveres.

We all got up early this morning. It's my court date. Mrs. Wheedler is happy to take Natalie for a few hours.

The other two children have to come with us. Why John didn't just offer to stay home with the children, I'll never know. They're going to get fed-up with him telling them every two minutes to be quiet. I expect he wants to know the ruling as soon as it happens. I may go to prison, and he'll be stuck with the children. The suspense would kill him if he stayed home until Mother got back. I've packed them two books each and Steven has a truck, Lizzie, her doll. Mother wants to sit in the public balcony with relatives of other cases and 'nosy parker' members of the town. She tried to persuade him to stay home, but he insisted. She even advised him, he would be in an outside corridor with them, as they could not have the children in court. She told him she wanted to make sure the Solicitor covered all the points well, so she needed to be in court to listen to the proceedings. He agreed. Mother looked astonished.

Later she had a quiet word with me. Then I understood.

The Solicitor she hired, who I met with once, said he thought he could stop me from going to prison, but Mother wasn't happy with that less-than-confident answer and so, unknown to me, or John, she hired the firm's Barrister. She swore me to secrecy and said I had not to mention anything about a Barrister in front of John. Apparently,

John had found out from someone at work that Barristers cost lots of money, and he tackled her about it. She played dumb. She convinced him that she would only hire a Solicitor.

So now I know what it is she's been up to, I suppose I should feel thankful that she's trying to keep me out of prison and keep the kids with me, rather than in foster care.

I'm grateful, but there's a secret part of me thinks they'd be better off in foster-care than with me. I have three kids. I'll probably be on my own with them for the next ten years. Who wants to get involved with a woman who has three children? I'm sunk. It's a prison sentence no matter what happens today.

And where am I going to stay? I have no job, no money, no long term plan, goals or ideas even. I've been out of the hospital for a while now, but I'm almost as depressed as I was before. I need to go back to the doctor and have him give me some higher dose tablets. Or I need to meet someone wonderful who is willing to take my kids on. Where am I going to meet anyone anyway? I don't work; I don't go out.

"You ready Beth?" Mother interrupts my melancholic thoughts.

"You bet Mother," I reply, "wouldn't miss it for the world." I've taken to sarcasm, or irony, lately. It helps me get through the day.

"You worried?" She asks.

"Me? Not a bit. What have I got to be worried about?" She gives me one of her looks like she despairs of me.

"Everything will be ok. We'll all go out for lunch after."

John has already started the car. Mother has Lizzie's hand, and Steven puts his in mine. He looks up at my face and says, "Come on Mummy. I bet we have a great day out today."
I can't help but laugh. "Yes, we will," I say. "It's going to be a hoot. You have to promise me one thing though, will you do that?" Steven frowns and looks earnest.

"Yes, Mummy, what?"

"Today, I want you to try to be the best and most good boy you have ever been. We're going into a big government building. We've all put on our Sunday best clothes. Now, do you think you can be quiet, not run around, and just be obedient today?" Steven nods.

“I promise Mummy.”

"Well if you keep your promise, Steven, we'll all go to a café for something to eat. Would you like that?"

"Yes, Mummy. I'll be good, I promise."

“Thank you. Now let's get in the car and let's all be very, very, quiet and good."

Mother sits in the front with John; I sit in the back with Lizzie and Steven. There’s silence all the way to town. John knows not to excite the kids with singing; he'll have to put up with them at the court house. The kids have learned to zip-up their mouths when they're around John unless he invites their participation. He rules supreme.

We arrive at the front of the Courthouse and John parks right at the steps. Not many people can afford cars, so I guess it's nice to be able to get out of a car instead of off a bus like most people. We climb the steps, and a man with a uniform and hat opens one of the big doors for us. We step into a large entry with some pompous looking Victorian men staring down at us from gilded frames. Another man in a similarly smart uniform asks for our names, and we are ushered toward a room down the corridor where we’re told to wait until called.

Mother reminds John and me that she needs to find our Solicitor and also ask where the Public Gallery is. There are numerous door-less rooms off the corridor. There's a hubbub of people coming and going all the time, with Solicitors meeting clients and talking in whispers. Occasionally men in wigs and gowns stride past our open room, then disappear never to be seen again.

Suddenly my mother appears in the corridor, tells us she has to go to the Public Gallery. She says she has spoken with our Solicitor and that we are first in court this morning.

"You'll be called in about ten minutes Beth. There's nothing to worry about; just do what we discussed. You must plead guilty when asked, as this is less time-consuming. Our Solicitor will work out a deal whereby you’ll get probation, and we’ll be out of here before you know it.”

John says, "Fine Mary. I've got the childer. I vish both you and Beth the best of luck."
Mother kisses him and leaves us. I look at John. I can't believe what I just heard.

"Do you mean that John?" He looks back at me.

"Do I mean vot?"

"That you wish me good luck?"

"Of course," he shrugs. "Vy not?"

"Thank you, John. I appreciate that."

"You're velcome. I like your childer. I don't vont them to have no mother for any amount of time. It's not good for them, or for you. I think this law is hard, to put a mother in prison when she gets so depressed. It doesn't seem like justice to me. I don't agree vith it."
I nod in agreement, and for the first time, John and I are having an authentic conversation where we both agree. I dare to believe that he does like Steven and Lizzie after all.

"Mrs. Elizabeth Caradine," a booming voice calls out.

I stand up and face the corridor. Another man in a suit looks directly at me. "Mrs. Elizabeth Caradine?"

"Yes, I'm Elizabeth Caradine."

"You are to go through those court doors, and someone will show you where to sit to be sworn in."
I leave John and my two children without even looking back. I hear Lizzie call out. "See you soon Mummy." I go into the courtroom and feel instantly unnerved by the scene before me.

There is polished wood everywhere; on the floors, half way up the walls, on benches and elevated desks that are so huge, they look like pub bars. The Judge sits behind one of the high wooden counters; his long white wig frames his stern face. He stares at me over tiny spectacles. An Usher touches my elbow and guides me to a seat behind what looks like a polished, three-sided box, lower down and right next to the Judge. I'm facing the center of the courtroom where two men with white wigs stand and face me. It all feels surreal. The Usher picks up a Bible and holds it in front of me.

"Please place your right hand on the Bible." I do as he asks. He speaks loudly as though making an announcement. "Please raise your left hand, Mrs. Caradine and repeat after me."
I do it.

"I, Elizabeth Caradine do solemnly swear this day." He reminds me of a vicar in a pulpit.
My voice, by contrast, is flat and weak.

"I Elizabeth Caradine do solemnly swear this day,"

"That I will tell the truth, the whole truth, and nothing but the truth, so help me God."

"That I will tell the truth, the whole truth, and nothing but the truth, so help me God."

"You may sit down."
He nods at me, backs away two steps then turns on his heel and retreats to a chair at the back of the courtroom. Gosh, I feel nervous. My hands are shaking and so are my knees. I place both hands on my lap and take a slow deep breath.

The men standing and facing me on my right and left wear black gowns that sway as they move. The left-side man speaks first.

"Please stand up Elizabeth Caradine so you may hear the charges against you. You may answer these charges only as directed by this court, as Guilty or Not Guilty. Do you understand?"
My voice is barely a whisper.
"Yes, I understand."
The Judge speaks, his voice is polished like he's addressing the bloody Queen of England.

"Elizabeth Caradine, You are charged with the following: The attempted murder of yourself and your child. Aggravated battery of yourself and your child with the intent to endanger life. Abandonment and neglect for the safety of your other two children, Steven and Elizabeth Caradine. How do you plead?" My head swims. It's the same words the policeman used in the hospital. I gulp for air.

"Guilty, Your Honor." My voice is croaky. The Judge speaks up again.

"We cannot hear you. You will have to speak up. How do you plead?"

"Guilty Your Honor," I croak louder.

"Thank you. You may now sit down."

He addresses my Barrister, the man on my left.

"Mr. Blackledge, you are representing Mrs. Caradine today. What have you to say about her guilty plea and her case?"

Mr. Blackledge, still standing, has a file in his right hand which he opens. He rocks back and forth from his heels to his toes as his voice with its superior tone addresses the Judge. His gown, floating to and fro with his movements distracts me for a moment.

"Your Honor, Elizabeth Caradine has had three children out of wedlock. Her situation is unfortunate in that she became involved with the father of her first two children while working as a store assistant on the American Air force base in Fairford. The American Sergeant, one, Lonnie Caradine, met Miss Elizabeth Borge, as she was then known, and they had a three year intimate relationship. According to my client, Mr. Caradine kept promising to take my client back to the United States where he said, he intended to marry her. The marriage never happened, and my client changed her name from Borge to Caradine when she was pregnant with her firstborn son, Steven. Your Honor, I refer to Exhibit One; the said change of name by Deed Poll on the 11th of October 1950. Also Exhibits One 'A' and One 'B,' the two children's birth certificates.; that is Steven and Elizabeth Caradine." He pauses for a few seconds and begins rocking and talking again.

"Lonnie Caradine and Elizabeth Borge cohabited together above the Arbor Café in Fairfield for almost two years. I refer to Exhibit Two, the rent book showing his name and her name on the front thereon."

He takes a deep breath, pushes out his chest and continues.

"I put it to you, your Honor that Lonnie Caradine acted as a scoundrel. He was not then, and still is not now, willing to fulfill his promise of marriage to Elizabeth Caradine."

He pauses again.

My mind seems to grasp the truth of his words, 'a scoundrel.' It hits me like ice-cold water on my face. My Lonnie is an absolute lie-telling, good-for-nothing scoundrel. It's as though I've been asleep for months and just woke up. I take a deep breath and nod in agreement.

"Your Honor, Lonnie Caradine has not yet paid one penny of support towards his children. My client's Mother, Mrs. Mary Krupp, has paid out sums of money and spent many months, tracing this fellow in the United States. I refer to Exhibit Three and Exhibit Four." The Judge lifts up papers and adjusts his reading glasses. My Barrister continues.

"Exhibit Three is the letter, addressed to Mrs. Mary Krupp, from the Whitehouse, signed by President Eisenhower himself, assuring her that Senior Officers are investigating.

The Judge lets out a tiny snort of laughter, examines the paper and looks over his spectacles at my Barrister before speaking.

"Well this is my first experience of having a letter from the Whitehouse in court, Mr. Blackledge. Do go on."

My mind's on fire. I stare at the Barrister as though he's a ghost. He continues.

"Exhibit Four is the letter from the United States Air force, showing Lonnie Caradine has accepted fatherhood of the two children and intends now to send regular payment checks every two weeks in the sums mentioned in the letter."

I gasp and stare up at my Mother in the Public Gallery. I'm astounded by what I'm hearing. Has she really been in touch with the Whitehouse? And how long has she had this letter signed by the President of the United States? When did she know that Lonnie will be sending regular payments? How? When did all this happen? Is this a hoax? Doesn't she know she can get in real trouble for perjury?
She doesn't look at me. Her eyes, steady and unblinking, observe the Judge who is reading the exhibits over again. He has a wry smirk. He looks up at Mr. Blackledge and says,

"President Dwight D. Eisenhower himself, hmm," he chuckles, "That's quite an achievement in itself."
He looks directly at me over his glasses and then addresses Mr. Blackledge.

“So what you are informing me and the court of, is that monetary relief for Mrs. Caradine and two of her children is pending. Is that correct?”

“Yes, Your Honor. The letter indicates that the money will be taken from Lonnie Caradine’s salary every two weeks starting next month. About my client, Your Honor. I would like to put it to you and the court, that my client was under extreme duress for quite some time and that this duress, is now significantly reduced by her present and future promised circumstances. It is, for this reason, M’Lud that I ask for leniency in this case, and that Mrs. Caradine be allowed to continue in residence with her mother and step-father, Mr. and Mrs. Krupp, who are overseeing the care of her and her three children.”

The Judge looks up, and his voice has lost its humor.

“Do we have a report from the Children’s Department concerning this arrangement and the welfare of the three children?”

“We do, M’Lud." My Barrister holds up a file, and the Usher takes it from him and gives it to the Judge.

The Judge adjusts his glasses and reads the report. He looks up again.

"Your Honor," says Mr. Blackledge, "The psychiatrist report indicates Mrs. Caradine, was released to her mother’s home three weeks after her baby was born. Her baby is doing well, and he does not consider Mrs. Caradine to be a risk to herself or her children. He supports two more visits before he unequivocally releases her from his care. The Children's Social Worker report states that the address of Mr. and Mrs. Krupp is in a local, well-to-do area and indeed, is in keeping with the standard of other professionals in the area. The report suggests that with continued care and support, the Children's Department think the children and their mother are in good hands. They say both of the older children will be attending school by this September. They too, support a lenient sentence for Mrs. Caradine, together with further visits from the Children’s’ Welfare Department until any Probationary period has been served.”

I take a deep breath. He continues.

"M'Lud. If it pleases the court, I would like to recommend the following.” He holds up another piece of paper, which is taken from him by the Usher to the Judge who reads it quietly to himself and speaks.

"I'm ready to give judgment on this case. Please stand up Mrs. Caradine."

As I rise, a thought flashes through my mind.

'Aren't you even going to ask me what I think? How come I can stand in this courtroom, with everyone from the President of the United States of America, to you, a Judge who I never clapped eyes on before today, having a say about me, my children and our future, and no-one asks me for my opinion?' Not that I have anything to say, I'm bloody speechless; but it would be nice to be asked.

The Judge looks at me over his small glasses now perched on the end of his nose.

"Mrs. Elizabeth Caradine, you have pleaded guilty to all the charges set before this court. Before I pronounce sentence, I want you to listen very carefully to my next words. Attempted murder, grievous bodily harm, and child-abandonment are serious charges and can put you in prison for some time. I have looked at the particulars of this case and its different reports and viewpoints from other professionals. I have concluded that your hand in life is not an easy one and that you also were abandoned in your dire circumstances.

However, I caution you to make much wiser decisions in life than you have done so far. A third child out of wedlock can only hinder your progress. However, I'm happy to hear that you have parents that have gone above and beyond to help resolve your problems and I'm satisfied with the Children's Department Report that you are a caring and loving mother and that you are all thriving in your present circumstances.

For these reasons, I give you a sentence of two years' probation with the proviso that you continue to see your psychiatrist until he deems you healthy in mind again. You must follow your probation officer's directions and not deviate from them, or you will find yourself back in my court. Do you understand Mrs. Caradine?"

"Yes your Honor," I say confidently. "Thank you, your Honor."

"Court is adjourned for ten minutes." He slams down his hammer.

"All rise," shouts the Usher.

Everyone stands and the Judge leaves. Mr. Blackledge comes over to me and shakes my hand. I can't help smiling at him.

"You are free to go home today Mrs. Caradine, but first I want to introduce you to your probation officer, Mr. Daniels. Do step down; we'll meet him through there in the corridor."

I get down from the raised dais, and Mr. Blackledge leads me out of the courtroom and waits for Mr. Daniels to join us in the corridor. By this time my mother is making her way towards us too.

A thin-faced, middle-aged man with a high forehead and weasel features introduces himself to me, congratulates Mr. Blackledge on getting a gracious sentence and stares at my mother who joins us. Mr. Blackledge introduces her, they shake hands, and she then proceeds to embarrass me with a huge hug and a smacking kiss on my cheek.

"Congratulations Beth and thank you so much, Mr. Blackledge. You did us proud today."

She then sees John enter the corridor from the side room and rushes off to tell him the good news. My Barrister bids me farewell and shakes my hand again before he turns away and disappears down the corridor into an anti-room with a door. Mr. Daniels addresses me.

"I have an appointment with you first thing in the morning in the building next to the Police Station. My office is on the second floor. Please be there by nine o'clock sharp tomorrow. I'll be explaining everything to you then, but it is of extreme importance that you're not late for, nor miss your first appointment. You can be re-arrested if you violate any of the probationary rules and regulations. Do you understand?"

I nod.

"I understand."

"Tomorrow, at nine then."

I just stand, dazed by the speed of everything, shell shocked by the power and audacity of what just happened. All the people who can decide my fate in an instant without any other words to me except, 'do you understand?' Just like that policeman in the hospital.

But I don't want to scream again. This time I want to laugh. I don't understand anything anymore, except that I'm free and Lonnie, 'The Scoundrel,' must still love me, as he is willing to support our children. And my mother? What on earth just happened?

She's hurrying in my direction with John, Steven, and Lizzie. I have a million and one questions for her too. President Eisenhower? Really? Money coming from Lonnie? Are you certain? How much money? When? How did you track him down? How and when did all this begin? My head is reeling.

Steven reaches me first and throws his arms around my legs. I start laughing. Lizzie reaches up for me to pick her up. I lift her up and kiss her cheek three or four times. John pats my back; he's smiling.

"Congratulations Beth, it's good news today."

I kiss him on the cheek and then kiss my mother. I'm overjoyed by our new circumstances.

"Thank you Mother; you have done so much for me."

I look at John's beaming face.

"Thank you again, John, I really appreciate all you have done for us."

He pats my shoulder again. Mother in her best cheery voice says,

"So let's go eat something. You ready for lunch Hinnies?"

"Yes, we are," says Lizzie as I set her down.

I hold both her and Steven's hands, and we all almost skip down the courthouse steps towards John's car.

"This calls for a celebration," says John. "Let's go to that new chicken place on the Main Street. What's it called Mary?"

"Kentucky Fried Chicken," she says. "Let's splash out and get a bucket."

"Right," answers John. "Is everybody happy?"

Steven, Lizzie, me and Mother shout at the top of our voice,

"Yes."

People stare at us as we bundle into the car laughing out loud. This day is one of the best days of my life in years.

CHAPTER 14: LIZZIE: STAY WITH ME.

Psalm 84:3, Even the sparrow has found a home, and the swallow a nest for herself, where she may have her young.

When Mummy first came out of the hospital, Steven and I moved out of the small room above the kitchen. Mummy and both of us now sleep in a much bigger room upstairs, looking out onto the front street. It has a small bed where Steven and I sleep head to toe and a larger bed for Mummy. There is a chest of drawers and the dressing table with the arch mirror. There is a built-in wardrobe in the wall next to the fireplace. This room is one of two bigger rooms upstairs with fireplaces. The other two smaller rooms do not have one.

I like that we have a fireplace in our bedroom. It has a gas fire sitting on its hearth and Mummy says we can use it when winter comes around. I like it because it reminds me of our fireplace in our other house. The one Daddy sat next to when he would pick us up onto his knees and talk to us.

There's a ticking clock on the mantle and Mummy has a few of Nana's little glass animals on both sides of it. I love them all, dogs, cats, ducks, elephants and two swans. There is a happy clown and a sad clown. We are never allowed to touch the glass ornaments. Mummy says they are her favorite ones. Steven broke one once. It was a dog and Mummy smacked his bare bottom. She had tears in her eyes, and Steven screamed.

We must never touch the flappy metal turn-key on one of the pipes going into the fireplace. I watched Grandpa tape it up, we cannot see it, never mind touch it. Only adults can move the key, as gas can be dangerous if not lit properly.

Today, everyone's talking in the kitchen. Grandpa is writing a list of things, and they are discussing something about furniture. I listen, quiet as a mouse. They talk about sofas, tables, chairs, dressing tables, coat stands, beds, dining tables, and armchairs. Usually, I like to listen, but this talk seems boring. Mummy sees me and tells me to go outside and play.

Later on in the day, after watching lots of adult activity and wondering about where all the lovely furniture in our house is going, I sit down for a drink of milk and some cake at a different kitchen table. This one has what Mummy calls 'leaves' which pull out either end to make the table bigger. Grandpa has delivered six chairs. Four fit around the table, but six can when the leaves extend out.

So much seems to be happening just lately. There has not been a day for the past week when some piece of furniture wasn't either leaving or coming in. I don't like the bustle. Grandpa and Grandma barely talk to me because they're always so busy barking orders for me to move out of the way as I watch them carry things through doorways. Mummy helps with some pieces too, and there is a man I have never seen before, helping Grandpa with the bigger things.

Suddenly I realize that Grandma, Grandpa, and Mama are all moving out of the house. It hits me. I stand still. I'm shocked. No one told me, and I have no idea where they are going. I run to Grandma and tug at her sweater just as she's about to exit the hall.

"Where are you going, Grandma? Can I come too?" She bends down and plants a big wet kiss on my lips.

“Not this time Hinny.”

“But why Grandma? Please don’t go. Please.”

"We are moving into a different house, but I’ll come visit you every week. One day soon, I’ll come and bring you over to stay for a weekend. Would you like that? Come to Chorley for the weekend?”

“What’s Chorley?” I ask her.

"It's where I live Hinny," is all she says before kissing me once. She turns and leaves. Tears sting my eyes.

“Stay with me, Grandma. I like living with you and Grandpa." She looks back.

"Don't cry, Lizzie. It's for the best, you'll see."

Then she's gone. I just stand still because I feel like I can't move. Tears stream down my cheeks.

"I thought you loved me and liked living with me," I say to the empty hall.

Mummy comes back in after waving them off. She sees my face and says very softly, but with a laugh in her voice,

"Are you crying, Lizzie? Don't cry. Grandma will be back soon."

"You didn't tell me she was leaving. I didn't know."

"Now come on Lizzie. Stop this and I'll make you a nice cup of hot chocolate. Ok?"

She takes my hand and leads me into the kitchen. I sit at the new kitchen table. It will never be the same without Grandma, not in this kitchen, not in this world. I look at how different this room looks. Two spare chairs sit idle against two other walls. Natalie has a high chair. It's yellow with a picture of a teddy on the backrest. It sits in a corner next to the door leading to the cupboard under the stairs. I stand up, wanting to sit near the stove on my favorite chair. I can see rings on the flat surface of the arms where Grandma always rested her hot cup of tea. I rub them with my fingers hoping the wood will still feel warm, knowing it won't. A thought comes to mind, and I catch my breath.

"Mummy," I call, "Please can we always keep this chair, don't let them take this one."

She comes into the kitchen from the back.

"That chair is staying here Lizzie; it's not going anywhere."

She's carrying a small teacup and places it right where Grandma's cup would be, on the arm.

"Hold the handle; it's not hot, just warm."

I look at the still swirling chocolate.

"Thank you, Mummy for being kind to me."

She smiles and says,

"You're welcome, sweetheart, I love you, you know."

She returns to the back kitchen.

I sip my chocolate and think. There's a clothes-holder hanging down from the ceiling. Grandpa put it up a few days ago. It's for wet clothing and has a rope which lowers and lifts it. A knot in the rope hooks under a metal loop on the door frame to hold it tight. It's one of my favorite jobs. Mummy helps me. She lets me take off the dry clothes and hang up the wet ones before I tug down on the rope to lift the whole thing up to the ceiling again. I love it. I have to stand on one of the kitchen chairs to do it, but Mummy says I'm growing so fast, soon I'll not need to.

We have a metal cage-like fire guard that stops us getting too close to the stove. It also serves as a place to put Natalie's nappies if they need to dry quickly. We usually hang them on one of three washing lines in the back yard to dry, but if it's raining the fire guard helps a lot. The guard has an upper flap that completely covers the top from one end to the other. Lots of socks can dry on it. Whenever she bakes bread, she puts the guard back after she has placed all her dough tins around the stove to rise.

Natalie has started to get around quite quickly on her own now, shuffling on her bottom from one area to another. She often uses the guard to pull herself up, so Grandpa added a holding piece on the side walls so she can't move the guard or pull it over. I like seeing how different things in the house are for special purposes. I never tire of thinking about how this catch works or that bolt holds things tight, or how that wheel holds moving ropes in place. Mummy says it's a pulley.

Another thing that makes me happy is that Aunty Maureen stays with us. She sleeps in the bedroom above the kitchen where Steven and I first slept. She has a single bed, a wardrobe, a dressing table, one chair and one bedside table. All her furniture is different to the furniture that was once in there. Mummy's glad too. She likes Aunty Maureen being here; well who wouldn't? Aunty Maureen gives us lots of attention; she reads stories to Steven and me, helps us bathe at night and get dressed in the morning. So I'll miss my grandma, but at least I can have some fun with Aunty Maureen.

My thoughts and the hot chocolate help me feel better. I hold my cup with both hands and rest it on my chest as I cross ankles as Grandma does. I'll see her again soon. It won't be too long.

CHAPTER 15: LIZZIE: A ROSE BY ANY OTHER NAME.

Numbers 6:24-26, May the Lord *bless you, and protect you; May the* Lord *smile on you and be gracious to you. May the* Lord *show you his favor and give you his peace.*

Today, Aunty Maureen seems all excited. We have a breakfast of shredded wheat and hot milk, then she dresses me in some new clothes. I have a knitted, dark gray skirt with a red waistband and a red stripe border around the hem. There is a cardigan to match, and I wear it over a white blouse that has buttons down the front. I'm wearing new white long socks and black buckled new shoes. Aunty Maureen even puts my hair in a ponytail and fastens a red ribbon around it. She tells me I look very spruced indeed.

"Today you're starting school," she tells me.

"I know. That's why I'm wearing my new clothes."

She laughs. "Clever bugger."

"Are you taking me to school?"

"No. Your mummy is. Are you excited?"

I nod. I watch Aunty Maureen buckle my shoes. They had taken me out to get them a few days ago. I had wanted the red ones I saw in the shop window, but Aunty Maureen kept telling me, 'You can't have red shoes, you have to have the black pair.'

"I want the red ones. I don't like black." I insisted over and over. Frazzled, they gave up and tried a red pair on my feet, just to shut me up.

"These fit me better, the black ones hurt."

But much to my chagrin, they got another pair of black ones with buckles and asked how they felt. I said they felt alright because by this time Mummy was mad at me and threatened to take me home without any shoes. So I got these.

“Aunty Maureen. Why would Mummy and you not let me have the red shoes?”

“Oh don’t start all that again,” she says with a smile. “I told you, Lizzie. No one wears red shoes. I know you’ll understand when you get older. So let’s just get you ready for school please.”

Sometimes adults don’t seem to make any sense. If children can’t wear red shoes, then why do they sell them in the shoe shop?

Then Mummy arrives in the kitchen. She looks beautiful in a dark blue skirt and a pale blue sweater with short sleeves.

"You look darling, little schoolgirl Lizzie," she says. "Here’s your coat, I’ll get mine. I’m taking you to school now.”

“Is Steven coming with us?” Steven walks into the kitchen dressed in new school clothes. He’s wearing a cap with a small brim at the front. It's dark gray with a blue ring around the edge. The color matches his gray socks and pants. He’s wearing a white shirt under a new blue sweater Mummy knitted for him. His black lace-up shoes are gleaming.

“Ooh! Steven,” I say. You look handsome.” Aunty Maureen bursts out laughing.

“Yes he does, doesn’t he?”

I love how she laughs with her head thrown back and her mouth wide open. She always makes me laugh. Mummy hands Steven a gabardine coat; she gives Aunty Maureen mine. As Mummy puts on her black wool coat with a curly collar, I suddenly feel very excited and jump up and down.

"I'm going to school. I'm going to school." Aunty Maureen laughs and grabs my arm and shoves it gently into my coat sleeve and fastens my front buttons for me. I give her a quick kiss and hug and I race out of the house into the street. Other mothers are already walking towards the school down Eldon Street holding their children's hands. I count every street we cross. It comes to six; then we are at the school. Steven suddenly pipes up,

“Only two more years and I’ll be in this playground in the big school. You’ll have three more years Lizzie.”

"Well let's just concentrate on doing well in the infant's school first," says Mummy. "Your playground is down the next street Lizzie."

Steven is excited and shouts out. "The infant's school is joined to the big school Lizzie, but we never go through the door to the big school. We're not allowed."

As we turn the corner, through the iron rods of the fence, a group of older girls in the playground turn a rope and jump over it. They all chant,

"Lucy's in the kitchen, doing a bit of stitching, in comes the bogey man, and she runs out." I stop to watch, pulling Mummy to a standstill. First one girl jumps into the middle of the rope and jumps over it for the whole chant. Then another girl jumps in, and the first girl runs out, and the song repeats. I can't take my eyes off them.

"Will I be able to do that Mummy?"

"I know you will Lizzie. You learn new things fast. It's called skipping."

Steven starts to hop on one foot, then the other. He speeds ahead of us and calls loudly,

"Anybody can skip. It's easy."

He gets to the infant's gate very quickly and goes through it. When we step through the gate, I notice other children and their mothers gathering around the nursery door. We follow them in.

"Hello," says a woman with red wavy hair. "My name is Miss Anderson. I'm the nursery assistant teacher." She looks at my face and asks, "What's your name?"

"Lizzie," I say, noticing her green eyes like Aunty Maureen's.

"Elizabeth Caradine," says Mummy, "But we call her Lizzie for short. I'm Mrs. Caradine, her mother."

"Yes, I remember you, Mrs. Caradine, hello again. Well, Lizzie, let's show you where to hang your coat, shall we? You'll hang your coat on the same hook each day. Follow me."

She takes us to a row of hooks down the center of the bright yellow painted room and points to a picture next to a hook.

"You see this picture, Lizzie? This picture is how you know which hook is yours all year. Do you know what this picture is?"

“It’s a red flower,” I say.

"Good girl. It's a red rose. So you’ll bring your coat and hang it on this hook next to the red rose every day.”

“That’s a beautiful red rose Lizzie,” says Mummy, “Just like the red roses we grow up the wall in our front garden. You’ll remember that picture won’t you?”

“Yes.” I smile.

Already Mummy’s taking off my coat. The teacher shows me how to hang it up.

"Come to your red rose every day and put the hook through this hole in the cloth like this. Now on rainy days when you might wear wellingtons, you can place them under the bench where your hook is. They'll be here when you change back into them before you go home."

She looks at my mother.

“You can go now; we've got her until three o’clock. Will you come to walk home with her today?”

“Yes, I’ll be bringing Steven and her each day, just for this week and picking them up again. After that, I think they’ll be okay walking to and from school together.”

Miss Anderson looks at me and smiles.

"That's right Lizzie. You have a brother in infant's class two. Steven. He was in our nursery class last year. Well, I'm sure you’ll be ok.”

Mummy bends down; we kiss each other goodbye.

“I’ll see you later Lizzie, be good.”

“Bye-bye, Mummy. I’ll see you later.” And she’s gone.

A little girl starts crying. "Mummy, Mummy, don't go." Another woman holds her hand and starts to talk to her, but she howls even louder. Miss Anderson leads me through another door into a large room.

“This is the nursery Lizzie.” She calls over to a tall lady who is standing by a desk.

“Miss Norris, this is Elizabeth Caradine, we’ll be calling her Lizzie for short.”

Miss Norris comes to me with a big smile on her face and greets me,

"Hello, Lizzie. I'm Miss Norris the Head teacher here. We are all going to sit cross legged on the floor until all the children are inside the school. Okay?" I nod my head and sink down where I stand and join other cross-legged children on the floor. None of the children speak. We all just sit and look ahead, or watch others brought in. There's a fire lit in the fireplace on one wall of the nursery, and my eyes automatically settle on the red and yellow flames behind the fireguard. They remind me of home.

*

Later that day, after our sleep on our little beds, we sit cross-legged on the floor again. My first day of school is exciting. Miss Norris does most of the talking and tells everybody what to do. Another teacher from the big school appears and plays the piano for us. I've never seen a piano before, and I like the sounds very much. We have to tuck our skirts into our knickers and skip around the nursery until the piano stops. I look silly. My mummy never asks me to tuck my dress or skirt into my knickers. I'm glad she can't see me. She would say we all look ridiculous.

Thomas Titterington stares at me, but when I stare back, he looks away. The boys keep on their pants, so why as a girl, do I have to show everyone my knickers. I don't understand. I feel embarrassed. Why? I just keep skipping around the room, and I don't notice anyone else looking at me. Then the piano stops. Miss Norris calls out,

"Take your skirts out of your knickers girls." I'm glad.

We all sit down near Miss Rogers who pays the piano, and we learn a song. It's a rainbow song, all about colors. It's fun. Miss Norris asks us all a question.

"Does anyone know who made all the colors?" She waits but no-one answers. "Well it's God in heaven, and we call him our Father because he loves us all like his children. Does anyone know where heaven is?" She waits again. No-one answers. Then Miss Anderson puts her hand up, and Miss Norris says,

"Children, notice how Miss Anderson puts up her hand when she wants to speak. If you ever want to say something, you must put up your hand until we see you and then you can speak. Yes Miss Anderson, what is it you would like to say?"

“Well Miss Norris, you asked if anyone knows where heaven is. I think it is above all the clouds in the sky. We cannot see Heaven because it is so far away and it is invisible.”

"Thank you very much, Miss Anderson. Yes, heaven and God are unseen. The word for this is 'invisible.' Can you all remember the word ‘invisible' and what it means? So, children, I think it would be a good idea if we spoke to our Father in heaven to thank him for all the colors we all love so much. So let us kneel on the floor and put our hands together like this."

She kneels and puts her palms together with her fingers pointing upwards. We all copy her.

“Now children, we’ll all close our eyes, and I want you to copy what I say. Repeat these words after me.”

I'm confused. I've never done anything like this before. I'm unsure of exactly what I am to do. School sure does have some strange things going on. I shut my eyes as I kneel and put my hands together, careful to point them upwards.

“Our Father,” says Miss Norris

“Our Father,” I hear all the children say, but I missed the chance. I listen harder.

“Who art in heaven,” she says.

All the children copy her except me.

"Mines not, he's in America," I say with conviction. No one seems to notice.

“Hallowed be thy name.”

I giggle. It's a funny name, but I repeat,

“Hello’d be thy name.”

I giggle again. All the other children don’t seem to think it’s funny. I carry on like they do, repeating each sentence.

“Thy Kingdom come, Thy will be done on earth as it is in heaven. Give us this day our daily bread.” I think about all the loaf tins around the stove and think God must bake too.

“And forgive us our trespasses, as we forgive those who trespass against us. And lead us not into temptation but deliver us from evil, for thine is the kingdom, the power and the glory, forever and ever, our men.”

Now I'm puzzled. I have no idea what we are saying, and to say, 'our men,' at the end is silly. What about our men? As I open my eyes, I ponder all of many strange things that have happened at school today. We have never done these things at home, ever.

Miss Norris asks us all to sit again, and she explains to everyone in the class that we were talking to, or praying to our Father in heaven, who is also called God.

"He made the earth, all the trees, flowers, and butterflies and every single thing in the whole world, including you and I. Praying, is a way of showing God that we are thankful for everything he gives us. Every day in morning School Assembly, we will be saying this prayer until you learn it by heart."

It will take me a few more times to understand lots of the words. Grown-ups know more about these things than children. Like furniture. They talk about furniture and move it around all the time. Children don't.

Then we learn a lovely song, "All things bright and beautiful, all creatures great and small, all things wise and wonderful, the Lord God made them all."

I love to keep singing it over and over. I sing it to Mummy on the way home. I ask her why God is called 'Hello'd.' She laughs and laughs.

"Hallowed be thy name, means we hallow it, or make it holy. Praise God's name."

"Oh. Do you pray to God Mummy? "

"I pray to him sometimes before I go to sleep or if I go to church."

"What's church?"

"I used to go to church in the Lake District when I was a girl. It's a beautiful building where people pray to God."

"If we go to the Lake District can we go and see the church?"

"Well maybe, we'll see. So let's stop asking questions for a while and do 'my back door goes flip flap flew.'

So for the rest of the way home, Mummy calls out,

"My back door goes flip flap flew," and she picks me up by one arm and swings me. I like it when Grandma and Grandpa do it together. I fly up with my legs in the air. It's such fun.

At night in bed, Steven and I talk about prayers and God. We pray together and thank God for everything. We take turns. "Thank you for the trees, the flowers, the birds, the frogs, the sky, our toys, the sunshine, the moon, the stars and lots of things."

Steven stops praying and goes to sleep. My prayer seems to go on for a while longer, then I get sleepy and snuggle under my blankets. What an exciting day. I have learned so much.

I have a Father in heaven who I can talk to, and he hears me, so, with my daddy in America, I have two daddies. They are both invisible because I can't see them. My picture is a red rose. I can sing two songs about rainbows and all the creatures God has made, and I can thank God for it all.

Life is getting very interesting. I like school.

CHAPTER 16: BETH: STARTING A BOARDING HOUSE.

Psalm 50:14, 15, Make thankfulness your sacrifice to God, then call on me when you are in trouble, and I will rescue you, and you will give me glory.

At last, my life seems to be getting on an even keel. My two eldest children are both at school now. My mother is passing on the twenty-five dollar monthly checks she gets from America. The rate of exchange is about two dollars to every British Pound Sterling, which means I get about twelve to thirteen pounds a month, which is a great help. My youngest daughter Natalie is over a year old now, and social services helped get her into regular day care three days a week to give me a break. Mother wants me to take her father to court for child maintenance, but I want nothing whatsoever to do with him. I don't want him able to have visitation rights; I never want to see him again. I know I only latched onto him because I was so depressed about Lonnie. He was a big mistake in my life.

I pay Mother and John two pounds a week rent which doesn't leave me anything for myself after the food. The children get free school meals, and Mother brings us some meats each week. Plus we have the hens and some regular eggs from them. It's not as though I haven't lived on rations before either. I need to either go back to work or start up this boarding house idea of my mother's.

It's not that I don't want to work; it's just that I was in a real mess just before the overdose and it has taken me all these months to recover. The dreams about running after Lonnie haven't stopped. He still rounds a corner and disappears, but my reaction to them is getting better. Instead of the usual sinking emptiness and devastation; I cry a little, then get out of bed and make a good strong cup of tea with two sugars, and I feel better for it.

Since I've been receiving checks from him, I'm more secure, but I still hold a candle for him. At least we're connecting again if only by his child support.

I can't describe the emptiness that flooded my soul when I didn't know his address anymore. I never thought about the word 'anguish' before, but I know what it is now. Mental torture. I used to sit with a cushion pressed hard into my stomach all the time to try to stuff the empty place in my center. I would rock when it became too much. I never want to go through that again.

I'm in two minds. If I do start up a boarding house, I'll be able to stay home and be here when Steven and Lizzie get home. But a part of me will feel housebound, tethered. I'll probably have to make early breakfasts for shift workers and dinner every evening. Who wants to get up at four in the morning to cook? The evening meal's not a problem; it'll make sure we all get meat and two vegs into us daily.

Then there is the big question. Do I want strangers in my home? Certainly not in the next bedroom, that would be creepy. I'll have to make the downstairs our living space, the dining room into a shared bedroom for me and the kids. I want complete separation from them. So where would they eat? I could make the front room that was Mama's room into a dining room I suppose. I'd had dreams of having a formal sitting room in there one day, but we don't need that extra room. It's not as though I have any visitors unless I count the School Board Official or the District Nurse or the Social Worker who come by now and then. Boarders would only come into the front dining room for two meals a day, and I could have a couple of lounge chairs in there for any daytime visitors.

When I was a boarder in the South, Mrs. Maxwell was lucky in that she had two tidy, pleasant women, who were no trouble at all in her house. Maybe I can get a couple of women, who knows? The docks and Courtaulds are the big pull in this town, and while Courtaulds does employ some women, most are men. Not a happy thought for me, having males in my home.

I despise that they want selfish sexual pleasure and can leave as if nothing happened. I hate macho irresponsibility and lies, unfaithfulness to their wives and me. Do I want to look after and feed people I hate? Not likely.

I think how little I knew about my father. I saw him sporadically when his ship came home; he brought in the money, but I only saw him for a short while. What is a father? I have no idea.

Even my grandpa died just when we were starting to see more of each other. Grandpa would walk with me over the hills, along streambeds, up rocky outcrops and we would finally look out over the whole lake and mountains in the distance, and I would know the beauty of creation and relationship. He had a magic smile, thick white hair, a white mustache that curled up at the ends, smiling at me. Then his brown eyes glowed warm and crinkled. He was older than Gran and had a son two years older than my mother. He said he was Anglo-American, born in the United States to an English father and American mother, but that when his father died of TB, he decided to come back to England with his mother, wife and small son. He was scholarly, had been to school and knew about bridges, engineering, and machinery. He worked in Newcastle.

Gran met him in South Shields a year after his wife died. She was at the fish market and apparently, so she told me, he was standing behind Gran and was listening to her talking to the fishwife about how she loved smoked finny haddock and how she cooked it for breakfast sometimes. He started a conversation with her telling her it sounded good. They got on like a house on fire. She asked him how often he came into the Shields; he said it was his first visit. He heard how lovely the beach was, how fresh the fish was and he wanted to experience it for himself. He said he loved the place and that he would come back on the Sunday train next week. His name was William; she always called him 'my Will.' He continued to work in Newcastle but then was able to get a job in the Shields with a ship builder and they got married, and all lived together. Gran had two children, Albert and my mother Mary, to her previous husband who died in a mining accident. Grandpa Will's son lived with them until at twenty years old, after Will's mother died; he returned to the United States.

When Gran evacuated to the Lake District with Maureen and me, Grandpa Will stayed behind to work. He visited monthly; he loved the mountains and lakes. He had been offered a job in the wheelhouse of the tin mine and was looking forward to moving in the autumn. Tragically, he had something in his bowel that caused him pain, and he died before the trees turned russet. Poor Gran had to go back to Shields to bury him. I believe my Grandpa was the first and last decent man I ever knew. They broke the mold after he died.

So, back to my present dilemma. What am I to do about starting this boarding house? I'm hesitant, but I'm going to give it a try. I hadn't thought of this before. If I find the meal times too difficult, I can maybe have cookers fixed into the two bigger rooms. They could at least have the facility to warm up soup, or make toast, fry an egg and sausages. That way, I can offer to wash up their dishes every morning if they leave them outside their rooms before they go to work. I can maybe have another gas fire fitted into the other large room that looks into the backyard. That way, the boarders would become lodgers, and I do not even have to cross paths with them much. I'll change their beds, clean their rooms and cookers each week. Mother is due to come over and collect rent tomorrow. I'll ask her to put an ad in the paper.

*

The next day I get up feeling happier. It's a good walk, pushing Natalie's stroller all the way to the nursery past Eldon Street school. I say goodbye to my other two and carry on another five minutes up the hill. The walk back is leisurely. At home, as I take off my coat and scarf, I muse about my latest new ideas. I couldn't sleep last night for thinking about starting a boarding house. I could expect three pounds a week, each. It's a realistic charge, especially if they are having meals and I'm paying the utility bills. If I get two boarders to start with, I can see how that goes. After all, I did learn how to cook bigger meals when Mother and John were here.

Then I could save up some money, buy some new clothes and get one of those new twin-tub washing machines that wash and spin clothes. My mangle washer is okay, but sheets are a blasted pain in the neck to mangle. Water spills all over the floor. Besides I'm always scared the children will get their fingers in it one day, especially Steven. He's a typical boy, always in the wars, cut and scraped knees and lumps on his head. The last thing I need is for him to get his fingers crushed.

I decide to have a cup of tea and cook beef stew for Mother and me. The kids can have some when they get home from school. I'll make a big pot.

Just as I walk into the back kitchen, the doorbell rings loudly. It makes me jump; I'm still not used to its shrillness. Who on earth can this be at half past nine in the morning? I peep through the front room curtains. If it's that man with the turban on his head and his brown suitcase selling household cleaning stuff, I'll not answer the door. He won't stop talking or leave. I tell the kids he stuffs children into his suitcase and runs off with them, so to never answer the door to anyone.

"Goodness me. It's my damned Mother already. What's she doing here so early?"

I tap on the window, so she doesn't ring the bloody bell again.

As I walk through the hall, I muse about my lovely new home. It feels posh stepping into the Victorian yellow and green tiled vestibule and closing the door behind me so that whoever is at the front door can't see into my house. It sets me apart from the commoner who opens their door directly onto the front street for all to see what they've got. Even though I know it is Mother, I still close the door before opening the front one.

"Good morning Mother. Did the cockerel get you out of bed too early? Come in; I was just about to put the kettle on."

"Just what I need Beth, I must have known."

As I turn and open the vestibule door and step over the shiny brass plate across the step, she says,

"Speaking of cockerels Beth, I think it would be good for your hens to have our cockerel, it will improve egg laying."

"Really? What about your hens?" I lead the way through to the kitchen.

"We are chopping a head off one every Sunday, and when they've gone, we are not getting any more."

“Really? Are you fed up of plucking feathers or just the smell?" I help her off with her coat. She ignores my dig.

"How are you, Mother? Anything new happening?”

"I'm going to start working a couple of night shifts a week as an auxiliary in a nursing home. John says I can bring in extra money. Besides, it will get me out of the house a bit. The Chorley house is small in comparison to this one, and I get claustrophobic at times, but it means I’ll still be in the house sleeping during the day if Mama needs me while John’s at work.

I hang her coat over one of my upright chairs. We no longer have the coat stand in the hall, and I hate going into the dark cupboard under the stairs.

“I’m not staying long Beth. I've got a hundred and one things to do today."

“Oh, like what?”

“Put the kettle on, then I’ll tell you.”

"What you up to now Mother?" I ask as I enter the back kitchen to make two cups of tea. There's no answer but I hear her open the green door, and her footsteps recede. The vestibule door opens and the front door. What's she forgot to bring in? By the time I have warmed the pot ready to put the tea-leaves in, she is in my back kitchen with a hen carrier, and her bloody cockerel is looking at me.

“Mother? You’ve brought the bloody thing today? What’s the big hurry? I might not want that thing at all. You could have asked me first.”

“I think it will help with the hens laying eggs and you might thank me for that soon.”

“Oh, and why’s that?”

“Let me put it in the back yard.”

She opens the back door, and it crows fit to waken the neighborhood.

The kettle starts boiling. It matches my internal temperature. Mother never asks me anything; she always does what she has set her mind to do. That old exasperation is building inside me. I pour the water steaming hot into the teapot and stir it vigorously. I then get two cups and saucers and put them on the drop-leaf cabinet with some custard creams. I grab two teaspoons and place them on the saucers next to the biscuits. As I pick up the tray, she has already gone ahead of me and is sitting on a chair next to the table. She smiles and asks,

"What happened to the china cups and saucers you brought from your Gran's house? These are good, but there's nothing like tea from a real china cup."

"Steven climbed on to the drop-leaf of the cabinet, trying to get at the biscuits. It fell over on top of him, and every single cup, saucer, and tea-plate broke. The jam and sugar made a hell of a mess everywhere.

"That boy. I hope you strapped him."

"He was pretty badly shaken and had a big lump on his head. Believe me, I wanted to kill him, but he was already screaming the house down. I don't think he'll ever do that again. I just got cheap cups and saucers at the weekend. We were drinking out of empty jam jars for days."

"Why's he so naughty Beth? He wouldn't be naughty if John were still here. He needs a man in his life. Teach him what's what."

"Well he hasn't got a man in his life Mother, so he'll just have to make do, like the rest of us. We don't need a man in any of our lives." That was an old dig at John, which was below the belt. I'd been getting on with him better lately. She blocked my verbal punch.

"Well anyway, I haven't come to get into an argument, Beth. I want to put something to you that I think will help get the ball rolling in bringing in a little bit of money for you."

"And I have something to put to you, Mother, so let's hear yours first."

"You remember the woman who took your old house, the one Ellen told me about?"

"What about her Mother? And before you ask, no, she's not moving in here, over my dead body." My venomous reaction surprises me. I still harbor anger at Ellen for colluding with my mother over it.

"Calm down Beth. Let me finish. She put me in touch with a family man her husband met on the docks." I breathe angry air out of my nostrils. My mother has once again run ahead of me and put the proverbial cart before the horse.

"I want to be the one in charge of my house Mother. I want to choose my boarders; but no, you've beaten me to the post yet again."

"Now please hear me out, Beth. My idea is only going to be a temporary arrangement, for about three months, no more."

“Oh, so it’s all arranged then. You’re not asking me for my opinion or what I think; you’re just telling me it’s happening.”

"No Beth. I ask you to hear me out. If you don't agree, then it won't happen. I promise you."

"Well, it will be the first time Mother."

"I promise you, Beth. I’ll not put you into a situation that you’re not happy about.”

"This is a first then. But what I was going to say is that I've thought the whole thing through, and I’m ready to have a couple of boarders. To try it out. I was going to suggest you put an ad in the evening paper. I wanted to see if any women might need a place to stay. I'm not too keen on the idea of having men here."

“Just as long as it’s not the woman from our other house then?” She digs.

"Show your hand, Mother."

"Well, this is what I propose, see what you think. This family man wants to get himself established. He works on the docks and lives in one small room right now. He earns good money; there's lots of overtime. He says he's enough money to get a bigger room, or maybe two rooms. He intends to be in a position shortly, to rent a house for his family, but he needs time. He wants to bring his family over from Ireland.”

“They’re Irish? How much family? Are they Catholics? Those bloody Irish Catholics are trouble with a capital T. I’ll not have Irish Catholics living in my house Mother.”

“They’re Protestants. Give me credit for some sense girl. It would not be like having single men in the house either. You know that not many single women are looking for lodgings. At least you would have a woman, his wife, living here too.”

“Do they have children?”

"They have two boys. One is six months younger than Lizzie, and the other is eighteen months younger than Lizzie. Maybe Steven will enjoy playing with them too."

"So neither of them will be at school yet then?"

"No, and I told the father, it can only be a temporary arrangement. I told him straight, 'We are not in the business of having children board in our house. We are not set up for that, and we don't want it.' I told him that I first needed to talk to you. You're my daughter, and it's entirely up to you what you think about the whole thing."

"Well, it's one thing to have to cook for two single boarders, Mother, and entirely another to expect me to cook for a whole family."

"I know, which is why I'm asking you to think about it first. I told the husband that they would have to sign a contract. They would have to leave by the end of three months. He is more than willing to do this Beth. He just wants to get his family over. He hasn't seen them in six months as it is."

I look at my Mother in disbelief. Don't tell me she cares about some 'Paddy' who's lonely. She doesn't have one single charitable bone in her body. But there again, I reason; She's done so much for my children and me lately. I don't know how I would have coped without her help, but this is something else. I know there's some other catch to this. I just can't see what it is right now.

"So this family needs to rent two rooms? A separate room for the children then?"

"Yes. I told him, we have one larger room, but he said he wants the kids in bed early in another room, so he and his wife can have some time together."

"How much should I charge them, Mother?"

"Well, I talked it over with John. He looks at it this way. This house is larger than our latest one. We bought it with a definite purpose of renting out all the rooms to boarders and making some decent money."

Here comes the catch. My stomach does a flip.

"Well, John says that you bring in two pounds a week and so he thinks that we could charge this man five pounds a week. John says you can either keep all the five pounds a week or twenty pounds a month, pay for all the food and bills and everything. If this is the case, he wants to put your rent up to three pounds seventy-five a week. Or, you can keep your rent the same, and take half of this man's rent, two pounds fifty a week and just buy the food. John will continue to pay the utility bills."

I sit quietly for a minute, mentally working out all the computations. I need time to think it over.

"What happens when the man leaves, what then?"

"Well, you'll know better how you want to run the house. You'll have had three months experience to see if it's what you like and have more idea how many boarders you can cope with. It'll give you positive experience all round."

"I get the feeling that John isn't happy just allowing me to live here for two pounds a week. Am I right?"

"We're paying a mortgage on the house, Beth. We need to find that money somehow, and we still need to do all the repairs on it. If anything goes wrong, it's still our house. Think about it for a few hours. I've lots of errands to run today while I'm here. I'll come by again this afternoon before I go home. Let me know what you think later.

I raise my eyebrows, "Oh, so no rush then?"

"Beth. John and I need to run our houses like a business. Here is a way for you to make some more money, feel like you're busy and involved. You may like his wife, who knows? You might make a friend. But more than this, it keeps John off my back. He wanted me to run this as a boarding house, which is why we bought it. When we talked about you living here and having boarders, it was like a godsend. It helps you, and it helps me. What's wrong with killing two birds with one stone?"

"Oh, I get it alright. Okay Mother, no need to prolong the inevitable. I'll accept your offer of getting this man in with his family. I won't, however, pay you three pounds seventy-five rent. I want to keep my rent at two pounds. I want you two to have the responsibility of getting this man's money and giving me two pounds fifty of it, out of which I'll feed them one evening meal a day and wash their sheets once a week. Any residual is mine."

"Good. I'm very pleased you're willing to look forward. I want the best for you all."

"Me, Steven and Lizzie will move downstairs, and we'll have the dining room as our bedroom. Maybe John could put up a wall, so there is a passage from the hallway to the kitchen instead of having to go through what will be our bedroom to get to the kitchen. I need another dining table for the front room; it's where they'll eat. I want to keep our lives separate; their children will not be interacting with mine. They're boarding in my home; I'll be their landlady, not their friend. Mother, when you come over for my rent, I want you to collect theirs and give me my two pounds fifty. When do they move in?"

"I'll tell John you agree. He wants to get all the furniture in place this weekend. They will probably move in early next week."

"You do not need to move my bed out of that large bedroom. I want a new double bed for me and a pull-down sofa for Steven and Lizzie. I can then have more space throughout the day in there when I put the sofa up. I deserve a new bed with a comfortable mattress; the one upstairs is hard. I can be out of the room by the weekend." Mother puts out her hand to shake mine.

"Done, it's a deal."

I shake her hand briefly. It's the first time I've held her hand in years. My mother drains the tea from her cup, wipes her lips with a hanky from her pocket, picks up her coat and smiles at me.

"Thank you, Beth. I appreciate your willingness."

She leans towards me and kisses my cheek. As she turns to go through the door, I wipe it off with my hand.

"Goodbye. I guess I'll see you and John soon."

I walk her out and shut the front door before she has started the car. I return to the kitchen and pour myself another cup of tea.

"Congratulations Beth," I say aloud. "That told her."

Then the cock crows.

"Darn her," I say aloud, "She always has to have the last word."

CHAPTER 17: LIZZIE: WHEN IRISH EYES ARE SMILING.

Ezekiel 47:22, 23, You shall divide it by lot for an inheritance among yourselves and among the aliens who stay in your midst, who bring forth sons in your midst. And they shall be to you as the native-born among the sons of Israel; they shall be allotted an inheritance with you among the tribes of Israel. 'And in the tribe with which the alien stays, there you shall give him his inheritance,' declares the Lord God.

Our house is getting full of people. Mummy says they're Irish. They talk funny. They speak English, but it's different to our English. It's Irish. I can't understand all their words. There are Patrick and Siobhan and their two little boys, Patrick and Sean who have blonde hair just like Steven. They have two rooms upstairs, the big one with the fireplace that we slept in, and the small bedroom next door. The boys share a small bed, head to toe like Steven and me used to. We are bigger than they are and they are not going to school yet.

Grandpa and Grandma bring in more furniture. When do they ever stop? Today, Grandma and Mummy are talking about some more Irish family moving in next week. Mummy laughs out loud,

"Mother you take the biscuit, you really do. You knew this when you first talked to me about it right?"

"No Beth, I swear on a stack of bibles, he only asked me yesterday morning."

"And? Where did I come into the conversation?"

"He said he needed to know in a hurry because they had to book the ferry in advance. It gets full quick as there's so many Irish coming over daily. It's just two women, his mother and his wife's sister. So I didn't think you'd mind so much, it'll be extra money for us all."

“How much extra Mother?”

“Another five pounds a week that we can share.”

"My rent's not going any higher Mother, we already agreed."

"No Beth, the same arrangement we discussed. I'll be giving you five pounds a week from their rent, and you'll still be paying two pounds a week."

“Who’s sleeping where?”

“I said they could share the other big bedroom, but they want separate rooms, so all four bedrooms will be used.”

“Great. More cleaning and sheets to wash every week. You’ll wear me out Mother with six more mouths to feed as well.”

I feel invisible, so I interrupt their conversation and stare up at my mummy.

"I can help you, Mummy. I'm good at washing up dishes now aren't I?" She looks mad.

“Oh, it wouldn’t be a show without Punch would it?”

"Now Beth, don't be mad at Lizzie, you'll do a fantastic job and just think of all the extra money. It'll only be for three months, and then they'll move into a rented house."

"Let's bloody hope so, or I'll be moving out."

Mummy flounces past us all into the back kitchen, and I can hear her banging the kettle and cups in a temper. Grandma takes me by the hand and leads me outside to the front step to watch more furniture move into our house.

“Let’s try not to get under your mummy’s feet hinny. She’s very busy today.”

“I know Grandma.”

Suddenly, Mummy flies out the front and looks at me hard.

"I'll say this only once Lizzie, and I expect you to do it. You're never allowed to go upstairs apart from going to the bathroom. You’re not allowed in any of their rooms, even if they invite you. Do you understand me?"

“Why Mummy?”

“Because I say so. Do you understand?”

"Yes, Mummy."

“Good, now come in Lizzie, I’ll make you a sandwich and milk. Then you can play in the backyard out of our way.” I follow her into the house and stay quiet as a mouse.

After lunch, I hear Mummy talking to Mrs. Wheedler over the back yard wall; she's speaking quietly. I don't know if it's because she doesn't want the Irish family to hear, or me. The back door is slightly open, and I have my ear to the opening. I love to listen.

“So how long have they been in England then?” asks Mrs. Wheedler.

“They haven’t. They’re straight off the boat. Bog Irish.”

“I thought you told me Patrick was here first.”

“Yes he was, but only a few months.”

“So how do you feel about having all these Irish people in your house then?”

“I’ll be running a boarding house Mrs. Wheedler. I’ll keep myself completely separate from them. I’ll make them their breakfast and dinner and change their beds once a week. I’ll be giving Siobhan a broom; they can keep their own rooms clean. The only time I'll see them will be in passing. They’ll not be allowed past the hall door. If they want me, they can knock on the door and wait for me to open it.

*

A week later, while Mummy is in the backyard, I'm in the back kitchen, I hear a loud knock on our green door. I run to open it, and Mr. Patrick fills the whole doorway.

“Is your Mammy home?”

I nod and run to the back door as fast as I can. “Mummy, Mr. Patrick wants you.”

“Ok, I’m coming.”

She stops hanging washing on the line, passes me and goes to greet Mr. Patrick who speaks first.

“I’d like to introduce you to Mammy. Mammy, this is Beth Caradine. Beth, this is Joan. Siobhan's sister Catherine is here. Come on in Catherine and Danny; they don't bite."

I watch them all shake hands and listen to their very different voices. Catherine is young and pretty. She has brown, wavy, shoulder length hair, the biggest blue eyes I have ever seen and two lovely dimples in her cheeks. It's strange to see blue eyes and dark hair together. I stare at her.

Mummy then steps through them all and says,

"Let's talk together in the front dining room. As you know Patrick, you're not allowed to come past the hall door. Just knock there if you need me."

Mr. Patrick apologizes.

"Yes, sorry for the intrusion Mrs. Caradine, I was forgettin' meself."

They follow my mummy along the recently created dark passage that only lights up when the hall door opens at the other end. Grandpa built a wood partition wall with a sliding door in it so we could have a private bedroom in the old dining room, but apart from a couple of small windows at the ceiling, it cuts off most of the light. They all go into the hall and turn left into the new front dining room, and the door closes. I'm never allowed in that room if the adults are talking in there.

I feel excited about having more Irish people in our house; this makes three women, two men, and two children all living upstairs. I sit in my favorite chair, entwine my fingers on my chest like Grandma does and think about it all.

I remember hearing their music last Saturday afternoon as I came out of the bathroom. It sounded loud, and there was a thumping on the floor and a clapping of hands. Mr. Patrick was singing, and every so often the children and Mrs. Siobhan would join in too. I was mesmerized and wanted to get a closer look. I knocked on their door, twice, to make sure they could hear me. One of the boys opened the door, and everyone saw me standing there. I asked if I could listen and they invited me in. I sat on a chair in front of the fireplace and watched enthralled as Mr. Patrick pulled first one side of a musical box out, while pressing sparkly red buttons with his left hand, then pulling both sides out and playing the little piano keys with his other hand. I was amazed at how the cream and sparkly-red box could make such joyful sounds. The music was fantastic. He sang lots of songs, all the while tapping his foot and squeezing the accordion. I never knew there was such a thing called an accordion, but he told me all about it and showed me what it did in more detail, between songs. The boys and their mother invited me to clap my hands in time to the music, and soon, I was clapping along with them all. I started to copy some words in the middle when everyone else sang. It was the most fun I ever had. I loved their music.

At the end of one of the songs, Mummy shouted up the stairs,

"Lizzie are you up there? Come down here at once."

Mr. Patrick asked me if I should leave and go downstairs. I shook my head and put my finger to my lips and waited until I thought Mummy had gone from the hallway. Mr. Patrick laughed and said,

"I don't want you gettin' into any trouble."

"I don't care," I said quietly. "I want to stay here for a bit longer. Can we sing some more?"

I can't remember how much more we sang and clapped, but I needed what they had. I needed the joy, the fun, every vibrant beat of his feet and the clapping of our hands. Every so often his wife would let out a whoop, and I would too and laugh. I could have stayed there for many more hours with them, soaking in everything they offered that filled me up. I was sorry when it was over, and I had to go downstairs again. I thanked them for letting me into their room.

I did get in trouble when I went downstairs. Mummy put her face close up to mine. She grabbed my arm and squeezed. It hurt.

"You're a very, very, naughty little girl Lizzie. I told you, you must never go into their rooms, didn't I?" I looked into her eyes and nodded. She shook my arm. "Well, this is your last warning my girl. If you ever go into their rooms again, I'll ask them to leave the very same day. Do you understand me?" I nodded my head, and she slapped my legs twice.

"Now sit down and read your books. I don't want to hear another peep out of you all afternoon."

She pushed me to my favorite chair and handed me a book. I cried and held my book up to my face so she couldn't look at me. I thought in my mind,

'Mr. Patrick is clever. I wish I could have a daddy that's such fun. I would love someone like him.'

I never did go in to see them again, but whenever I heard their music above my head, it brought such a smile to my face. It was something inside my heart that no-one would ever be able to take away from me. Like a treasure. Like Grandma and Aunty Maureen.

Mummy says Aunty Maureen has married an old man. He's German, and whenever he and Grandpa get together they speak German, and we can't understand a word of it. He even speaks his English like Grandpa. They both put V's where W's should be. It's funny. His name is Otto. I met him a few times. He's always kind and smiles when he talks to me. Anyway, Aunty Maureen married him, and they live in another house I haven't seen yet. I miss Aunty Maureen with her loud laugh that always makes me laugh. I miss snuggling up to her in bed and listening to her stories.

She once made up a song for me about the time I got hold of Steven's ears and pushed his head hard against the bathroom wall, twice. He had been his usual disagreeable self, and he pushed me. He called me names. I had seen a cowboy film on television, and one cowboy got on top of another on the floor, picked his head up with his ears, and bashed his head on the floor. He won the fight. I told myself that the very next time Steven bullied me, I would do the same thing to him. I didn't know a way to get him on the floor, but I saw an opportunity with the wall. I held his ears really fast and bashed his head twice. He screamed the place down and ran downstairs to tell Mummy and Aunty Maureen what I had done. They roared laughing. So I went downstairs, and they commended me for sticking up for myself. Anyway, Aunty Maureen made a song up, all about it and we laughed lots more. I do miss her.

My thoughts are interrupted when the Irish people all come out of the front room.

I know there will be lots of commotion up and down the stairs as they move in. I go outside to play because I know Mummy will be busy preparing food, setting the table in the dining room, and in and out of the kitchen all day. I'll keep out of her way.

CHAPTER 18: BETH: THE LUCK O' THE IRISH.

Zecharia 3:10, 'In that day,' declares the Lord of hosts, 'every one of you will invite his neighbor to sit under his vine and his fig tree.'

Danny and Catherine have gone out as usual this morning with Patrick. Danny goes to the docks with Patrick, and Catherine is working in town at one of the many new café's opening up everywhere. Once again, Mother sprang the two on me very late in the game. So now all four bedrooms are taken. I feel as though my world has been taken over by Irish. I told them they'd have to pay an extra ten shillings directly to me every week because it was not part of the original bargain Mother struck with me. They are good with it, and Mother knows nothing about it. Patrick gives Mother the rent, and I get half of that each week.

I can still hear Siobhan moving around upstairs, and soon she'll go out with her two children and her mother-in-law, Joan. They go out most days. Where? I have no idea. Hopefully, they're looking for a house to rent.

Their stay is now at almost four months, and I've just about had enough of them. I don't like Siobhan or her two children. She has that hard-bitten Irish look to her and whenever she speaks, her accent grates on my nerves. She sounds softer when she speaks to her husband or her children, so I think she must not like me either. Who cares?

I've told my kids half a dozen times, not to knock at their door to see if her two boys can play with them. I forbade them from speaking to their kids, and they must walk away if they meet on the street. That's no problem for Steven: he's older than they are and he couldn't care less. Lizzie is another one altogether. She has a will of her own and chats with the boys as if they are her bosom buddies.

Thank goodness she's in school. All her questions drive me mad. She always wants my attention, and when she doesn't get it, she whines. I'm sure that half the time she cries and tells me Steven is mean to her, it's for attention.

When she asks me why she can't play with the two Irish boys, my usual short answer, 'because I say so,' isn't enough for her. 'Why Mummy, why?' Her questions are incessant. I slapped her legs the last time she started; she got me so frustrated. I told her why.

"Because Lizzie, they should be back in Ireland, growing potatoes and cutting peat from the bogs. That's why. And never ask me again lady. When I tell you not to do something, you just damn well don't do it. Do you hear me?"

She's stayed out of my hair since.

I don't regret it, not one bit. As a child, I had to obey Gran, or I got 'what-for.'

She has the bloody 'luck o' the Irish' when she's around Mother. I don't know what Lizzie's done to bewitch her, but my mother dotes on her; Fawns after her on purpose, in my opinion. She knows it gets on my nerves. Mother dislikes me as much as I do her sometimes. I'm beginning to feel like I'm not too keen on Lizzie these days either.

And talking about the luck o' the Irish. What have the Irish ever done to have such luck anyway? They come over here with their entire families and have the likes of me waiting on them hand and foot. Patrick looks at Siobhan like the sun shines out of her backside. Catherine can't put two sentences together without 'Danny this,' or 'Danny that.' I never hear a peep out of those kids either. It's unnatural for them to be so quiet. I'm sure it's not because they're any better than mine. I'll bet Patrick rules over them with an iron rod.

I barely see his mother, Joan. She's not always down for breakfast, and whenever they have dinner, she's always the first one up and out of the way. She seems timid to me. Like a mouse. I wonder how old she is. Her hair's gray, maybe fifty years old. Who knows? Who cares?

Yesterday Steven put an earthworm down the oldest boy, Patrick's shirt. All hell broke loose. Siobhan charged outside to the front street waving her finger at Lizzie and Steven, asking them why they are so cruel to her two boys. I heard her raised voice and went outside. Lizzie and Steven didn't say a word. I called them in. Then I told Siobhan, "If you have a complaint about my two children, you need to come to me with it, and I'll deal with it. Don't be shouting for all the world to hear. Just come and tell me about it."

Siobhan reacted like the Irish trash she is. "Oh yes? Where do you think they get the idea that they are above my children and can treat them like they do? They put a worm down Patrick's back. It comes from you, Mrs. High and Mighty. You think you're above all of us. You won't even let Lizzie come to our door, I've heard you."

I just smiled. I was standing on the top step; she stood below me on the path. I had all these feelings inside me that just wanted to burst out, but I kept calm. I answered her.

"That's because you are what you are Siobhan. It's not because I think you're below me, it's because I'm your landlady. I don't mix my business with social hob-knobbing. It's just how things are. Now if you'll excuse me, I'll go and talk to my children about what just happened." I turned my back on her and closed the vestibule door.

I went into the kitchen where Steven and Lizzie were sitting on their behinds, hiding them.

"Steven?" I asked, "Why did you put a worm down Patrick's back?"

"I didn't Mummy. Lizzie did."

"No, I didn't Mummy. I don't like worms. Steven did it."

"Well," I said and paused. I looked at each of my children, and I wanted to laugh. They probably just did more for me to get those Irish peasants out of my house than they will ever know.

"I know we don't like them very much, but I don't think it's alright to put worms down their back. Do not do anything like that again. Do you understand?"

They both nodded.

"Now I'm going to make a cake for dinner, so go and wash your hands and you can help me if you promise to be good in future."

They jumped up and rushed into the back kitchen. Scraping the bowl, and licking the cake batter off fingers is a favorite treat.

Anyway, that was yesterday. Today's another day.

The cake's gone. The Irish finished it all off. Mother is coming tomorrow to collect their rent. I'll get half of it. Maybe I'll go into town and buy myself something nice to wear. It's a good excuse to put my make up on and wear my favorite skirt. I'll put on some stockings and my high heels. I love getting dressed up; it doesn't happen too often these days.

I dreamt about Lonnie again last night. He's been on my mind lately. I almost got to him this time in my dream, but he disappeared around the corner as my hand went to touch him. I called his name, but the wind took it away. As I rounded the corner, he was gone. I woke up crying. My usual cup of tea didn't fix it either.

What I need is a good night out with a girlfriend. The trouble is I don't have any friends. I'm not likely to meet any either. I live like a hermit in this house.

I hear myself sigh. "Oh well. I'll have one more cigarette and a cup of tea. There's no rest for the wicked, as Gran would say. My life will get better one of these days when my ship comes in."

My life is just one long string of every saying Gran ever used. I never realized before just how many sayings she had. I miss Gran, but I've no idea when I'll be able to visit again. Not soon, that's for sure. This boarding house steals my every waking moment.

CHAPTER 19: MARY: NEVER TRUST AN IRISHMAN.

Jeremiah 4:18, Your actions have brought this upon you. This punishment is bitter, piercing you to the heart.

I'm sitting in the Solicitor's office again and looking at dishing out more money.

"It's my stupid fault," I say to Mr. Wilkins.

"I should never have rented my house to Patrick and his family. They've not paid their rent in three weeks. The first week, he gave me half-rent. He said they were looking for a rented house and had some unexpected expenses. I told him I wanted it made up the following week."

Mr. Wilkins interrupts my flow. "How many did you say are living in your house?"

"Seven."

"Do they pay their rent individually?"

"No, Patrick pays it."

"Why do you think he's stopped after all these months, you say he paid it on time for four months?"

"He always did, but the whole family was out of the house when I came for the rent. My daughter says they came back in after eight o'clock at night. They were staying out of our way alright. The third week, he told me that they could no longer afford to pay the rent. No reason, no excuses, nothing. You should never trust an Irishman my mother always used to say. They have a twinkle in their eye and a bludgeon up their sleeve."

"So what did you tell him?" Mr. Wilkins asks.

"I told him to pack up all of their stuff and get out, or I would be throwing them out. He said I needed to give him a written notice.

So I did. I went downstairs, wrote him a day's notice and told him they had better leave by morning."

"And they are still there."

"Yes. I want them out, Mr. Wilkins. I already told my daughter she is not to cook one more breakfast or dinner for them. And I want what they owe me. At ten pounds a week, they owe me twenty-five pounds. By this weekend it will be thirty-five pounds."

"Mrs. Krupp. It's easy to see what they're doing here. They probably can't afford a private, bigger house to rent, so they have probably approached the council to try to get rehoused by them. The council will not rehouse them because they have a roof over their heads, and they are not overcrowded. What we need to do is get a court order to get them out. When the council sees that the children will be made homeless, then they'll probably rent them a house, if they have one. Otherwise, they'll have to book a couple of hotel rooms, or the children will have to go into foster-care while the adults sort themselves out."

"When can you get them in court? I ask.

"In about three weeks."

"Three weeks? My god-fathers. Okay. Let's do it. I'm not shilly-shallying around. I want them out as quickly as possible. I'll never rent to a family again. No boarders either, eating our food and not paying for it. Lodgers are what I'll have in future. Just single men."

"Right then Mrs. Krupp. I'll start it up right away. Can you come back in the morning to sign some paperwork for me?"

"Yes. I can."

We stand up and shake hands. "I'll see you tomorrow Mr. Wilkins. Thank you very much."

"Goodbye Mrs. Krupp and thank you very much too."

I leave his office, say goodbye to his secretary and step out into a very wet and windy street. I put up my umbrella, and straight away it's sucked inside out. I feel foolish as a man passes by and asks if he can help me with it. "No thank you. I can manage," I tell him. I try to wrestle it back into shape, but one of the prongs has snapped and hangs down limp. As I go towards my car, I reject my first idea of getting a nice cup of tea and éclair. I decide instead to drive to Beth's and have tea and toast there. I'll bring her up to date on the court order. There's a bin on the telegraph pole near to where I'm parked. I shove my broken umbrella into it and curse.

There is nothing more infuriating than tenants who will not pay their rent. Now that I realize these Irish people are just playing the system so that they can get a council house, I'm even more furious. It's at my expense. It will just serve them right if their kids go into care until they can offer them council accommodation. Thirty-five pounds they owe me by the weekend. If they are in their rooms today, I'll give them 'what-for.'

As I drive over to Beth's house, or should I say *my* house, I tell myself to calm down and focus on the road and street signs. I ruminate about how I allowed myself to get into this mess in the first place. I got soft, first with Beth and her children and then with the Irish family. I allowed my heart to rule my head. I trusted the Irish bloke, Patrick. I trusted that he would do the right thing and be grateful for what I was doing to help him and his family. I was even willing to extend their stay until they found what they needed. And this is how they repay me.

I'm also mad at the woman who took over Beth's smaller house in Edward St. It was on her recommendation that I took this family in. Well, I'll show her too. I'll give her two weeks' notice on her house this weekend. I'll spruce it up a bit and put up the rent for another tenant. I'll show them all that they are messing with the wrong woman when they mess with me.

Then I remember that I'm not getting any rent except hers and Beth's. So I'll wait to throw her out until I get more lodgers ready for Beth's house. John will have my guts for garters if I do anything rash right now.

Soon I'm at Beth's. She opens the front door with a surprised look on her face and no welcome. You'd think that after all I've done for her, she'd at least smile at me from time to time.

"Hello Beth, I've been to the Solicitors and have come to see if those Irish buggers are in their rooms today."

"Siobhan and Patrick's mother are in with the kids, but they're usually out and about by now, so you may have come just in time."

As I step into the hallway, little Lizzie stares up at me with a smile on her face.

"Hello, Lizzie. What are you doing home?"

"We're going to get some new shoes, Grandma. My other ones hurt me now."

Beth speaks before I can.

"Yes, I hadn't realized her feet had grown so fast. The school sent her home with a note saying they let her walk around in her socks all day because she was limping. She said her shoes hurt. I was going to go on the market and see if I can get some cheap ones for her. She can wear her wellies today."

"You'll do no such thing, Beth. I'll give you some money towards it, and you get her some Clark's shoes."

Beth raises her eyes to the ceiling, turns and struts off into the kitchen. Lizzie puts her hand in mine. She feels cold.

"Come on little Lizzie, let's get you sat near the fire, and after I've been upstairs on some business, I'll come and sit with you." I sit her on the chair next to the stove.

"Put the kettle on Beth. I'll be down in a minute."

I walk up the stairs quietly. They probably know I'm here already. Sure enough, I no sooner get near their door when it opens and Siobhan is hushing the children. They're leaving. Siobhan is startled when she sees me and stops in her tracks.

"Hello, Siobhan looks like I caught you in time. Are you going out?"

"Yes, we have an appointment in town. I'm rushing to get there." I put out my hand.

"Oh, so before you spend all your money on a taxi, I'll be asking you for what you owe me."

"I can't afford taxis Mrs. Krupp, we are rushing for the bus and my husband Patrick handles all the money."

"Now don't tell me you don't have any money because I know better. You're at least twenty five pounds better off than I am right now because that is what you owe me."

She opens her handbag, then her purse. She has some money squashed into her purse with lots of change. She takes out the crumpled bills. She thrusts them into my hand.

"Two pounds is all I've got. You can have that."

Just then the bedroom door at the top of the stairs opens and her mother-in-law, Joan, says out loud.

"Now you just stop bullying us, Mrs. Krupp. Patrick will get you the money as soon as he has it. Have a heart for the children at least."

"I had a heart for the children, Joan, and look where it got me." I shove the money into my pocket. "Now I've been to see my Solicitor today, and I'm taking you all to court to get you out. Don't be surprised when you get back tonight if I haven't changed all the locks."

With that, I turn and go down the two steps from the upper landing, then turn again to go downstairs. I see Lizzie run from the hallway. Beth must have sent her to spy on me, to see if I got any rent. As I start to descend, Siobhan and her kids stare at me from the other side of the wooden banister. Then she pulls her two boys back towards their room. She's taken me seriously. They go inside and shut the door. I hear the bolt slide on the other side. Joan closes her door too and locks it.

I smile to myself. "Yes, let's just see who's really in charge here, you bloody Irish pigs," I say under my breath. Then I go downstairs and into the kitchen. Lizzie is looking up at me with big eyes, wondering if I'm going to scold her for spying on me. I go over and sit her on my knee for a cuddle.

"Hey Beth, where's this child's sweater? She's freezing."

I hear Beth sigh and reply in exasperation. "She knows where it is. Go and get it, Lizzie, it's on your bed."

I get up and sit her down again. I wink at her. "I'll get it for you hinny, you just stay here and keep warm." I go down the dark passage and pull the wooden sliding door that John installed in the partition. The room smells of urine. Before I know it, Beth's in the bedroom with me. She must have flown out of the kitchen behind me.

"I'll get it, Mother, look it's here. Now can we just sit down and have a cup of tea and stop fussing around Lizzie for once. You're spoiling that girl, and I can't do a thing with her after you've gone. If you love her so much, why don't you just adopt her and give me some peace."

I know she flew in here because she didn't want me to see the disheveled state of her bedroom. She's trying to distract me. I say, "What's that smell of urine? Is one of them wetting the bed?" I look at the sheet on the unmade pull-out sofa. It looks dry to me.

"It's Steven Granny," a little voice behind me says. "He's been going wee-wee behind the sofa against the wall. I saw him."

"He's been doing what?" I look at Beth.

Beth stares at Lizzie. I can see murder in her eyes.

"Yes, and he got a big spanking before he went to school this morning Mother. I'm going to pull the sofa out today and clean up whatever I find. His backside is raw. He won't be doing that again."

I tut three times, speechless. The world is heading into cataclysmic disorder; the boarders have a mutiny, my grand-daughter can't go to school because she's no shoes, Steven is using the wall behind the sofa-bed as a urinal, my daughter's not coping again. I shake my head in disbelief. In my head, I'm saying, 'No wonder I never wanted to be a mother.' From my mouth come the words,

"Let's all just sit down and have a nice cup of tea and some toast shall we?"

I turn around and walk out of the bedroom, down the passage and into the kitchen. I sit on my chair and wait for everyone else to come through. I'm in a bad dream. Lizzie walks sullenly into the kitchen with her cardigan on inside out and sits on my knee. Beth goes into the back kitchen and calls out, "Did they give you any money Mother?"

"Not a penny," I reply.

Lizzie turns her head quickly to look into my eyes. I put a finger to my lips and she looks away. She knows to keep quiet about what she heard about the two pounds.

CHAPTER 20: BETH: OUR SUNDAY DINNER CELEBRATION.

Leviticus 16: 21-22, Then Aaron shall lay both of his hands on the head of the live goat, and confess over it all the iniquities of the sons of Israel and all their transgressions in regard to all their sins; and he shall lay them on the head of the goat and send it away into the wilderness by the hand of a man who stands in readiness. "The goat shall bear on itself all their iniquities to a solitary land, and he shall release the goat in the wilderness."

Well, 'it's all over bar the shouting,' as my Gran would say. I never really understood that saying until I went to a concert and the audience was up on their feet at the end shouting for more. The Irish family is finally out of our house. I don't know whether the council helped them or not, nor do I care. They've gone for good and I have never felt more relieved about a situation in my life unless you count my day in court.

Talk about tension in the house. They all kept their doors locked out of fear that someone may come and change the locks. That's what I wanted to do, but the Solicitor said it was against the law, that we could end up having them for a lot longer if we did that. We had to take them to court.

I kept our doors locked out of fear they may get mad and murder us all in our beds or our kitchen. Lizzie and Steven sensed the tension and would no longer go upstairs to the bathroom without me. They said the corridor to the bathroom made noises and scared them. It was just some brown paper in the skylight that shifted with the draughts going through the house, but to the children it was unnerving.

If ever we were about to go upstairs, and we heard one of their doors open, we slipped back into the dark corridor until we were sure the coast was clear. I had no intentions of ever passing them on the landing or stairs. Lizzie and Steven would grab hold of me in the corridor until I opened the door again and some light from the hallway poured in. I never want to go through another day of that, never mind a whole four weeks of it, as we did. I felt trapped. I don't know, or care how they felt. They held us to ransom in our own home and for that, I don't care what happened to them after they left.

But now, we can all breathe; they've gone. I went upstairs to see if there was any damage in the rooms, but everything seemed to be fine. The sheets were in a big pile on Joan's bedroom floor. They must have bought themselves a mop, as their floors were all swept clean and smelled of pine disinfectant. I'm going to take all the blankets outside, hang them over the washing lines and let them air out all day. What doesn't fit on the line today, can wait until tomorrow. There's nothing like fresh air to blow away unwanted odors. If they are too bad, I'll have to wash them. I I just need to clean the windows, wash the lace curtains and wipe the picture rails over with a damp cloth. I found the rubber sheets I had put on the children's bed intact and free of odor.

It was so good to be able to walk from one room to the other, that we did it over and over for a good ten minutes after they had finally left. Steven and Lizzie ran from room to room like freed prisoners. I know exactly how they felt. It was such a relief.

Today, John and Mother will be over to take a look at things and discuss what comes next. If I didn't have to do it, I would never let another stranger in my home, but we have to make some money somehow. The last few weeks have been brutal financially, for Mother and me.

John was so angry over the Irish family that he evicted the Edward Street family too. He told them he was going to sell the house and he wanted them out within two weeks. They didn't hang around; they knew what was going on. They left that same week leaving the house in a disgusting state. I was surprised by how much more self-pride the Irish had than them. So John was out of rent for Edward Street almost three weeks until he got someone new. He had to clean and repaint most of the house inside and spend more on new carpets and mattresses. Who'd want to be a landlord?

John's going to kill a hen for dinner today. They want to celebrate and are bringing Sherry for the adults and fizzy pop for the children. I've made a cake.

Lizzie's up early, feeding the hens and playing in the little pool that has formed where the rain pours off the end of the shed gutter. She says it holds shiny treasure. When I went over to see, there were tiny stones in there that Mother must have put in. They were all different colors and looked nothing when dry, but beautiful when they got wet. She's a funny little thing. She notices things I would just pass by without a second look. She runs inside.

"Mummy. I've been talking to Sally, and she says she'll lay two big eggs every day for my breakfast. I can eat two boiled eggs before I go to school."

"Oh. Did Sally say that? I tell you what Lizzie, you have a great imagination."

"She said it, Mummy. She said, Cluck-cluck-cluckety-cluck."

I laugh out loud. Lizzie sounds just like a hen.

"Well, that's wonderful Lizzie. Because you're such a good girl today, how would you like me to take you to the park for a couple of hours?"

"Yes please, Mummy. Let's go on the swings again. Hooray."

She runs off to tell Stephen the good news. The park is only a fifteen-minute walk from here. I put a note on the kitchen table, in case

Mother gets here before we get back. It'll be good to let them run around for a bit, calm them down. Later, maybe they'll take a nap and not be under our feet all the time. I fasten Natalie into her push chair and call out for them.

"Steven, Lizzie, come on let's go for a walk in the park. I'll take you all to the swings if you're good."

They come running.

"I'm ready Mummy," says Lizzie. "Can we take a picnic?"

"Not today. Your Grandma and Grandpa are coming over. We're having a party later."

"A party," shouts Steven. "Will we have some cake?"

"Of course we will. If there's no cake, there's no party."

"Hooray," they shout running towards the front door. We have been in such a good mood since the Irish left. All the tension has dissipated.

They skip most of the way to the flashing beacon crossing just before the park. We have practiced this enough times, so they know the drill. They look right, then left, then right again and no-one steps onto the crossing until all cars have come to a full stop. As we get to the middle island, they wait and this time look left for all cars to stop before crossing over. I'm proud of them.

"You two are so obedient when you want to be," I tell them as we enter the park. They're too excited to take any notice and run ahead.

I love this park with its half mile avenue of English-lime trees and ornate Victorian railings. We take the first turn to the left. There are other paths we could take, but this one is flanked endlessly with long rectangular beds of the sweetest smelling red roses. Lizzie starts to pick up the dropped petals immediately. I make a suggestion.

"Let's pick them up on the way back Lizzie so you don't lose any while we go to the swings." She places a little pile of them near the edge of the flower bed.

"Okay then. We can get these on the way home." I know she will not forget about them either.

I've lost count of the dozens of petals that Lizzie's collected and put in clothing drawers at the house. Lizzie will take a rose petal and examine it so thoroughly and carefully, stroking its velvet softness for many minutes, before she deposits it in the drawers. Steven likes to wait until she's out of the room, then he'll sneak them all out again and throw them away. I stop him if I catch him. He seems to be jealous of everything Lizzie has or does. The District Nurse told me it often happens when another baby comes along. "Just give him some extra attention," she said. But really, when do I have time for that?

Soon, we are at the playground. One thing they both love and enjoy together is the swings and slide. I take them there first. Then it's the roundabout until they're dizzy. Then it's the see-saw where they sing their see-saw song. I listen. They're so sweet when they're getting along.

"See-saw, Marjorie Daw, Johnny shall have a new Master. He can saw for a penny a day because he can't go any faster."

I choose a swing, sit Natalie on my knee and gently swing back and forth. Natalie is such a good baby. She's always happy, never cries, unless she's wet or dirty, which isn't as often these days as I'm slowly potty-training her. The nursery day care is a great help in this too. It's been a godsend.

Natalie wants to go on the slide when she sees Lizzie up there. So I wait for Lizzie to slide down and catch her at the end. She's never fallen off before, but my presence there gives her a little more confidence to let go and slide. Then I walk up the steps, clutching Natalie. It's awkward, but I manage to sit down at the top and put

Natalie on my knee. I'm not the first mother to do this, nor will I be the last. I get fun out of it too. Natalie says, "Again," when we get to the bottom but we need to be heading back home soon.

She wriggles and fusses when I place her back in her push chair. Steven and Lizzie just have to have one more go at the roundabout before they follow me. I slowly make my way through the gate of the playground enclosure. Then they run ahead of me and run after each other in a game of tag until I catch them up, then they run ahead of me again. Gosh, I wish I had half their energy.

It's a good twenty-minute walk back to the entrance because Lizzie stops to pick up her rose petals and then some more. She gives Natalie a few but snatches them away when rose petals end up in Nat's mouth. They're good children, just a bit too energetic at times. I wish they would get along with each other as good as they have today. Life would be so much easier.

By the time we get home, we have been out of the house for well over one and a half hours, and John and my mother are already inside. They have a key. Steven and Lizzie run right through the house shouting,

"Grandma, we're home."

My mother comes out of the back kitchen, and they fling themselves at her legs, which surprises her and me. Steven seems to have missed her too. He's not usually so demonstrative.

"Goodness me you two," she exclaims, "I'm glad to see you both too. Now go on upstairs to the bathroom and wash your face and hands. Go on, off with you. I'll see you back down here when you're all fresh and clean." And, wonder of wonders, they do exactly that, rushing around like little banshees.

As soon as they are out of earshot, Mother says, "John has killed the white hen for dinner. I would have stopped him had I seen, but I was in the bathroom when he killed it. I don't think John knows it's Lizzie's favorite hen, and I haven't said anything to him. He's in too much of a good mood. Let's not spoil it. He's almost finished plucking it outside in the backyard. So let's keep it a secret from her for today."

"Well, she's going to find out soon enough. She'll notice it's missing." I reply.

"I know, but let's at least eat the bloody thing before she finds out. It might turn her into a vegetarian if she knows it's Sally."

"Okay. I'll give the kids a snack, and they can go on the front step to eat it and play for a while. That way they won't even know about a dead hen."

Soon I hear little thundering feet racing from the bathroom, down the stairs and along the passage to the kitchen. I stop them at the door.

"Hey, you two, as a treat, go and sit on the front step. I'll bring you a snack and some milk."

They race back along the passage, through the hall, and outside. Mother's right, there's no need to spoil Lizzie's day.

All our moods are elevated. I can hear John whistling to himself in the back yard. I determine that I'll not let anyone or anything spoil my joy today. The Irish have gone, what could be better than that?

"Did you see the upstairs rooms Mother?" I ask.

"I did, yes. It looks like you gave them a good cleaning."

"I did, but in all fairness, they left all the rooms looking good as new. I was surprised. I thought the Irish might damage them before they left."

"Huh. Patrick probably figured out I could find them if I needed to, and I'm not afraid of taking them to court either."

"Did the courts say anything about the rent they owe us?"

"Oh yes. Patrick and Danny have to pay me one pound and ten shillings a week until it's all paid back. Mr. Wilkins is staying on top of them for a small fee. I'm happy to pay it."

For a moment I almost ask her when I can expect my portion of the rent, but I'm learning to pick my battles. Why spoil the day? That battle can wait a few days.

"I must say, Mother, that Solicitor has done well for you, hasn't he?"

"Well, I do most of the work anyway, but yes, he helps out a bit. What are you making for the bairns' snack?"

"Just two Farley's rusks each and a glass of milk."

I note the sudden change of subject. Mother likes me to keep out of her business, and this includes the Solicitor. We never even discuss the checks that are sent to him in my Mother's name from Lonnie. She just hands over the checks with a letter permitting me to cash them. Why they are in her name is a mystery to me, but she says it has to do with her letter to the President of the United States. They just use her name.

Mother takes control of the conversation.

"Right then, I'll deliver their snack to them and spend time on the front steps. You clean out the hen, Beth if you don't mind."

"It's my greatest pleasure Mother; you know that."

*

We have a fun afternoon. Everyone's jolly. I wish it could be like this more often. John plays 'Fee Fo Fi Fum' with the kids, and they squeal with terror and delight as he hunts them down after they hide. Mother pours the sherry. We toast ourselves and our latest good luck. Then toast Gran, Maureen, and Otto, for no other reason than we are slightly merry from the alcohol, so feel generous. Finally, Mother offers a toast for those no longer with us. The kids join in shouting 'Cheers' and clinking their little cups of lemonade and soda water up against our glasses.

We talk about another ad going in the paper this week for two single men for two separate rooms. We're letting the two biggest rooms out. Mother has agreed to allow me to choose any prospective lodgers. They will be bed and breakfast only. Mother says this protects her if she wants to give them notice. It's not like they are tenants just renting, they are getting a service and are therefore weekly only. No binding-contracts this time.

Steven finally calms down and rests his head on his arms on the kitchen table, and Lizzie is sitting on the chair next to the stove. I think she senses that it's time for 'goodbyes.' She looks deep in thought. I hear Mother and John coming down the stairs after their final inspection of the rooms.

"Well Beth," says Mother as she enters the kitchen. "We'll be on our way. The ad will go in the paper for Friday, which should bring some people out over the weekend."

She hands John's coat to him, opening it with both hands. He takes the cue and allows her to help him on with his coat. Then he takes her coat and returns the favor. He looks over her shoulder at Lizzie with a big golden-tooth grin.

"Well, Lizzie is everybody happy?"

"Yes," she shouts out. I join in. Steven doesn't stir.

"Did you enjoy your party?" John continues.

"Yes," she says just as loudly.

"What did you think of the dinner you ate?"

"I liked it."

"Well so you should. You ate Sally." Then he roars laughing. So he did know Sally was her favorite hen. She looks shocked. Her little face stares up at each of us. Then she looks down again. She doesn't say anything.

I don't know why John waited until the very last moment to tell her. I would rather he didn't say anything. I had forgotten about it. But then, to him, a hen is only dinner on the table, he's from Poland. It can never be anything else. Lizzie speaks at last.

"I thought you said you wouldn't kill Sally."

"She's the only one I could catch," replies John still laughing. She doesn't say another word. She gets up and passes through us all, opens the kitchen door and calls back.

"I'll see you to the door, Grandma," then opens every door until she's standing on the top step outside.

We follow her out in silence. Mother bends down and kisses her. Lizzie wipes off her kiss with the back of her hand, right in front of her, turns and goes back inside the house, shutting the vestibule door behind her.

"Oh, Oh, She's mad at me now John. You killed the bloody hen, not me," says Mother.

"She'll be alright." He shrugs. "Every child learns that food means animals die." His tooth glints and I can't help but think he is being malicious. He gets in the car with Mother still saying things to him. She slams the door hard. She waves at me, still scowling. I wave back.

"Good riddance to bad rubbish," I say under my breath, my happy mood dissolving like stomach powder in water. I'm so angry. John took great pleasure in telling Lizzie that she had eaten her pet hen.

"He's a sadist *and* a peasant," I say to myself audibly. I feel sad for Lizzie and guilty because I ate Sally too.

I walk to the kitchen. Lizzie's sitting on her chair with a sulk from here to next Wednesday on her face.

"Why did you let them kill Sally Mummy?"

"I wasn't here Hinny. He killed her while we were out in the park. I didn't know."

"Why didn't Grandma stop him then?"

"She didn't know either. Grandpa just went out there and did it. She wasn't even out there."

"I don't like Grandpa *anymore*," she says, her little fists all bunched up and banging on her knees. Then her tears fall, soaking her cheeks. I pick her up and place her sobbing body on my knee, rocking her gently.

"I don't like him either Lizzie."

She cries for a long time.

CHAPTER 21: LIZZIE: SOMEONE ATE MY CHOCOLATE DIGESTIVE.

Exodus 20:15, 16, 17, "You must not steal. You must not lie against your neighbor. You must not covet."

I love it when it's windy, especially when it's behind me. My hair is everywhere and I feel like I'm being blown all the way to school. I look up, and the white clouds are moving and changing shape in a beautiful blue sky. This morning when I got up, the toilet seat was so chilly, I was glad to get off it. Mummy had the stove burning, and made us toast with strawberry jam on one slice and marmalade on the other and a nice cup of sweet tea.

I arrive at school and all the girls hair is in the air. I wonder if my nose is as red as Alicia's. I see she is wearing woolly gloves. The bell rings, and everyone lines up according to their class. With our three lines and the four lines of big boys in the next playground, there are seven lines of whispering children. A teacher from each side of the school whistles and tells everyone to be quiet. Mrs. Whiteside is our playground monitor, and when we are completely silent, she allows us to go into school. The nursery children go in first.

I find my rose and hang up my coat. It's always a happy feeling I get, when I go into the large nursery room. I head over towards the fire and sit on the floor with my legs crossed. Each child, first of all goes over to the snack table and places their snack on it, then sits down on the floor too. Mummy doesn't give me a mid-morning snack, but that's okay, we don't have much money, she tells me.

Miss Norris asks us to kneel and says prayers. Then we stand and sing ‘All things bright and beautiful,’ which I love. I’m always singing it, even at home. ‘Each little flower that opens, each little bird that sings, He made their glowing colors, He made their tiny wings, All things bright and beautiful, all creatures great and small, All things wise and wonderful, The Lord God made them all.’ It makes sense to me that someone made everything on the earth. I’m still not sure who made God and it irritates me to think that no one did. Miss Norris says he’s always been God from millions of years ago, and no one made him. She says he had no beginning and will never have an end. So He’s up in heaven forever.

Every night before I go to sleep, I tell God, thank you, for everything he has made. I still thank him for Sally, even though she's been eaten. Mummy says God put animals on the earth to be eaten mainly, if not by us then by each other. She says dogs and cats are our pets. She says she doesn't like cats, but that she may get a dog as a pet one of these days.

Yesterday, we learned a hilarious song, all about who eats who. I love singing it. I hum it to myself and say the words in my head.

“There was an old woman who swallowed a fly, I don’t why, she swallowed a fly, perhaps she’ll die. She swallowed a spider to catch the fly, she swallowed a mouse to catch the spider, she swallowed a cat to catch the mouse, she swallowed a dog to catch the cat, she swallowed a horse to catch the dog." Suddenly Miss Norris's voice interrupts my thoughts.

“Children,” says Miss Norris loudly, “we are going to read a book this morning, called Janet and John. Miss Anderson will bring each of you to my desk to see how you’re doing. While we do that, I want each of you to sit at your tables in groups and color in the letters and pictures you'll find at your table."

I get up and go to my chair, the same one I sit on every day and start to color. Then half way through coloring, Miss Anderson lifts me up and carries me over to Miss Norris. She asks me to read the first page. I recognize the words, 'Janet and John,' because there are pictures of them on the walls with their names underneath. Anyway, something magical happens. I know my alphabet both in the way adults read it A, B, C with long sounds, and in the way Mummy taught me that children must read it first, in short sounds. Miss Norris shows me that as I say letters the short way, that all the letters flow together, so c-a-t is easy, cat. I read three more pages. She tells me I'm a good girl and that I can read. I never knew that before. I go back to my desk. I have just realized the secret of reading. It makes me feel like I do when I have just eaten a big ice cream cone. Happy.

After this, Miss Rogers from the big school comes in and plays the piano. We all skip around the nursery room for about ten minutes, first going one way then another. I see something shiny blue as I pass the snack table. On my next go round I stop off at the table and look at it. It's perfectly round and the blue shine is coming from the paper around this flat round object. I skip around one more time and stop again. I wonder if anyone notices. No one does. So I open a part of the shiny blue paper and see chocolate on one side and what looks like biscuit on the other side. I take a bite, put it back down and carry on skipping; amazed that absolutely no one sees me. As I skip I munch on the most delicious chocolate biscuit I have ever had. Mummy's biscuits never have chocolate on them and this one is twice the size of any I have ever seen. I pass the table as I munch and skip and know that on my next go round, I'm going to have one more bite. Still no one notices and I wrap it back up. It tastes delicious.

Then soon, it's time for break and we each are given a small bottle of milk with a silver shiny top on that we poke our thumb into, so we can peel it off. As I drink my milk, I realize that nearly all the children have some sort of snack to eat. Cold toast seems to be the favorite snack, or a small sandwich, or a couple of small biscuits, like the ones we sometimes have at home, custard creams. I think of that chocolate biscuit I just ate and go to the snack table to see if it could possibly still be there. It's gone. The taste is still in my mouth, and my milk is not satisfying me like the biscuit did. I feel cheated. So I decide to make a little fuss about it.

I walk over to Miss Anderson and tell her that my snack has gone off the table. She then asks me what it looks like, and I tell her it's wrapped in blue shiny paper. She tells Miss Norris, who then shouts out,

"Children. Stop what you are doing now and listen to me."

The whole world goes quiet. I can hear the crackle of the fire.

"Who has taken a blue wrapped biscuit off the snack table?"

I think to myself, 'Wow, she's going to find it for me.'

"I'll ask you all once more. Who has taken a blue wrapped biscuit off the snack table?"

I look at all the children, still and silent. It's a big thing going on, and no one knows what to do about it. Everyone's just staring at Miss Norris.

"Children, I want everyone but Lizzie to go and get their hats and coats and come back in here. Don't put them on, just bring them back in here and line up, quickly now, off you go."

I start to think, 'Oh, oh, what's happening. Why can't I go and get my coat too?'

Miss Norris sits on a chair, and one by one, has each child hand over their coat to her. She looks in their pockets. When she gets to

Anne Turner, she brings out a shiny blue circle and calls me over to her.

"Is this what you brought, Lizzie?"

By this time, this whole snack thing has gotten a little out of hand for my liking and I know that something does not feel right, but I can't put my finger on what it is.

"Yes, Miss Norris."

I know it's not mine but what can I do? This is a big time fuss and now I have to go along with it. She gives me the biscuit.

"Well, go and put on your coat and hat and go outside."

She then tells everyone to put on their coats and hats and go outside.

"Not you, Anne," she says to Anne Turner.

So we all go outside and I get to eat my delicious chocolate biscuit. Somehow, it's not as delicious as it was when I was skipping around. The atmosphere in the nursery has changed and I think Anne may be in trouble. I feel a bit uncomfortable about that. I don't like that I said it was mine. Anyway, I push it to the back of my mind. When we get back inside, Anne Turner is sitting on a chair. She's crying.

*

Today is another day at school and as I go into the playground, Anne Garstang comes over to me and says,

"Ah, you're in trouble with Miss Norris. She told me I had to look for you. She said I had to tell you to go and see her as soon as you got to school."

My heart falls into my tummy. I feel like I do when Mummy is mad at me. I like Miss Norris and I don't want her to be mad at me about the chocolate biscuit. Anne Garstang is the tallest school-girl in the nursery, and she has a large head. She is very bossy in the way she is telling me, and her bigness makes me feel even worse. She marches ahead of me and knocks hard on the nursery door. Then she opens it and says,

"Miss Norris, Lizzie Caradine is here." Then I hear a sharp voice.

"Tell her to come inside."

"You have to go inside," says Anne, like she's a teacher too. I pass her and she closes the door behind me.

"You know why I want to see you Lizzie. You stole Anne Turner's snack yesterday and told me a lie, that it was yours. Sit with Miss Anderson until I'm ready to deal with you. I'll be smacking your bottom three times on either side."

I burst into tears.

"I'm sorry Miss Norris. I'm sorry."

Miss Anderson sits me on a chair facing her and Miss Norris ignores my pleas and walks to her desk and starts to write. I follow her with my eyes. I love Miss Norris, she has always been so lovely and kind to me, now she doesn't like me anymore, she is going to smack me. I'm scared and feel like I want to be sick. My whole world is in a jumbled mess in my head. I appeal to Miss Anderson.

"Please tell Miss Norris, I don't want a smack. Please tell her I'll never do it again, that I'm sorry." Miss Anderson looks at me with genuine concern. Her brown eyes look sorrowful.

"Miss Norris," she says, turning to look at her, "Lizzie says she doesn't want a smack and that she is sorry and will never do it again."

"It's too late for that Miss Anderson; she's going to get a smack."

I feel terror. I know that this smacking is inescapable. I know that my beloved Miss Norris is going to become not so beloved in the very near future. I know that when she smacks me, it's going to hurt my bottom, but most of all, it's hurting my heart. I don't want to lose Miss Norris. If she smacks me, it will be the end of her love for me, and I'll never be able to look at her again because she'll have changed her mind about me. She calls me over to her.

"You've been a very naughty girl. You must never steal and you must never lie again."

Then she bends over me, pulls me into her legs, lifts up my coat and skirt and pushes one side of my knickers away and smacks me three times. I scream the place down in terror. Then she pushes the other side of my knickers away and smacks me three more times. I scream even louder. It really hurts. I never thought Miss Norris would hit me so hard, it stings. Each smack feels like I'm in the middle of horrible things. My happiness shatters. I'll never be able to look at her face again. My whole tummy and chest heaves in and out and I can't stop my loud crying.

"Now go outside," She tells me and walks away. I don't know what this terribleness is but I don't want to go anywhere near other children. I frantically wipe my eyes with my hands and coat sleeves. I clench my teeth together so the noises from my throat will stop.

Anne Garstang is standing outside the nursery door. She stares at me.

"You got smacked," she says with a smile.

"No, I didn't," I say. "I got told off."

"I saw you get smacked," she says. I feel so bad, like it would be better if I could deny to everyone around me that I got smacked. But Anne Garstang saw it all happen. I want to run and hide. I don't want her to tell everyone. I want it all to go away. My thoughts are a jumble. I feel so unhappy. Miss Norris has changed towards me. Things will never be the same again. I can never tell anyone about this, ever. Especially not Mummy.

I don't go outside when Anne does. I sit on the bench below my rose and just stare at the floor. Today will be a very long day. I don't want to see Miss Norris again, or Miss Anderson, or Anne Garstang. Then the bell sounds outside and soon everyone files in.

"You got smacked," says one boy after another as they take off their coats. I can feel my face get hot. I can't look at them.

Steven didn't come to school today. He's sick. There's a tiny thought in my head, 'I'm glad.' I stand up and walk into the awful, crowded nursery room. I hate school.

CHAPTER 22: BETH: A COLORED MAN NEEDS A ROOM.

Romans 12:19, Never take your revenge, beloved, but leave room for the wrath of God, for it is written, 'Vengeance is mine, I will repay,' says the Lord.

The doorbell rings at ten o'clock in the morning.

"Please don't say it's the Social Worker. She's not due for a couple of days, and I haven't cleaned up yet," I say to myself as I make my way through the hall.

It could be someone looking for a room. Mother put an ad in the paper yesterday. I look at myself in the mirror of the new hallstand. I look presentable. The very act of opening a front door, while standing in a beautifully tiled and lead glass paned, vestibule, makes me feel important, so I like to look at least poised.

I find myself looking down at a colored man. He has stepped back off the steps after ringing the bell, as is the custom for visitors who respect one's privacy. He's dressed smartly in a white shirt and blue tie. His trousers are impeccably pressed, his shoes, black and well-polished. I'm not shocked, just surprised.

"Hello, how can I help you?" I ask

"Hello." He smiles. "I saw your advert in the newspaper. I'm looking for a room."

He's brown-skinned, greased back hair, neat mustache. I smell a quick scent of his aftershave. His English is good, but I can't place his accent.

“Where are you from, if you don’t mind my asking?”

"I am from India. I have come to the Mother Country to live and work at Courtaulds. My name is Mr. Patel."

He’s a skinny looking man around five foot, five inches tall. His brown eyes have a cautious look. He isn’t good looking to me. No-one is in comparison to my Lonnie. I’m thinking he reminds me of the Punjabi man with the turban who comes by selling housewares. A similar coffee color. I can't have a colored man living in my house. I think he can tell by my face. He looks a little uncomfortable and shifts his feet.

“Do you still have a room to rent?”

Realizing I've been scrutinizing him, I lift my head and look over his head at the house across the street as I answer.

"Yes, yes I do. But I have another man coming to look at it later." I nonchalantly look back at his upturned face and smile, "He'll probably take it."

“I’m on two-to-ten shift this week. So I can’t come back this afternoon. I can come tomorrow morning again if you’re willing.”

I take a couple of seconds to let his words sink in. His accent throws me off guard. I don’t want him to come back at all.

“I don’t want to put you to any inconvenience, Mr. Patel. I’m almost certain the man coming back this afternoon will be taking the room.”

He shakes his head in a cockeyed sort of way, which I think means ‘No.’

“Okay,” he says, still moving his head, “I’m coming back in the morning. It is okay if the other man wants it. Just tell me then. It is no trouble."

He smiles at me and puts his two hands together and tips them prayer-like, once, towards me. He's going to be harder to get rid of than I thought. He can tell I'm hedging. I'll just ignore his return in the morning, not answer the door.

"And please to tell me, who I am speaking to?" He wants my name.

"Mrs. Caradine. Alright then, thank you for enquiring about the room." I step back and start to close the door.

"I'm an excellent worker, Mrs. Caradine. Always punctual. I have this reference from my foreman, Mr. Jarvis." He pulls a white envelope from his inside jacket pocket and hands it to me. Persistent beggar, he is. He wobbles his head some more.

"Please keep this and read it at your convenience Mrs. Caradine. You can give it back to me tomorrow when I'm coming back." I take the blasted letter.

"I'll let you know," I say. "Goodbye." I shut the door and pause. I hear the gate clang shut. He's gone thank goodness.

"He can have it back tomorrow," I say out loud. "Pushy bugger."

Maybe I've been naïve about being a landlady. There's much more to this business than cooking and cleaning. I have to interact with people, almost interview them. I have to make hard decisions about who is okay and who is not. I can't see into the future and how do I know who is going to pay their rent? As Lonnie might say, 'It's a crap shoot.'

I still have a lot to do. I finish the last dregs of my tea and take a tea leaf off my lip. I look inside the cup and see it has a wavy line of tea leaves all the way from the bottom to the top. Gran used to visit a lady in the next village who read tea leaves. According to Gran, who's a born skeptic, the reader was always accurate. I went with her once, and she said that Gran was not living in her final home and to expect a move out of her house. She also told her to cut down on her daily beer a bit. I had laughed at that because every day Gran would fetch a jug of beer from the pub up the hill. She liked nothing better than to sit in the back garden on a kitchen chair and sip her beer and smoke two or three cigarettes one after the other. I would sit with her in the afternoon sun, and we would look up at the fell behind our house, taking occasional glances at each other and discussing whatever news we had read recently. She had a weekly paper delivered, and that would keep us going every afternoon. The Cumberland and Westmorland Herald had local births, marriages, and deaths and she would sometimes comment on local people she knew or had heard of in those columns.

She loves the new Queen Elizabeth crowned in 1953. 'I'm not too keen on her husband though,' she would say. 'It's all Greek to me why she married him.' Prince Philip is dashing and I know he's Greek, so I would always laugh at her sarcasm. I think Gran has a fear of foreigners. It took her quite a while to warm up to Lonnie, and she has never even seen a 'darkie' as she calls them, except in a newspaper now and then. There are certainly no colored people living in the Lake District.

Once, on one of my visits to her with Lonnie and our children, she showed us a magazine from the local post office. It showed a picture of Queen Elizabeth and Prince Philip riding on the back of an elephant in India. There were Indian attendants all around, dressed in what we supposed was their best ceremonial uniforms. I think that was the first time we had ever discussed 'colored people.' The photo was very colorful with red and gold adornments on the elephant's square box-seat.

"Pomp and circumstance indeed," said Gran, to which she added, "Looks more like a circus than anything."

I could not help but see that our Queen looked apprehensive all the way up there on an elephant's back. I thought her very brave.

Gran loved that magazine. She said, "It's the nearest I'm ever going to get to Royalty." In her mind, there was not even a glimmer of hope that one day she could go to London and visit Buckingham Palace. Some areas of life seemed out of bounds to Gran, and although I had traveled further away from home than she had, I think I felt the same way too. So, yes, in Gran's sheep covered world, Indian people are an anomaly. I think if one turned up on her doorstep, she'd have a heart attack.

That visit to Gran also sparked a bigger discussion about Lonnie's views on those in America who are not white. "There are Asians or Niggers," he said. "And we don't mix with either."

I had replied, "In Britain, we call people from India, Indians or ‘coloreds,' but so we don't confuse them with the 'red Indians' in John Wayne films, we mostly call them ‘coloreds.’ Black people are 'darkies,’ but some call them 'wogs.'"

Call me a snob, but I'm not keen on foreigners either. I'm from Great Britain, and we conquered half the foreign world.

When Lonnie told me about segregation in the United States, I was shocked. It was hard for me to understand because I had no experience of it here in Britain. I suppose I was ignorant of any other USA facts, other than President Abraham Lincoln had a lot to do with outlawing slavery. Slavery to my mind was cruel and heartless, but it was not that long ago that richer people here had servants, which is a step up from slavery I suppose because they did get a small wage. Even if it was a pittance.

Lonnie's views were very entrenched, and it had to do with the harsh life the early pioneers endured I suppose. He said his grandfather was the meanest man he ever knew and used to own an ice house where he had slaves working for him. So Lonnie grew up with a lot of mean influences in his life.

I know what he would say if a man from India wanted to rent a room in our house, and it would not be eloquent.

Sometimes I still have imaginary conversations with Lonnie. It's like I cannot give up on him. Somewhere in my heart, I believe that our love will win out and he'll come back to England to look for me. He is and will always be the love of my life. Thinking about him makes me want to see him, hear him, touch him.

I walk into my bedroom and open the top doors in the wall cupboard to the left of the black marble fireplace. He was in the Navy before he joined the Air Force. I didn't know him back then, but he looks handsome in his Navy uniform. I pull out the fancy cardboard box that once held some expensive toiletries, but now holds my letters and pictures of Lonnie. I haven't looked inside this box since before my breakdown, but I'm feeling stronger now.

As I pull them out and arrange them on the counterpane. I notice they smell of my favorite perfume, Chanel NO5. Immediately I'm transported to being in his arms again. I close my eyes and hold the images, scents, and touches for as long as I can. I love him still. Part of me just wants to put it all back in the box and hide it again in the cupboard, but I prefer torment to forgetting everything we had.

I pick up his last letter to me in its white envelope and open the page. Those blue lines look unimportant now. I wonder how long it took him to find the paper and rip it out of a notebook. Was it ripped out in haste, in anger, in pain? Or is everything we had just one big lie?

I can still remember Lizzie handing his letter to me and jumping up and down in excitement.

“What does it say Mummy?”

"If you wait a minute Lizzie, let me read it first, then I'll tell you, and we'll both know."

I remember very clearly how I felt that incomprehensible morning.

'Dearest Beth, my sweetheart, my beautiful girl, please hug Steven and Lizzie for me. It's been a while since we were together and I miss you all honey. I hope they still love their gifts I got them and that you have plenty of chances to wear your pearls.

I can still smell your scent on the scarf you gave me. I keep it in a plastic bag in my closet. When I miss you, I take it out and hold it to my face. I ache for you, Beth. I have never longed for anyone more in my life. This letter is the hardest letter I ever had to write. It's killing me.

I fell in love with you honey, hook, line, and sinker. I want you to believe me. But I was not honest with you. I knew if I told you the truth, you would have nothing to do with me and I wanted you so bad.' Back then, my heart jolted. I gasped out loud.

"What's wrong Mummy?" Lizzie asked, but her words became muffled in a fast descending fog.

'I'm married, Beth. I have three children. I don't know how else to wrap this.'

"No," I screamed. "My godfathers, Lonnie, no. Married? Three kids?"

"Mummy. What's wrong?" I heard the fear in Lizzie's voice, like a warning.

'I believed when I got home; I would divorce my wife and find some way to get you over here. None of what I ever said about my love for you is a lie, Beth you've got to believe me. I told my brothers, and they blabbed to their wives. They had a family talk. My brother Henry invited me over to his house, said we could go hunting. When I got there, my twin brother Jonnie and his wife were there too. They tore into me like they were skinning a deer. They told me if I divorced my wife and left my three kids they would disown me. They said I would be a family outcast and none of them would ever have anything to do with me again. They told me to keep quiet about any of it to my wife. She never had to know. They said I would bring shame on the whole family. They meant it all Beth. I ain't never seen my family so fired up and bitter. I told you how religious they all are. Divorce has never happened in my family. I'm stuck where I am because of the Air Force. I can't move a muscle without their permission. I thought I could get a divorce in Mexico, but I know I'll be demoted when everyone finds out. Then I won't have enough money to pay my wife and kids and bring you over anyway. It just seems that the whole doggone world is against us, Beth. I never meant to hurt you. I'm a no good son-of-a-bitch with no spine. I hate myself right now. All I ever wanted was for you and me to be together. Please forgive me. I don't know how to put it right.

My brothers have made me change my PO Box number, so you can't get letters to me. They're as mean as snakes right now. They're watching my every move. I can't bear to write to you anymore Beth. It hurts too damn much. I'll send you money whenever I can. I promise.'

My knees went to jelly. Denial spewed from my lips. Lizzie was clinging onto my legs. "Mummy? What's wrong?" I continued to read.

'You once said to me it's better to have loved and lost than never to have loved at all. You're the best thing that ever happened to me Beth; I'll never forget you. I just can't ever be with you. Please forgive me. I'm sorry. I'll never forget you in your green dress and the great times we had together. Please don't hate me. I'll always love you babe, forever.

Lonnie xxx '

That's when I fell to my knees, pushing Lizzie away. That's when my whole world shattered like a bomb landing on Gran's metal shelter. I still can't believe what I read.

I still see him in my dreams. He's walking in his long warrior-like stride; we are on the street and I know I have to catch up with him before he gets to the next crossroads. I shout his name, and I'm running as fast as I can go, but he's getting further away. It always ends the same way. He reaches the crossroads and turns the corner. When I get there, he's gone. The streets are empty. I'm desolate. That's when I wake up sobbing his name.

I lost whatever power I may have mistakenly thought I had over my life, when I read his last words to me, on some lined paper he had torn out of a notebook.

For some reason, right now, I'm no longer tearful. I feel angry. I feel rage.

"You're so right Lonnie," I say to his photo. "You're a cowardly son-of-a-bitch. All those nights we spent together, you never once gave me any indication you were married. You gave me children and still kept up your lies. You betrayed me."

My heart twists and I feel physical pain in my chest and stomach. I refuse to give in to tears, and instead, spit out the words, "You traitor. We have a colored man living in our house now Lonnie, and your children say hello to him every single day. And guess what? We have to share our bathroom with him. So what about that, you sorry son-of-a-bitch?"

As I speak the words, I feel a depth of satisfaction, as though he is standing in front of me and I have just punched him in the face. It fills me up. I say the words over again and embitter each syllable with accusation and hatred. I use his word, 'nigger.'

How is it possible to love someone with all my heart and feel this hatred? Gran's words, 'Sticks and stones can break my bones, but words will never harm me,' come to mind. I'm seething. My bitter words dissolve into the air. Lonnie's not here to hear them. I want so much to make him feel my pain.

Suddenly it hits me. "Revenge is sweet Lonnie. You have no hold on me or our children. You lost the right to have a say in their lives when you left us. When Mr. Patel comes back in the morning, I'll show him the room, and if he wants it, he can damn well have it."

CHAPTER 23: BETH: TWO NEW BOARDERS.

Diaspora: India: The 1947 Partition resulted in the migration of millions of people between India and Pakistan. A simplistic definition might be: Hindus from Pakistan moved into India, Muslims in India moved to Pakistan. However many more people of differing religions were affected. The resultant religious and sectarian violence killed between one and two million people. It was a blood bath. Thousands of former subjects of the British Raj went to Great Britain from the Indian Sub-Continent after India and Pakistan became independent.

It's been almost four weeks since Dan Patel and Peter Snow moved into the two larger rooms upstairs. Mr. Patel works at Courtaulds, the textile mill, and Mr. Snow, at a furniture warehouse near the docks. I've managed it all rather well. They're no trouble. They keep their rooms clean and tidy, and they're out of the house nine or ten hours a day. Mr. Snow is out all day until around seven in the evening. Mr. Patel does shift work, so is out at different times every week.

When he's on the morning shift, I pack him a couple of sausage sandwiches and leave them on the hallstand the night before. He says he eats them on the bus going to work. I cook a breakfast of bacon and egg, or sausage and egg for Mr. Snow every morning. Sometimes I do fried bread, sometimes toast and jam to go with it. If Mr. Patel is on the afternoon shift, he gets his cooked breakfast at midday before he leaves the house. When he's on the night shift, he buys his food at

Courtaulds, so I don't have to cook late at night for him, then I give him breakfast when he comes in at seven in the morning.

I've gotten into a routine now. I get three pounds and fifteen shillings from each of them, a week. My rent to John and Mother has gone up to three pounds a week, so I let them just cash out Lonnie's checks to cover that. I manage to buy all the food and pay all the bills. It's tight sometimes, but I'm managing to keep house and home together.

Steven and Lizzie like school and Natalie still has nursery two mornings a week. I need to be a larger part of her life. It's not fair to have someone else looking after her when I'm quite capable now. Hopefully, soon, I'll have her full time. It depends on the social worker. Nat's quieter than my other two ever were. Mr. Patel chats away to her whenever he sees her. She doesn't say anything to him, just stares at him and laughs. Right now she's somehow managed to find Lizzie's old red Wellington boots and keeps putting them on. She looks hysterical plodding around; they're too big, so she keeps falling over. Lizzie and Natalie have bonded tightly. I think Lizzie thinks Nat is her child, not mine, the way she mothers her all the time.

Mr. Snow and Mr. Patel only interact with my children if their paths cross. Sometimes it's when the kids are setting the table.

Mr. Snow is aloof, but Mr. Patel's very chatty with them. Lizzie asked him why he talks funny; well she would, wouldn't she? She's little 'Miss, I-want-to-know-it-all.' Once she said to him, "If you scrape all your skin off, will you be white underneath?" I wanted to kill her. I said, "Lizzie, don't ask such questions of Mr. Patel." He just waved it away and said, 'It's okay. Let me ask you a question, Miss Lizzie. If I put mud all over your face, will you be brown like me?"

She liked that and laughed out loud.

"No," she said, "I would just wash it off."

Mr. Patel answered, "So you see, we are born as babies with white skin or browner skin. People in India have brown skin because the sun is hotter over there and our brown skin helps us not to get burned.

Lizzie looked at her pale arms, said, "I see." And that was the end of that.

Honest to goodness, I sometimes ask, 'What have I done God, to deserve Lizzie?'

She's learning to read and write and can count up to a hundred. Steven is doing well too, but he is more hesitant when it comes to writing. His reading has improved but sometimes he day-dreams. His second-year infants' teacher says she catches him looking out of the window at the sky. She asks him what he's looking at, and he says,

"Clouds and planes."

She says sometimes boys are a little slower than girls in maturity, but he'll catch up.

For his birthday, I bought him an airplane that runs on wheels on the floor. He loves to play with it and makes it take off and fly through the whole house with his arm held high and the noise of its engines buzzing out of his mouth. He's a chip off the old block, and he's growing to look more and more like Lonnie. He has similar mannerisms, and I can see Lonnie in him when he laughs. I'm glad he looks like his Dad, just as long as he doesn't turn out like him.

I don't know who Lizzie looks like the most. When she was born, Gran said,

"She'll improve with keeping." She was referring to how long and skinny Lizzie was. All my children have put on some weight. They look healthy.

Natalie favors me except for her father's blonde curls. She's a cutie-pie, and I love her dearly. I tell everyone, (by everyone, I mean the local shop owners, who ask me questions every time they see me),

I have three children to my first husband, Lonnie. I say I divorced him and he went back to America. It's no-one's business anyway.

I hear a key in the front door, it opens and closes, then, the vestibule door squeaks and there's a sharp metal sound as someone's foot stands hard on the brass plate across the hall step. I glance at the clock; it must be Mr. Patel. Then I hear a knock on the hall door. I go and open it.

"Hello, Mr. Patel."

He looks tired, his eyes have bags under them, and he's wheezing.

"Are you alright?"

"I have asthma and need my inhaler. I left it behind today, but I'm okay, I'll use it shortly."

"Okay. Did you want me for something?"

"If you wouldn't mind telling me where the nearest doctor is, please? I'll go and see him. My doctor's on the other side of town."

"Of course," I reply. "I go to Dr. Markowitz. He's just down the road. Cross over Hardwick St, and his surgery is the third house on the left. He has a sign outside his front door. He'll be open at four o'clock if you need to see him tonight. Just tell him Beth Caradine sent you and that you're boarding here. He's a good doctor."

"Thank you very much. I wonder if I might be able to get a cup of tea from you in about twenty minutes after I've washed and changed."

"Of course. I'll hear you coming down the stairs, and I'll bring your tea into the dining room."

"You're too kind Mrs. Caradine."

"Not at all, Mr. Patel, I told you. You just ask if you need anything."

He places his hands in front, palms together and does that funny little wobble-head movement. Then he goes upstairs, seeming to suck in his breath on every step. I go back to the kitchen and start to peel a few potatoes for our dinner. The children will be home soon, and we'll have fish and chips, home-made and delicious. We like mushy peas with them too. I have some left over from yesterday's ham-hock dinner.

Mr. Patel often goes out in the evening, presumably to eat, maybe to get a pint or two of beer. He's always back in by ten o'clock. It occurs to me that he may not feel like going out if he is not feeling very well. Maybe I should offer him some fish and chips.

I go and open the front door for the children. That way they needn't ring the darn bell. I hold back the door with the iron Scottie-dogs that Gran had let me keep from her home in South Shields.

I hear Mr. Patel coming out of the bathroom just as I stir sugar in his cup of tea, and the children arrive home. They speed through the vestibule as if a ghost is after them, and tumble into the hallway.

"I won you," shouts Lizzie.

"You cheated," screams Steven.

I halt them in their tracks while trying not to spill Mr. Patel's tea.

"Hey, you two. Be quiet when you come into the house. This is not a playground."

They stop suddenly and look up the staircase.

"Hello Mr. Patel," says Lizzie.

I turn and see Mr. Patel looking scrubbed and tidy, standing half way down the stairs.

"Good afternoon," he says with a smile.

"I was just bringing you your cup of tea," I say. I turn to the two ragamuffins with wild hair, scraped knees and socks all wrinkled down to their ankles.

"While Mr. Patel takes his tea in the front room, you two can go upstairs to the bathroom and wash and brush up. Your dinner will be ready in another half hour, so I want to see you sitting at the kitchen table as quietly as dormice. But before you go upstairs, just calm down and stand still. Allow Mr. Patel to pass and go into the front room first."

They stand still, smiling up at him. I think he's still a novelty to them. He disappears into the front room with his tea and biscuits; then they race upstairs.

“Slow down, you two,” I call. But they don’t.

I open the front room door and step inside. Mr. Patel is about to read the weekly newspaper and is sipping his tea.

"I apologize, Mr. Patel, they have far too much energy. I was going to ask you if you would like me to make you some fish and chips to eat this evening when you get back from the doctors."

“That is too kind of you. I do not want to put you to any trouble.”

"Well you seemed poorly when you first came in, and I thought that maybe you might not want to go out if you’re under the weather.”

"Thank you, Mrs. Caradine. I would like that very much. Tonight, I may retire early to my bed."

“Alright then. When you get back, I’ll start your dinner. It will only take ten minutes to cook. Do you want mushy peas with it and bread and butter?”

“That will be very good, Mrs. Caradine. Thank you very much.”

“No problem, Mr. Patel.” I leave him to his newspaper and close the door behind me.

I can hear water splashing in the sink upstairs. The toilet flushes. I go into the back kitchen to make our dinner. Natalie is in her playpen, busy with bricks and teething rings.

Steven runs downstairs and sits at the table. "I won again," he says. Lizzie is only seconds behind him. Then Lizzie leaves and goes back upstairs, returning five minutes later. Steven says, "Ah. I'm going to tell Mummy of you. What have you done to your hair?"

“I don’t care,” replies Lizzie. “I cut my hair.”

I turn my head and call out, "Er, you cut your hair, Lizzie? Come here and let me see it now," I can't leave the cooker, the chips are frying, and I'm cooking the fish in a separate pan of hot oil. So Lizzie comes into the back kitchen, and I just burst out laughing.

“Oh, my giddy aunt, what on earth have you done to your hair? There’s a big chunk missing out of the front my girl. What did you do?”

"I cut my hair, Mummy."

“Well, I can see that? What did you cut it with?”

“Some scissors.”

"What scissors?" I open the drawer, and my kitchen scissors are in there.

“I found some scissors.”

Just then Mr. Patel knocks on the hall door.

“Steven go and open the door for Mr. Patel; ask him to come into the kitchen, I’m in the middle of cooking.”

Mr. Patel comes to the back kitchen and looks at Lizzie’s hair. He is holding a piece of hair in his fingers and a pair of scissors in his other hand.

“I’m very sorry, Mrs. Caradine, I must have left my room door open upstairs. I think Lizzie must have gone in and cut her hair. I found this on my dressing table.”

He looks mortified. Lizzie smiles up at him as if butter wouldn’t melt in her mouth and says, “I did.” I burst out laughing again, and Mr. Patel sees the funny side to it, and he laughs too. Steven comes into the back kitchen and joins in laughing. She isn’t the least bit embarrassed. I shake my head.

“What am I to do with you Busy Lizzie?” I say.

Mr. Patel says, “You’re a great sport, Mrs. Caradine. I’m going now to the doctors. I’ll see you later.” He leaves still holding her cut of hair. Giggling, the children go and sit at the table waiting for their dinner.

The haddock I bought is fresh and tasty. We all enjoy it. I wash up, then sit with the children and tell them three stories from their bedtime book of fables. We sing 'ten green bottles hanging on the wall,' twice. Then I 'shoo' them upstairs for their nightly ablutions and let them color for a while in their pajamas.

Natalie eats well, and I bathe her in the kitchen sink which she loves. I sit her on a towel on the draining board to dry her off. I just finish putting on her nappy when I hear the vestibule door open and the brass plate rattle. Heavy footsteps go upstairs, and I look at the clock. It's already seven o'clock, and I know those sounds belong to Mr. Snow.

“Mr. Patel must have changed his mind about fish and chips and gone out for dinner," I say to Natalie. “Well that’s his loss. Come on angel let’s get you to bed.” I take her to our room and into her cot. She’ll be asleep soon. I tiptoe out and notice through the hallway that the front door is still partly open, so I lock it.

“Mr. Patel can use his key when he gets back,” I say aloud.
I’m feeling tired and decide to have an early night. I feel safe in our room. It’s quiet and looks onto the back yard. The view is an apple orchard beyond the fence. It’s very private.

By the time Natalie is asleep, and I've tucked in Lizzie and Steven, it's eight o’clock. I wait until Lizzie and Steven stop whispering, and Lizzie has said her super-long prayer, thanking God for everything under the sun. I lock the hall door, the sliding door, and snuggle into my comfortable double bed.

I don't say prayers these days, I’ve become an agnostic. Anyway, Lizzie says enough for all of us, with some to spare.

I fall asleep immediately, but a sudden loud bang has my eyes and ears wide open. It's dark and the clock shows quarter past eleven. I hear a key, and the front door closes with another bang. It's late for Mr. Patel to be coming in. He stumbles through the vestibule door hitting the brass plate across the step. Is he drunk? I hear the distinctive click of the switches that turn on the lights in the hall and the upstair's landing.

"Drat," I say, "I forgot to leave on the light. No wonder he's tripping over himself." Then, blow me down, Mr. Patel knocks on my hall door.

"You can get lost," I whisper in the gloom. "If you think I'm at your beck and call, bugger, you've got another think coming." He knocks again. This time I feel anger. I talk myself out of going to the hall door to give him a piece of my mind. His footsteps go upstairs.

"Yes. Too bad, you missed a great fish and chips dinner," I whisper. "Cheeky Bugger."

CHAPTER 24: LIZZIE: WHERE'S MY MUMMY?

Numbers 25:2-3, For they invited the people to the sacrifices of their gods, and the people ate and bowed down to their gods. So Israel joined themselves to Baal of Peor, and the LORD was angry with Israel.

I'm in the bathroom doing my ablutions thinking about what we ate yesterday. Mr. Patel cooked us some of his kind of food. Mummy put extra butter on mine and Steven's because she said we are not used to spicy food. It burned our tongue a bit, but we drank cold water with it. After, Mummy gave us some rice pudding she made in the oven. It was sweet and took away the burn.

We've seen a lot more of Mr. Patel. He took us to a Saturday morning picture show. It was fun. Batman and Robin caught all the bad people and put them in prison. When we came out of the pictures, he bought us a big ice-cream cone each.

As I brush my teeth, I hear Grandma's voice. I'm surprised and rush to finish. I wash and dress, then run downstairs as fast as I can and open the passage door. I bump right into Mummy who is coming through from the other side. I stare at her. She is wearing a pale pink jacket that has a wavy edge at her waist, a matching pink skirt that tapers and stops at the knee, just like the mummy-shape crack on the ceiling upstairs. She has a tiny petal shaped hat on; the pink net is over her eyes. She has on new pointed shoes and stockings. Her lipstick is lovely.

“Mummy. You look beautiful."

"Well thank you, sweetheart."

"Where are you going?"

"I'm going to get married." I know what that means.

"Can I be your bridesmaid?"

"It's not that kind of wedding Lizzie."

"I want to come with you, Mummy."

"Not this time Lizzie. Grandma will look after you until I get back, I won't be long."

"Who are you getting married to Mummy?"

"Dan."

"Who's Dan?"

"Mr. Patel."

"Mr. Patel? Why are you going to marry Mr. Patel?"

"Lizzie," says Grandma coming up the passage. "We'll sit and have a nice cup of tea if you like. Mummy will be back soon."

Mummy. bends down and kisses me. "Be good for Grandma Lizzie. Steven's out playing. We'll be back soon."

Just then Mr. Patel comes down the stairs in a dark blue suit, a white shirt, and a shiny blue tie. He looks nice too. He's behind me in the hall. I'm standing in the doorway between him and Mummy. I know that getting married is something special and I'm hurting that she does not want to share it with me.

"Please, can I come with you?" I feel hopeful.

She doesn't answer, but holds my arms and guides me behind her to my Grandma's waiting hands. She goes out through the doorway and closes the door behind her. Grandma and I are left standing in the dark. I look up at her and can barely see her face.

"C'mon Hinny," she says and guides me back to the kitchen where she sits me on her knee in our favorite chair. We don't speak, just sit and cuddle for a long time.

Eventually, Grandma kisses my cheek and asks if I want a cup of tea.

"Yes, please Grandma. Please, can I have three sugars in it?"

“Three Hinny? You need sweetening up do you?”

"Yes, Grandma. I do.” Not sure what to call the feelings, or how to explain them to her I ask a question.

“Mr. Patel’s a boarder Grandma, so why’s Mummy getting married to him?”

“Don’t you like him, Lizzie?"

“He’s okay Grandma. Why’s Mummy getting married to him though?”

“She must like him I suppose.”

I cannot quite grasp what’s happening. My mind feels jumbled.

“I’m sad that Mummy doesn’t want me to be a bridesmaid Grandma.”

“Well, they’re not getting married in a church. They’re just going to the registry office. Their witnesses will be two people off the street I guess."

“Who off the street?”

“Just a couple of people they don’t even know. It will all be over in five minutes flat.”

“When they are married? Who will I be?” She picks me up and hugs me.

“You will still be our lovely little Lizzie.”

We sit and drink tea and stare at the stove for a long time. Steven keeps coming in and out of the house; he looks at us still sitting together and walks away. When he comes in for about the fifth time, Grandma tells Steven,

“Look out on the front for your Mummy and Mr. Patel coming back Steven. Run in and tell us when you see them coming down the road.” Eventually, he runs in and says they have just come around the corner.

They seem to have been gone a long time. I run with him outside and see them walking arm in arm down our street. I run as fast as my legs will carry me.

"Mummy, you're back. I missed you."

She barely looks at me and continues her conversation with Mr. Patel. They’re smiling and chatting. Steven stays outside our house and just stares at us as we all approach him. I stop, but they pass him by and go indoors. I stand with Steven and call out,

“Shall we come in with you?”

She doesn't reply, and the vestibule door closes behind them.

Mummy is different. It’s like I’m invisible to her. Nothing I say has any impact on her. It’s like she went out as my Mummy and came back a different person. She doesn’t even look the same. Something has changed.

Later, when Grandma has gone, Mummy calls Steven and me over to her and says,

"Now you two, Mr. Patel and I are now married. My name is now Mrs. Patel. Mr. Patel is your new daddy. You can call him Daddy, or Dad if you prefer."

I’m feeling so mixed up in my mind. I think to myself, ‘Dad? He’s not my dad. My daddy's in America. He's inside the airplanes in the sky. He sees me when I wave. When I’m big, I’m going to find him in America.’

When Steven and I go to bed, we whisper about Mr. Patel. We both agree he’s not our daddy. Steven says, "Mummy said that tomorrow, Mr. Patel is moving into this bedroom with her, and we three are to go and sleep upstairs again."

"I thought his room is upstairs."

“Shush. Not anymore."

I can't take it all in. One day Mr. Patel is a boarder, now he's married to Mummy, and we all have to split up and not sleep in our bedroom together. He's going to sleep in Mummy's bedroom, not us? My head hurts. Eventually, I fall asleep. When I wake up the next morning, Mummy's bed is the same as it was last night. She's not in it. I wake Steven.

"Mummy did not come to bed last night Steven. She must have stayed up all night with Mr. Patel."

He grunts, "I don't care about Mummy. I don't care about Mr. Patel. I'm going back to sleep."

He turns away from me and pulls the covers over his head. So I turn away from him and do the same. I still don't know why Mummy would want to marry Mr. Patel. It seems like a nonsense thing to do to me. He's a boarder. We don't even know him that well. Just for a short time. He's not my daddy.

I pine for her. Things have changed. I feel muddled up.

Where is she?

CHAPTER 25: LIZZIE: GUJARATI: SPEAKING IN ANOTHER LANGUAGE.

Isaiah 30:1-3, "Woe to the rebellious children," declares the LORD, "Who execute a plan, but not Mine, and make an alliance, but not of My Spirit, in order to add sin to sin; Who proceed down to Egypt without consulting Me, to take refuge in the safety of Pharaoh and to seek shelter in the shadow of Egypt! Therefore the safety of Pharaoh will be your shame and the shelter in the shadow of Egypt, your humiliation.

It's a sunny day and Mummy is heading toward the vestibule door with Natalie's push-chair. Two shopping bags swing on her arm. I'm on my way downstairs from the bathroom. The sunlight through the glass gives her hair a soft outline of dark blue-black. She is wearing her check, green and black wool skirt that I like so much, and a fluffy sweater of the same green. She looks pretty today. She turns around and I can see another outline of pale cream glowing through the soft hair on her cheek. I put my arms around her legs and strain my head back to see her face.

"Can I go shopping with you?"

"Not today. I have to go and pay a few bills; it's just a quick trip. You can stay home; I won't be long."

Since Grandma and Grandpa had left and she had married Dan, I mean Daddy, I always feel lonely without Mummy. Anytime she goes out; I always ask her the same question.

"Who's going to look after us?"

She laughs and pulls me away from her legs.

"Daddy and his friend are here. You'll be okay. I won't be long." She bends down and puckers her lips to kiss mine. I hug her neck, and my lips meet hers. I make a loud kiss sound.

“Okay, okay, Lizzie,” she says as she pulls my arms away from her neck. “Anyone would think I’m not coming back! Now go into the kitchen and see if Steven wants to play with you in the backyard.”

She leaves. I watch her green fluffy shadow through the glass in the vestibule door. I note the beautiful curve of her back and shoulders as she carefully lowers Natalie's pram over the edge of each step. Her shape shrinks as she goes down the path and through the gate. I stare at the tiny, shiny raindrop patterns on the glass door. I feel sad. I lick my lips and taste her lipstick like I always do.

Since Mummy got married, she is different. Before Natalie was born, at the other house, she would always be doing something with us. She showed me one day how to sew with bright blue thread on material over a circle of wood. There was a picture of a house and flowers across the middle of it. She had given it to me to hold in my left hand, as she put a needle in my right hand. There was a hole in the top of the needle and it had blue, shiny thread going through it. Mummy showed me how to put the needle down through the cloth near to the place where the blue thread poked through. She said it was called making a stitch. Then she said I had to let go of the needle and put my right hand beneath the circle and pull the needle through gently. There appeared the blue stitch I had made. She let me practice for a few minutes doing the same thing again and again until I somehow managed to wrap the blue thread over the edge of the wood circle. She took it off me to fix it.

Or, she would sit on the floor with us and read Thomas the Tank Engine. She could make all the engine noises and whistles. We loved her stories. These days she always seems to say ‘in a minute' when I ask her to play with me. I wait a minute, which always seems to be a long time, then I ask her again. A few days ago, I was playing with my tea-set, and I kept asking Mummy if she wanted a cup of tea. At first, she drank one or two cups; then she told me she was too busy to play. "Play with your doll and your tea-set," she said. I got bored and sulked. In the end, I put my tea-set away and stomped upstairs to sit in my bedroom on my own.

Steven never seems to want to play with me either. He keeps telling me I'm a stupid girl. Since I started at the nursery school, I see him on the playground with his friends, but he always ignores me. He seems to be worse than ever.

Daddy and his friend are drinking tea in the kitchen when I go back there to find Steven. Steven looks at me, sticks out his tongue, then asks Daddy if he can go out to play. Daddy looks at his friend before answering. “Yes go out in the backyard. Don’t be running in and out. If you go out, you stay out.”

Steven takes his cricket bat and soft ball and walks towards the back kitchen.

“I want to play cricket too Steven,” I call.

“No, I want to play on my own.” I hear the latch go and the door slam shut. It’s not fair; he never wants to play with me. I sulk.

I look again at my daddy’s friend. I’ve seen him here twice before. He's always smiling. When he and Daddy talk to each other, I don't understand much of what they're saying. Mummy says they are talking in their own language, a language that people speak when they come from a place in India. Daddy says it's Good-Jarati. He sometimes asks me to repeat certain words, then tells me what they mean. I like listening to them both talk because now and then, they say an English word. I like trying to guess what they're saying.

"Kem cho," I say to Daddy’s friend.

“Saarun,” he says back to me. “You can speak Gujarati?”

I nod. “A little bit. Daddy tells me some words.”

“Ahi Avo,” he says to me lifting his chin to the side.

It sounds like a cat. Meow, without the m. I know that means ‘Come here.' I step towards him.

“You’re a clever girl,” he tells me.

He’s still smiling. His eyes are large and brown like my Daddy's, but he has long eyelashes and very wavy, black hair. I think he looks nicer than my Daddy.

Most of the time when they speak together, it's as if I'm not in the room. My Mummy does it too. I sometimes think that if I stay very still, they won't see me at all. I listen to every word they say. It's so interesting to me that other people can speak what Mummy calls ‘gobble-di-gook' and understand each other. It feels like they have a secret world and that's so great! When Daddy teaches me some words, I feel like he is letting me into his secret world.

Suddenly, I hear Daddy say ‘Lizzie' in the sentence. They want to give me some attention. I feel pleased that at least someone does.

“Now tell me your name,” says Daddy’s friend.

“You know my name. Maaru naam Lizzie che.”

I giggle. I’m showing off again. Daddy just mentioned my name to him.

"Well, you're a *very* pretty girl Lizzie. Come here and sit on my foot and I’ll give you a ride.”

He crosses one leg over the other, takes both of my hands and sits me astride his leg. I feel his upturned shoe behind me as he bounces me up and down for a while, all the time smiling and laughing.

I remember how the last time he had been here, my Daddy had picked me up and thrown me up above his head and caught me again. I hated it because my tummy felt sick inside, it scared me. The more I told him to stop, the more my Daddy laughed and kept doing it. Finally, I burst into tears, and Mummy told him to stop, that I was frightened. When he did the same thing to Steven, he liked it and kept saying, “Do it again.”

I like this new game though; it's fun. Then he stops moving his foot for a moment.

“What’s your name?” I ask.

“Gandhi. Remember I told you.”

"Gandhi. Yes, I remember now." I repeat his name to get used to it.

“Goosy, Goosy Gandhi,” I say, remembering a nursery rhyme I’d been learning. Gandhi laughs.

“Tell me the Goosy Gandhi story,” he says.

“It’s not a story. It’s a nursery rhyme. We sing it at school.”

“Well, sing that nursery rhyme. I’ll bounce you as you sing it.” I laugh because I can show off. I like to show people how clever I can be. I stare at his eyes and start the rhyme straight away.

“Goosy Goosy Gander, where shall I wander? Upstairs and downstairs in my lady’s chamber. There I met an old man, who wouldn’t say his prayers. So I took him by his left leg, and threw him down the stairs.”

We’re all laughing, even Daddy. Gandhi bounces me a few more times.

“Ok little girl, I’m tired now. We need to play something else.”

He helps me off his foot. Daddy stands up and offers me his hand. "Come with me," he says. "We will play more games." He opens the kitchen door leading into the dark passage.

“Where are we going Daddy?”

“You’ll see,” he says.

Gandhi follows us, and they exchange more words and laugh. Daddy opens the other door, and we step into the hallway. He lets go of my hand and turns the doorknob leading into the front room.

“What games are we going to play Daddy?” I ask him.

"You'll see," he says again.

This is a room I hardly ever go into. If visitors come and the adults want to talk to each other, Mummy and Daddy bring them into this room. If we disturb them, they lock the door. Once, I asked Mummy,

"Why do you lock us out, Mummy?"

"Little pigs have big ears," she told me.

"What do you mean Mummy?"

She told me I had big ears and adults don't like children listening to everything they say. So this is not a play room. I feel special.

Daddy locks the door.

"We are going to play some games Lizzie. Just you, Daddy and Gandhi. These are not games we tell Mummy about. We do not tell *anyone* about our games."

I'm puzzled and stop smiling. He places both his hands on my shoulders and puts his face very close to mine. He looks right into my eyes and smiles. The whites of his eyes look yellow.

"These are our secret games Lizzie. You understand?"

I nod, although I don't understand why the games have to be secret.

"Why Daddy?"

"Because if you tell anyone about our games Lizzie, Daddy will go to prison. You'll never see me again."

"Why Daddy? What's prison? Is it like Batman and Robin's prison?"

I feel perturbed.

"It's a place where you have to go forever. They take you away and lock you behind bars. They throw away the key. They *never* let you out."

His words and grave face frighten me.

"Your Mummy wouldn't like it if Daddy went away and never came back would she?"

Tears spring into my eyes and sting.

“No Daddy.”

“So promise me you won’t tell anyone about our games.”

“I won’t.”

He tightens his grip on my shoulders. It hurts.

“Not even Mummy,” he says.

“Ok, I won’t tell Mummy.”

He straightens up. He and Gandhi say a few more words I do not understand and then laugh. Gandhi rubs my hair.

“Okay. Don’t cry. Everything will be ok. Come on, smile little girl. Be happy. We are going to play games now.”

I wipe my cheeks with my fingers and sniffle. I feel silly.

“Daddy, it’s your fault. You made me cry. Don’t go to prison.”

He kneels down beside me and lifts up my skirt.

"Well you keep our games a secret, and I won't go away."

He pulls down my knickers and helps me step out of them. I feel alarmed. Then he turns me around and tells me to lie down on my back, on the floor with my head in his lap. He pulls up my dress and Gandhi kneels at my feet. Gandhi holds my ankles in both of his hands and pulls my feet apart. I realize that this is not a children’s game. I have no idea what this is all about.

“Open your legs Lizzie. That’s it.”

He reaches towards me. What’s he doing? Mummy had explained to me that wee-wee comes out of my front bottom, and poo-poo comes out of my back bottom. Is he seeing if I’m weeing? He smiles and unzips his pants at the front and pulls something out from inside his underwear. I don’t know what it is. I’m puzzled. I stare at his face.

“Do you know what this is Lizzie?”

“No.”

I know it’s attached to him but it’s too big to be a Thomas like Steven has.

He comes close and his knees are either side of my legs. He takes one of my hands and puts it on the thing.

"Hold it for a little while," he urges.

I hold it. It feels hard. He puts his hand over mine and starts to rub my hand up and down on his thing. He makes some noises in his throat and then stops. He then puts the end of his thing right where my wee-wee comes out and starts to rub it up and down slowly. Then he goes faster, and I cry out in pain.

"Don't hurt her," Daddy says.

Gandhi slows down. I feel very uncomfortable between my legs, like my wee-wee part of my bottom is stinging. Gandhi smiles.

"You're a very obedient girl Lizzie."

His face is changing.

"I like obedient girls. Do you like this game?"

I shake. my head.

"I like it very much!"

He looks down at my face and opens his mouth. I can see black fillings in his teeth. His tongue looks yellow and furry. He looks ugly. He makes a sound like a dog growling. He squirts my legs and tummy with some white stuff that comes out of his thing. I can smell something. Daddy takes a hanky from his trouser pocket and wipes it all off.

"Good enna?" Daddy says.

I don't know what 'enna' is. He must be talking to Gandhi.

He lifts me up to a sitting position and turns me to face him. He has his thing out from his zipper too. He puts both of my hands on it and tells me to squeeze. He then puts his large hand over the both of mine and starts to shake our hands up and down violently. I don't understand what he's doing, and it's uncomfortable. He goes fast, and my arms are hurting. I don't like it. I'm scared. He opens his mouth and sticks out his yellow tongue. His breath stinks of cigarettes. He stares at me and laughs very loud and cries out. White stuff squirts up and lands on my face. I don't like how it smells.

"Yuck Daddy! What's that?"

I try to wipe my face with my hand, but Daddy grabs my hand and says,

"Don't touch. I'll wipe it off with my hanky."

He wipes it off, but I can still feel it, sticky on my hands and face.

He stands up, says something in his own language and goes out of the room, returning with a wet face cloth. He locks the door again and stands me up. He wipes me from my tummy to my legs, then my face and hands. He also wipes some off the carpet. He offers the cloth to Gandhi who waves it away.

"I don't need it."

They speak to each other in Good-Jarati again. Daddy looks at his watch and shrugs his shoulders; he wobbles his head slightly which I know means the opposite of what it seems. It's not quite a shake, more like his chin swings from side to side. I can't do it. Once, I asked him if it means, 'no.' He told me it means 'yes.'

I feel something I cannot name. It feels like I felt after I had swallowed a drawing pin that Steven had told me was a sweetie. Not the pain part as it went down into my tummy; no, the other feeling. My head hurts, and I can't believe what just happened. I want to lie down and have Mummy stroke my head and tell me it will be okay. Steven lied. Today, I believed Daddy about the games, but he lied too. I want to shout very loud, but all I can manage is a big swallow.

I remember being very careful of Steven after that. I knew he'd tricked me and hurt me by telling me it was something sweet when all the time it was something dangerous and painful. Mummy had taken me to the hospital to some doctors and nurses. I had to have a big photograph taken, and I could see the drawing pin on a big white square on the wall. Mummy told me not to take anything from Steven or anyone, who said they had a sweetie. Steven got a big spanking too.

Daddy leads me by the hand to a space in front of the fireplace. This time he pushes me down on the floor and lays me on my back. He then goes down full length in front of me on his stomach with his head over my legs and feet. Then he lifts up my legs and puts them over his shoulders. I don't know what is going to happen next. I just have to let them move my body around as they play with me like a doll. They chat again, in their own language, laughing and smiling.

All I can think is, 'I want my mummy to come home. Now.'

"We are going to have a competition," Daddy says, he laughs out loud. "Wait until the end and then tell us which one did it best. Okay?"

I have no say in this. I know they will do, whatever it is they want to do. I know that these games aren't games at all. I don't know what they are. These adults are in their own adult world. They speak their own adult words, they've got their own secret language, and they're tricking me. I don't know what a competition means. It's a big word to me. All I know is that I can't tell anyone about this. I wish my mummy would come home, so this would stop. Something in my mind tells me that Mummy would not like them doing this to me. She would say,

"Stop it. She's frightened."

It feels nasty and uncomfortable and a stupid thing to do. My head hurts, and I don't feel happy. I can't name the feeling. Why would Daddy want to do this to me? It's horrid. I stare down at the top of Daddy's head, I look across at Gandhi, and he is grinning from ear to ear.

"Do you like it?" He asks me.

I turn away. All I keep hearing in my head is what Mummy says is my favorite word. 'Why?' It doesn't feel like my favorite word anymore.

Why are you doing this to me? *Why* do you call it a game? *Why* are you smiling? *Why* are you laughing? Why don't you speak in *my* language, so I know what you're saying to each other about me? *Why* is it called Good-Jarati, when it's Bad-Jarati. My head's aching more now. They swap places. Then after it's all over, Daddy says,

"Who's better? Is it Gandhi or me?"

I don't know why they are even asking me this question. They're waiting for me to answer. I say in my head, 'If I say, Gandhi, Daddy might be upset. If I say Daddy, Gandhi might be upset.'

"Both of you," I say.

Only Gandhi laughs. Daddy speaks harshly to me,

"No. You have to choose. Do you like Daddy or Gandhi doing it best?"

His eyes have changed, he looks mad. I feel like unless I answer, they won't let me go. I'm scared.

"It's you, Daddy."

"Good girl. You're right. Daddy is best!" He gets up, claps his hands and dances around in a circle.

Then we hear the front gate creak open and close with a metallic bang. Daddy springs into fast movements. He puts my knickers back on and holds my arms very hard. He whispers, but his voice has real anger in it.

"Mummy's back. Don't dare tell her anything about this ok? It's our secret."

"I won't," I say, but inside my head, I say, 'I'm *so* glad Mummy's home again.'

Then I'm whisked through the door, through the dark passage and in through the green kitchen door as fast as my legs will carry me. I hear Mummy in the hallway with the pram, then her footsteps, Natalie's baby chatter. She's standing in the kitchen with us all, Natalie in one arm, a shopping bag in the other. Daddy and Gandhi are sitting in their chairs, holding their tea-cups like they just finished their tea.

I run to her and put my arms around her legs.

“Have you missed me?” She asks. I nod and keep hugging her.

“Ok then, let me through. Let’s put this shopping away. Dan, can you take Natalie?”

I step away quickly as Mummy offers Natalie to him. He stands up and takes her.

“You’re back soon,” says Daddy.

“Yes, I decided not to go pay the bills after all. I can go on Monday. So I just did a bit of food shopping. Have the kids been good?”

“Yes very good. Steven’s in the backyard. Lizzie’s been sitting with us.”

Gandhi looks straight at me and says,

"Yes, she's been teaching us some nursery rhymes. She's a very clever girl."

I follow Mummy into the back kitchen, glad that I don’t have to see Daddy and Gandhi staring at me. Mummy puts the shopping away and tells me to go outside to play.

Later, I venture back in and feel relief that Gandhi has gone. I don’t like him anymore. Daddy and Mummy are in the back kitchen cooking. I can smell the spices. It seems to be everywhere; it's pungent. My head throbs.

“We’re having curry,” he says. “I know you both like that enna?”

Daddy is flip-flapping a flat, round chapatti over in his hands. There is that word again, ‘enna.’ Steven just pulls a face and walks away.

Steven and I listen to the radio while all the cooking is going on. Then Mummy asks us to set the table and get glasses of water from the tap. We know we’ll need plenty of water.

Soon, everyone's eating, no-one speaks. Mummy says it's bad manners to talk at the table. The curry is not as hot as the last time we ate it, thank goodness. Steven seems to like his food. He puts big spoonful's in his mouth.

I hear sounds from Daddy's mouth and look up. He's eating in a way that Mummy would never allow me and Steven to eat. His mouth is open, and he is swishing curry around in his mouth with his tongue and chomping very loudly. The sight and sounds are nasty.

The sloppy sounds make me think about what happened in the front room, and I suddenly feel sick. I look at Mummy and silently will her to look up and see what I'm seeing. Surely she'll tell him not to eat like a pig. Surely she can hear him. I can't look away, and I feel madder and madder. Why won't Mummy say something? She's ignoring him.

Now I'm really mad. I hate his face. I hate his mouth. I hate his bad manners. I hate that he can get away with doing whatever he wants just because he's an adult. I feel his wrongness and terribleness in our home. And I hate *him.* I hate him so much that I can't stay at the table, yet I can't move. Mummy never allows us to leave the table until we've all finished eating.

This man I have to call Daddy will be sitting at our table and eating like a pig forever. My head feels like it's splitting. My body lurches. I grip my tummy and try to get off my chair. Mummy says,

"What are you doing Lizzie?"

I throw up on the floor. I retch and retch, and the taste is horrible. My throat burns. I bawl. This is the worst day of my life.

Mummy whisks me off my chair and runs me into the back kitchen to get my mouth over the sink. She's very kind to me and turns on the tap and puts her hand under the cold water. She places her cool hand on my forehead and says,

"Poor thing. You'll feel better soon."

I stop being sick but the sting in my throat makes me cry. She guides me through the kitchen, past Steven and Dan and upstairs to my room. "Let's get you in bed darling," she says as she places my nightie over my head.

“My poor little Lizzie. You’re all out of sorts today. Look, you’ve even put your knickers on inside out and back to front.”

"No, I didn't," I insist.

I'm just about to say, ‘Daddy did it,' then I catch myself and remember I'm not supposed to tell her. I feel miserable. I start to cry again. Mummy nurses me on her knee for a while and sings me the rainbow song. I start to calm down. Then she leads me to the bathroom, gently brushes my teeth, washes my face and hands and carries me back to bed. She places a cup of water on my nightstand and strokes my head gently.

“Now try to close your eyes and go to sleep. I’ll come back in a little while and check on you, okay?”

"Stay with me a bit longer Mummy. I don't feel tired yet."

“Well let me go down and wash up the dishes first then I’ll be back, okay?”

"Okay," I agree, and she leaves.

I lie here looking up at the white ceiling. I find the crack I love. It gives me peace when I see it, except the shape has no knees and no legs. "Mummy needs legs and feet," I say aloud, "so she can walk." It's like magic having a mummy-shape on my ceiling. I see her forehead, her nose, her lips, and chin.

Then Mummy comes into the room to tuck me in, I point at it to show her.

“Look Mummy. There is a shape that looks like you on the ceiling.”

“Where? Oh yes, clever girl, it *does* look a bit like me. Fancy you finding that. Are you feeling better?”

I nod my head. She kisses me.

"Well goodnight, God bless. I love you,"

"I love you too, Mummy."

She starts to close my bedroom door. I shout out,

"Don't close the door."

"You usually have your door closed Lizzie. I don't want the landing light to keep you awake."

"It won't Mummy. Please?"

"You've always slept in the dark."

"Please leave the door open just a little bit. Please?"

She pulls the door slowly towards her.

"Is this okay? Tell me when it's okay."

I sit up as my bedroom gets dimmer and dimmer.

"That's right Mummy. Just like that please."

There is an orange 'L' shape showing around the door. She leaves the landing light on for me. The warm orange glow makes me feel happier. I close my eyes, but something in my head keeps talking. I can't stop it. I keep thinking about the front room, and I keep asking, 'Why? Why? Why?' I feel very irritated. I keep turning to one side and then to the other. I kick my legs like I'm trying to get something away from me.

Later, Mummy comes back. I see her peep her head through the door. She starts to pull the door quietly to close it.

"Don't shut the door Mummy."

"Aren't you asleep yet Lizzie? It's after ten o'clock." She again leaves the door open a crack. "Try to go to sleep, Hinny. It's very late."

The voice in my head won't stop because I know there's no answer. I can't ask anyone about it, ever. It has to be a secret. I don't know what time it is when I go to sleep, but when I wake up the next morning, I'm still repeating the same word in my head. 'Why? Why? Why?'

I feel an urgent need to wee-wee. I almost don't make it to the toilet. I scream out in agony.

"My wee-wee is hurting me."

It stings so much I scream again,

"Mummy, Mummy, help me. My wee-wee hurts. Mummy, help me."

She doesn't hear me. I know she's in the kitchen, I hear her running the taps.

Suddenly I cover my mouth with my hand to muffle my crying and squeeze my wet eyes closed.

What if it's not Mummy?

ACKNOWLEDGMENTS

My two nearest siblings, more comfortable with anonymity, are named Steven and Natalie in my book. They each had a big part in saving Mum's life. Steven's intelligent insight and persistent bad temper at the tender age of four got Mum help when she was free-falling off a cliff, unable to help herself.

Natalie's birth, her will to live and sweet personality gave Mum a new light in her life, just when her light had faded to not even an ember. Natalie awoke Mum from living in the past to the hope of a brighter future.

Some children invent imaginary friends when they are lonely. My siblings were my real honest to goodness friends; always a constant in my turbulent childhood. Like Steven, my brother taught me to stand up to adversity, especially when I was always the American Indian squaw who got tied to lamp posts when his friends were the cowboys. Like Natalie, my sister gave me someone to love. The imaginary part of my relationship with her was that I was her real mum and she was my daughter. I took her everywhere with me and practiced being a mother before I ever learned to be a child. She saved my life when I was falling. I just never told her before.

Thank you, both. I love you dearly. Probably more than we ever knew.

I would be remiss if I did not thank all my friends at the Atlanta Writers Club for their thoughtful and very much appreciated constructive critiques and encouragement. A special thank you to George Weinstein, Mike Brown, Kimberly Brock and Tinderbox Retreat enthusiasts. You kept me going.

I also thank my daughter and my husband for all their patience, love and unending belief in me. They show me the kind of love that can move mountains. I have not been the perfect person, no-one can be, but I daily face my truths and meditate on how to improve in my walk with others and with God.

My Heavenly Father and I have had quite a journey together but God is so good. Thank you, for helping me in my writing and for your great Word. You gave in to my requests to have all my memories back. Our past makes us what we are in the present, so we can move forward to our future. Thank you, Jesus, my daily Shepherd, Savior, Healer and King. Thank you, Holy Spirit for your ever present inspiration, insight, power and witness to God's love.

I could not have written this book without you.

Finally, my Mum. I was squeezed from your womb and suckled at your breasts. I loved you so completely as a child. Thank you darling.

Dear Readers,

If you have taken the time to read my book, a huge thank you. If you love Lizzie and her family and want to know more, please look out for Lizzie's Life: Book 2. A website for comments and blogs is being developed and I hope you soon find it engaging and useful.

I rely on you to recommend Blow Me Over With A Feather to others. So please be so kind to tell your friends and fellow readers and to write a review on Amazon. I will be indebted to you. Reviews are so important to get the word out.

The last chapter was very difficult to write. A lifetime's silence over matters of sexual abuse is a hard habit to break. I want my book to open up discussion of this taboo subject and allow children and adults to have a voice. It's time!

Thank you all.

Made in the USA
Lexington, KY
20 August 2018